Mary Imlay Taylor

The House of the Wizard

Mary Imlay Taylor

The House of the Wizard

ISBN/EAN: 9783744649278

Printed in Europe, USA, Canada, Australia, Japan

Cover: Foto ©Andreas Hilbeck / pixelio.de

More available books at **www.hansebooks.com**

THE
HOUSE OF THE WIZARD

BY

M. IMLAY TAYLOR

AUTHOR OF

"ON THE RED STAIRCASE," "AN IMPERIAL LOVER,"
"A YANKEE VOLUNTEER"

CHICAGO
A. C. McCLURG AND COMPANY
1899

CONTENTS

The House of the Wizard

CHAPTER I

THE CAREWS OF DEVON

In the days of King Henry VIII., between Honiton and Exeter, at Luppit, stood Mohun's Ottery, the great house of the Carews of Devon. Built like a fortress, it was too strong to be reduced, save by cannon, and its walls had sheltered for many years a race of gallant gentlemen, while its gates were ever open with a generous hospitality that welcomed both the rich and the poor. Its furnishings and tapestries were so magnificent that it was commonly reported that they would grace the king's palace at Greenwich and not suffer by contrast with any royal trappings.

The Carews were famous, both at home and abroad, and had been since the first Carru came over with the Norman Conqueror. There was never a quarrel on English soil, or for the English cause, that a Carew was not in the forefront of the battle. One had been Lord Lieutenant of Ireland, one a captain of Harfleur

for King Henry V., and another fought for
Henry VII.   A proud and valiant race, claim-
ing kindred with the Geraldines, loyal and courteous to their friends and ready with sword and
dagger for England's foes and their own.   Sir
William Carew, the head of the Devon branch
of the family, held noble sway at Mohun's
Ottery, and day by day a hundred poor and
more were fed by his open hand, for in those
times there was no niggardly charity, although
the king's laws spared not the valiant beggar.
Every gentleman's house was in itself a tavern,
and men of all conditions came unbidden to the
board, finding, too, a night's lodging, even
though it might be but a bed of straw upon the
stone floor of the hall.   The food was neither
scanty nor of mean order; cooks who fed a hundred or so at one meal were accustomed to
serving in a day beef, mutton, venison, pigs,
geese, plovers, curlews, besides pike, bream,
and porpoise, and of ale and wine there was
no lack.   A plentiful, free feast that drew a
multitude of pensioners; the odors that floated
from the kitchens, even on a fast day, brought
a retinue of visitors to the doors, and after
meal time the sounds of revelry told their
own story, giving ample proof that there were
no empty stomachs.

It was Shrove Tuesday in the year 1535, and the midday dinner was over at Mohun's Ottery, as great a company as usual having been entertained. Upon the doorstep stood Sir William Carew and his guest, Master Raleigh, the father of Sir Walter, who was then unborn. These two worthies were engaged in deep and grave converse upon public matters, for the Act of the Supremacy had been followed by the Treason Act, and Sir Thomas More and Bishop Fisher were in the Tower, having refused to take the oath without conditions. So there was no lack of matter for discussion, and the faces of these two were neither unruffled nor jolly, though they had so lately dined. However, their conversation was doomed to a sharp interruption. A horse and rider came suddenly in sight upon the highroad, advancing at so mad a gait that both men paused in their talk to watch the approach. A great bay horse, flecked with foam and with blood upon his flank, showing a cruel spur, and on his back a large and handsome man, gayly dressed, his velvet cloak embroidered with gold and his hat beplumed, but reeling in his saddle, keeping his seat, as it seemed, only by a miracle.

"It is Sir Thomas," Raleigh remarked, after a second glance at the red face of the rider.

"Ay," retorted Carew, bitterly, "my worthy brother and, as usual, in his cups. A naughty rogue it is, and like to be a disgrace to his blood."

As he spoke, he fixed a scornful gaze upon the drunken man who was now coming to the door, trying, too, to sit straight in the saddle, as if he knew that his brother's disapproving eyes were on him. A little way from the entrance stood a large stone horse-block, from which the women of the household mounted, and toward this Sir Thomas Carew urged his horse.

"He has been gaming at Exeter," Sir William remarked coldly; "he is ever thus after he has been brawling and drinking in a public house. I have not seen him for a twelvemonth, and I doubt not that he comes to borrow a hundred pounds; such is like to be his case. 'Pon my soul, a meritorious beggar!"

The words were scarcely spoken ere Sir Thomas struck his spur again into his horse's bleeding flank. The great brute plunged, swerving madly to one side; his tipsy rider, reeling from the saddle, fell headlong upon the stone block, rolled over and lay in a hideous heap at his brother's feet. The horse turning about as suddenly, trampled him under foot and rushed back toward the stables, clearing a wide path in the crowd of spectators who had come out to view the accident. Sir William and Raleigh both hastened to the fallen man, but something in the limpness of his figure told its own story. He lay face downward, and they turned him over to find a lump of mangled flesh, his neck being broken just below the skull, and his drink-blurred eyes stared into space.

"Stone dead," Carew said sternly; "cut off in his sins. God pity him, for he is like enough to be damned!"

"Here is a sad end," rejoined Raleigh, looking gravely at the dead man; "a gallant gentleman brought into such a case by evil communications. Lend a hand, good fellow, and we will carry in this body," he added, addressing the nearest bystander, for the curious crowd had gathered in a constantly narrowing circle around the central figures.

"Let be, Raleigh," Sir William interposed coldly; "these grooms shall take him up; he deserved less for the dishonor he has brought upon his name."

With the same proud indignation, unforgiving even to the dead, he directed the removal of the corpse, and then he and Raleigh followed it into the house. Without, all tongues were loosed at their departure and gossip flowed on every hand, and there was food enough for it in such a life and such a death as this.

"I told Sir Tom 't would be so!" one of the spectators said, with the air of a man who felt justified; "that brute was like to end some man's life, and who but a Carew would back him in the state of liquor that yonder poor gentleman was?"

"That horse? Why, man, he held him above all else he had," cried another; "he valued the beast above his daughter."

"Like enough," was the reply; "certain it is that he valued him above his wife, poor lady!"

"She has been dead these many years, I take it," said a third; for, after the fashion of all such leeches, they were eager to discuss the affairs of the family whose substance they devoured.

"Ay, dead enough, good luck to her!" rejoined the first speaker. "They do say Sir Thomas wagered her at dice the very night on which his daughter was born, and lost his bet, too; but his opponent levied not the debt, and the poor lady, dying not many years thereafter, perchance never knew it. Howbeit, it is certain that had she known it, she could not have hated him more heartily than she did."

"That's true enough, my masters," said an ancient crone. "I knew her woman, and a sorry death the poor thing made. Even at that hour her husband was as tipsy as he was but now, and came into her chamber blubbering, as a sot will sometimes, and with great oaths, that he would guard her child. My lady heeded not his voice, but cried out to her tirewoman that the end was near, and she thanked the dear God for it, and to let her go in peace! She looked but once at her little daughter and then fell to weeping and blessing her, saying that the queen would care for this lamb, and so turned her white face to the wall and died."

"The queen, — did she commend her baby to the queen?" they all exclaimed.

"Ay, ay," the old woman answered, "to the queen's grace; there was but one queen then, but now there is the old queen and Queen Nan Bullen, and God wot how many queens there be!"

"Hold thy tongue, mistress!" cried one;

"thou wilt be up by the Treason Act, and hang at Tyburn, if thou hast so foul a tongue!"

"Belike I shall, and all of ye," the old creature laughed shrilly; "but it would not profit much to twist my shrivelled neck, there be fairer ones that would furnish a better entertainment."

"Where is Carew's child?" cried one whose thirst for knowledge was not yet slaked.

"Hidden somewhere in that old nest of his," returned one of the gossips; "a sad life she's had of it and is like to be in a worse case yet. Sir Thomas never did her a good turn until this day; the worst he did was to father her. An ill-favored wench, too, when last I saw her, thin and yellow and with a cold way that made no friends."

"Then ye have not seen her lately," the old woman said with a chuckle; "she has shot up like a young sapling, and has eyes like two stars, and a smile that will turn many a young fool's head, albeit her purse is empty and her kirtle patched."

"Poor wench, poor Mistress Betty, my heart doth ache for her," a kinder woman said, shaking her head.

Strangely enough, at that same moment Mistress Betty Carew was spoken of within the house by Sir William and his wife. He turned from his brother's corpse, a certain stern relenting in his face, and said to Lady Carew, "There is the child."

"Ay, we must have her here, William," his wife replied at once; "you may not leave your own blood in so poor a strait as he is like to have left the maid."

Sir William mused. "How old is she?" he asked.

"Seventeen, come Michaelmas," Lady Carew replied, watchful of her husband's face, her own heart full of compassion for the orphan.

"I know not how she may be bred up," he said doubtfully; "she was a plain wench when last I saw her, but that is five years since. Well, well, she must even come and follow this wretched man's funeral, and then you and she will doubtless find a way to settle it to your own liking."

So it was that Mistress Betty came to Mohun's Ottery; a tall, slim girl in a black gown and with a calm look on her young face that startled her uncle, so unlike was it to anything in youth. Sir Thomas was carried from the home of his ancestors with all due state and ceremony, but there was no pretence of mourning, and the well-born rogue was laid in

his narrow house without a tear.   After it was
over, the affairs of the orphan were soon disposed of by Sir William.   Finding that she
was dowerless, save for a beauty of which her
childhood had given no promise, he kept her
under his own roof, and she lived there until
other events took her to far other scenes.   She
was then in her girlhood, growing every day in
beauty of a strong and striking type, and carrying her head like a queen rather than a penniless maid living in dependence at her uncle's
house.   Her form, though slender, gave the
promise of a richer outline, and as she grew
happier in her new home, a color came into
her cheeks, a sparkle to her eyes that made
her lovely in the sight of many who marvelled
that so plain a child should grow so beautiful.
Lady Carew fretted much, however, at the
will that Mistress Betty showed, which brooked
no crossing, and the tongue that could, in
anger, cut like a whip, for this beauty was no
saint.   There was, however, that in her lordly
nature which scorned all meanness and baseness, a nobility that shone through the imper-
fections of her temper like a star, and looked
out through the windows of her great eyes, —
eyes that were clear brown, heavily fringed
with black lashes, and set beneath two straight,

black brows. Her mouth closed, perhaps, a trifle too firmly for so young a woman, and her chin was clear cut as a man's, but her voice was sweet and low, and there was witchery in her smile.

2

CHAPTER II

MICHAELMAS had come and gone, and it was past the middle of October when a messenger came down post-haste from London. It was after supper, and there was revelry among the retainers and visitors at Mohun's Ottery. In the great hall, however, there were but few; Sir William had only his favored guest, Master Raleigh, and besides these two were Lady Carew, her daughter, Mistress Cicely, and her niece. There were three sons, but none were home. Peter, who ran away to France, was even then with Sir John Wallop; that same Sir Peter who made the barns of Crediton smoke for the Lord Protector in after years. That evening the little company sat about the fire, the women working with their needles in a group at the left, and at the right sat Raleigh watching his host brew a posset. It was a matter of grave import to Carew, and he let no other hand mix the rare composition, but stood over it; a noble figure, a man in middle life, having a fine head and grizzled hair, with the keen, bright eye and strong jaw of a resourceful and stubborn nature. His rich dress of Flemish velvet, dark as the dregs of wine, his great lace ruff and heavy chain of gold, set off his person and made it the more striking in contrast to the darker, plainer garb of Raleigh. The guest watched his friend stir the beverage and smiled at his ardor.

"What secret lurks in it," he said, "that you let no man brew it for you, Carew? I should scarce be willing to take the pains that you have this night, though I do heartily acknowledge you the king of posset makers."

"If it be not worth the pains, it is not worth the drinking," replied Sir William; "'t is like a fine child, it may not come into the world without some travail and a good leech. See you, friend Raleigh, there is a secret in stirring it aright and putting in the parts in due season. If the cream and almonds be not wisely boiled with the amber and musk, and if you heat not the sack before you put in the eggs, then is there confusion, worse than these late troubles have brought upon this realm, and caused much in the same way, too, by a domestic disagreement."

Master Raleigh shook his head gravely at this, his mind slipping away from the posset as his next words betrayed.

"It will be happy for the realm if it prove but a domestic quarrel," he said thoughtfully, "since the Act of the Succession there can be no doubt that there is much foreign meddling, and, I fear me, plots against the king's majesty, made over seas, are foster-mothered here at Bugden; albeit, I do not greatly blame that noble lady that she will not yield. To her it must seem a sore and bewildering visitation of evil."

"God help her!" cried Lady Carew; "she was a good wife to the king, and deserveth better at his hands."

"Hush, madam!" retorted her lord, sternly; "a woman's heart is more full of pity than of wisdom. It is not for us to dispute the matter; there is talk enough, and no little harm from it. The marriage hath been set aside, and let us hear no more of it while there is another queen and an infant princess."

"Ay, it is an easy matter for a man to forget his wife for a pretty face," replied the good dame, hotly; "this is a policy that men like, since it favoreth their own slips upon the road; but no good will come of it, I warrant."

Raleigh laughed, looking from the husband to the wife; and even Sir William smiled, though a little grimly.

"The women are all alike," he said; "there is a great cackling amongst them over this, and if the petticoats could set the kingdom in order, I doubt not one fair lady would hang as high as Haman."

"I blame them not for their pity for one we know," Raleigh answered quietly; "it seems, forsooth, a great wrong, yet would I not see the Lady Mary come to the throne to bring back the Bishop of Rome and the Spaniards. These last I loved not ever; albeit there is cause for mourning that we lose with them the Flanders trade. Yet my heart has not been in all these acts; the fall of Sir Thomas More was, in itself, grief enough to me, for I had much friendship for that virtuous gentleman."

"Could it not have been averted?" asked Lady Carew, sadly; "he and Fisher both consented to swear to the Act of the Succession, with an exception, as I heard; could not this suffice?"

"Nay, madam," Raleigh answered quietly, "since the very clauses they excepted to were those which did declare the king's first marriage illegal, and his present one legal. Of what profit would it be to swear allegiance to the Princess Elizabeth and, in the same breath, to refuse her legitimacy? It may not be. We must have a settled succession; if the king have not male issue, I fear me there will be war in any case. Besides the Lady Mary and the troubles that my Lady Salisbury is like to hatch in the cause of the White Rose, there is the King of Scots, and verily no English stomach can digest him and not vomit."

"Nay, forsooth!" exclaimed Sir William; "there shall be no Scotch dressing to an English pudding while there is a sword in Devonshire. If the king could but get a boy there might be an end in peace, but as it is, one girl child set up against another, and one-half the kingdom crying ' Mary,' the other ' Elizabeth,' and so blood and fire from Land's End to the Tweed, and, eftsoons, the King of Scots!"

"Friend Carew, let not thy posset burn, for all that," said Master Raleigh, smiling, for in his vexation Sir William had well nigh forgotten his brewing.

"'T is ready," Carew answered, taking it from the fire; "Cicely, wench, hast ground the amber and sugar for it?"

As he spoke, there was a great stir without, the sound of hurrying feet and voices. The group by the fire paused in their talk to listen, and looked down toward the door at the lower end. In a moment it was opened and an attendant came swiftly across the hall and addressed Sir William, who still stirred the posset while Mistress Cicely sprinkled the amber over it.

"A messenger from London, your worship," the servant announced hurriedly, "and he craves leave to speak with you at once."

"From whom?" asked Carew, shortly.

"My lord privy seal," replied the man, in an awestricken tone.

Sir William's face showed both surprise and anxiety, but his manner changed but little.

"Where have you got him?" he asked.

"Without, sir; shall I bring him here?"

"Nay, I will go to him," Carew replied, after an instant of thought. "Raleigh, drink thou the sack, I will return again;" and he followed the servant from the hall.

Lady Carew glanced nervously across at her guest.

"May it be trouble?" she asked in an anxious voice.

Raleigh shook his head. "In these times we cannot know, madam," he replied, "but I take it that Sir William stands well with the king's highness and with Cromwell."

"Ay, so we believe," she said, speaking low, "but which of us can know how soon change may come? Wolsey, More, Fisher, the unhappy and gracious lady at Bugden! Why may not my good lord be caught also in the toils?"

A shadow crossed Raleigh's face, but it was only for the moment; after it came his ready smile.

"Madam," he said gently, "I know not how it may be, but I am sure that Sir William's honest heart and clean hands are truly valued by the king's grace; you know the saying is that ' King Harry loves a man,' and nowhere in this realm will he find a more valiant soldier or a more honest and God-fearing gentleman than your husband; albeit, Sir William may — from his own frankness — have made some enemies. A great-hearted man who dealeth honestly is like to have them, for there be many who do hate the odor of the truth."

Lady Carew sighed. "It may be that my heart is over-anxious," she said; "these be troubled times, and Sir William hath often told me that my outspoken sympathy with that good queen is like to bring him into evil straits."

There was no more time for the good dame's fears and misgivings, for at this moment Sir William returned, followed by a young man of fine bearing, whose rich attire was besprinkled with mud from hard riding.

"Madam, I bring you a welcome visitor," Carew said briefly. "My wife and Master Raleigh, this is Master Simon Raby, the son of Lord Raby of Sussex."

The young stranger made his obeisance with the easy grace of a courtier, drawing near to the group by the fire, and at Sir William's invitation laying aside his cloak and disclosing a gallant figure. A tall man, broad-shouldered enough, yet graceful, with a fine, frank face, which had in it the pink and white color of a girl's, but bold and brave enough to bear this dainty touch of nature. His hair was chestnut color, and his dark eyes were keen, but with a merry glance in them. He wore the rich dress of the court, his velvet doublet slashed with satin and edged with fur, Flanders lace upon his ruff, and in the side of his velvet cap were set three crimson feathers, clasped with a great jewel, while his velvet cloak was lined with crimson sarsenet. Certainly a figure for the two young girls to look at in some amazement, being little used to court gallants down in Devonshire; and while they viewed him, no doubt approvingly but in discreet silence, his eyes rested in some wonder and manifest admiration upon the glowing face of Mistress Betty. All the time, however, he talked with Master Raleigh, while Lady Carew and her husband spoke apart. Sir William held in his hand a letter, of which he evidently had much to say, and both he and his wife glanced frequently at the two young maidens by the fire. At last Carew turned abruptly to his niece.

"Betty," he said, "what say you to a brief absence from home, that you may attend upon a great lady, who is in poor health and — unhappy, and so has need of your service?"

Mistress Betty looked up amazed, with a pretty deepening of the color in her cheeks, and it was noted that Master Raby listened to her answer with much attention.

"I am so happy here at Mohun's Ottery, good uncle," she said, "that I love not the thought of quitting it; yet so deep am I in your debt that it is for you to direct me as you will, and for me to obey with love and cheerfulness."

Sir William smiled. "Wisely and modestly spoken, wench," he said, "and I have so little wish to part with you that I would fain find an excuse to my lord privy seal, but there is none. Therefore prepare for the journey; to-morrow morning you will ride with me."

Mistress Betty's bright face paled a little and her eyes clouded. "Where go we, uncle?" she asked quickly.

"Of that you shall know hereafter," he answered shortly, his own brow frowning slightly; "it is enough that you attend a noble lady by order of the privy seal."

Mistress Betty bit her lips, casting down her eyes, a sudden chagrin in her manner. Young as she was, she had no love of orders that were unexplained, and Master Raby, seeing her expression, addressed her with a pleasant courtesy.

"I fear your service may be sad, mistress," he said gravely, "but, happily for you, it is like to be a short one, if rumor saith the truth."

"Is it so, indeed?" exclaimed Raleigh, a sorrowful surprise in his kindly face. "I heard it not, ere now;" for he understood the reference, although Betty did not.

"True enough, I fear me," Raby answered, "although we know it not at Greenwich."

"How goes it there?" asked Sir William, anxiously.

"Gay, marvellously gay," his guest replied, "though the king's grace has been troubled with the swelling in his leg again."

At this Sir William shook his head.

"And no boy yet," he said; "pray Heaven this realm may see a prince before his highness yields further to these troubles, and so leaves us with our swords at each other's throats!"

"What other tidings?" asked Raleigh, eagerly.

"None of late importance," Raby answered. "Fox has gone to talk to the Lutheran princes against the French intrigues; Master Latimer is made Bishop of Worcester; the parliament has passed the vagrant act, and the universities will pay no more tenths and first fruits; there has been a great mask at Greenwich and a wizard has come to London who promises to show the king his own successor, but his grace will none of him."

"It may be that he dreads to inquire into so grave a matter," suggested Lady Carew.

"I know not, madam," answered Raby, smiling; "it is a much mooted question, even now that the little princess is proclaimed."

"Ay, but we have had already enough of such fancies," retorted Carew, stoutly; "we have not forgot the Oxford conjurer, nor the prophecy that he made whereby he declared that none of 'the Cadwallader blood' should reign long, and would even have raised an heir to Lancaster from the bloody field of Tewkesbury. All such matters be but the beginning of treason;" and the good baron turned to his posset in open disgust of the sorcerer's arts.

Far other thoughts ran in the mind of his elder guest; Raleigh sat looking at the fire with much perplexity upon his face.

"Latimer a bishop!" he said, at last; "I do remember the time when they would have burnt him but for my lord cardinal; strange, too, that Wolsey's hand should have plucked such a fagot from the fire. Verily, these are days when swift changes come upon this realm."

CHAPTER III

UNDER a gray sky and over moors, brown with the frost, rode Mistress Betty Carew upon her first journey into the great world. She and her uncle were escorted by Master Raby and a few stout retainers, all being well armed, for travellers encountered some perils upon those lonely roads. The young girl, going out upon an unknown errand and feeling herself almost a stranger even to Sir William, spoke but little, her mind being full of many thoughts and fancies. She had as yet no intuition of her destination, and marvelled not a little at the peremptory summons coming to one so little known as she was. Happily for her, she had been bred up in the school of misfortune and had profited by its early and sharp lessons. Naturally imperious in temper, she had learned to submit to the inevitable, and accepted this sudden and unwelcome change as part of her uncertain destiny, knowing that her poverty and dependence made her a plaything in the hands of fate. She had learned also in that early school to be a close observer of men and women, and was not unskilful in reading character, although so young.   Therefore she smiled a little when she heard her uncle's sharp comment on Simon Raby's groom.

"What hangdog knave is that thou hast there, Raby?" Sir William asked, when they were leaving an inn where they had stopped for a few moments.

"You mean not my groom surely, Sir William?" said Raby, smiling; "an honest fellow, who has served me two years or more."

"I marvel that he stayed so long out of gaol," Carew answered dryly; "a crop-eared villain, who will hang some day at Tyburn."

The younger man laughed gayly.   "A sorry prophecy, sir," he said lightly; "the man has served me faithfully, as far as I know, and seems free enough of bad habits, — drinks less, thieves less, and quarrels less than most."

"Ay," retorted Sir William, with a grim smile, "he would not quarrel openly, but keep a knife for your back at midnight; I would give him short shrift if he were mine."

"Verily, I must look for another knave," Raby answered, still laughing.   "I shall scarce ride in comfort after this with the fellow at my heels."

"Take my word for it," Carew returned; "I have been magistrate and provost and chief executioner — as it would seem — here in Devon, for all things are shifted on my shoulders, and it is such-looking rogues as that one who keep the hangman from forgetting his trade."

"Your uncle is a hard judge, Mistress Carew," Raby remarked; "I should not wish to stand trial at his hands unless, perchance, he liked my face. Here is my poor groom, Thaxter, already doomed to hang for his."

"To speak truth, he has an evil countenance, Master Raby," she answered quietly, but with a smiling glance at her uncle.

"You are prejudiced by Sir William," Raby declared. "I am willing to wager that the poor fellow is as honest as many with a fair exterior."

"I will take the wager, Raby," Carew remarked calmly, "and you will be the loser, therefore make it not too heavy on your purse."

"Fifty pounds, and I do not fear to lose," the other cried, still much diverted by the matter.

"I am that much a gainer," Sir William said, "but I will pray you not to test the affair at the moment by making him our guide.   I am not willing to trust my neck and Betty's to his mercies."

"Mistress Carew shall take no risks," Raby replied; "you and I will settle the wager when we are not in so fair company. Indeed, I trust that we shall make this journey safely and with expedition, since my lord privy seal was urgent that the matter should be speedily accomplished."

"Will they be ready for our reception? Has yonder lady been notified, or is this the act of Cromwell only?" Carew asked gravely.

Raby shook his head. "I know not," he answered. "I am but the bearer of certain instructions, but I fear that the — that her grace is little consulted in the affair."

Carew did not reply, but seemed to muse over some grave subject, for his face became almost stern in its repose; and Raby, seeing his preoccupation, took his place at Mistress Betty's bridle, guiding her horse and talking lightly and pleasantly of those matters that he thought would amuse his young companion. He had been but lately at the court, and told her of the jousts at Greenwich, when the knights tilted before Queen Anne Boleyn.

"It was a beautiful sight," he said; "they wore white velvet, embroidered in silver, and the lists were surrounded by the gayest ladies of the court; there was a sheen of gold brocade, and jewels; it was a scene worth seeing, and 't will be remembered long by those who saw it."

"And the queen?" Betty asked, with a little hesitation, "is the queen as beautiful as they say?"

"She was thought to be the most beautiful woman at court when she was Marchioness of Pembroke," Raby answered; "and she is still fair to look upon, though I do think that there are others more lovely. I doubt not she would call it treason did she hear me say it," he added, smiling.

"I should like to see her," Mistress Carew said thoughtfully.

"You have no need to seek so far to find a fairer face," Raby answered, with the gallantry of a courtier.

And so they rode on, talking in a friendly way until they seemed no longer strangers, and were but little interrupted by Sir William, who was wrapped in his own thoughts, which were apparently not altogether pleasant ones. Thus the three made the journey together, and still Betty knew nothing of her destination, though she marvelled more and more as the way lengthened, and they stopped at first one tavern and then another. But in those days young girls were little considered and were expected to submit, with implicit obedience, to the guidance of their elders. More than once Betty thought that she was likely to come to her journey's end without knowing her errand, but it was not to be so. The last day of her travels brought her enlightenment. Toward evening, when they were riding along at an even gait and had just passed through a small village, Master Raby fell back, leaving uncle and niece alone, as though he gave them opportunity for a last talk together, and Sir William, almost at once, availed himself of it.

"Fair niece," he said, "you are truly a jewel among women, for you have not yet asked me a question. Did your aunt tell you whither you were bound?"

"Nay, uncle," Mistress Betty answered quietly, "but I remember my cause for gratitude and am willing to do your bidding, though I should like to know where we are going."

Carew smiled. "There spoke the woman," he said, "yet I fear you will be little pleased; it is no lively errand for a girl. We are riding to Kimbolton, where they have but lately taken the princess dowager."

"What, sir, do I go to the queen?" cried Betty, in amazement.

"Mind thy tongue, young mistress," Carew said sharply; "not queen, but princess dowager."

"You mean Queen Catherine, uncle," Betty retorted, some excitement in her voice; "I cannot think of her as less than the queen."

"Then must you learn to speedily," Sir William said, "for you are sent down to Kimbolton by my lord privy seal, and you must not transgress the king's commandment in this matter, whereby we are bidden to hold this lady as only the widow of Prince Arthur."

"I cannot see how that may be," the young girl cried; "she was surely the king's wife, and there be many who declare that there is no divorcement."

"But ye are not of them, wench," her uncle said sternly; "his grace of Canterbury hath declared the king's first marriage null, and we have naught to do with the opinions of the Bishop of Rome, albeit this lady clings to his judgment and will none of the king's."

"Uncle, do you believe that she is fairly used?" asked Mistress Betty, with the fearful honesty of youth; "think you they had a right to treat the daughter of a king with such contumely?"

"'T is not for you to ask, or for me to answer, niece," Sir William answered sharply; "it is done, and the Act of the Succession hath set aside the Lady Mary. Mind, therefore, that you fall into no error in these matters, but do your duty, leaving these questions to the bishops and the king's grace."

"But wherefore do they send me thither?" she asked, her voice betraying her discontent; "what need is there for me?"

"Now listen well to me, Betty," her uncle said sternly; "you are young to be sent on such an errand. The princess has been surrounded only with her own creatures, there has been some plotting, and my lord privy seal would have one woman there who, being not of it, will be a check upon them; and he sent to me, because he puts some confidence in me, and was recommended, too, by our kinsman, the master of horse, Sir Nicholas Carew."

For a moment there was silence, and then Betty spoke with passionate feeling.

"See you not, uncle, that they would make a spy of me?" she cried; "how can you bear that this should be? Surely you are too honorable to see your niece sent to watch and betray a noble and an injured princess!"

"Hark ye, fair niece!" said Sir William, in a low tone, "I am not without sympathy for yonder great lady; she has been hardly used, though it is my peril to say so, and if you go not to her, my lord privy seal will surely send another who may, being tempted, work some deep mischief to her. See ye not how grievously an enemy might hurt her?"

"I see, I see," Betty answered, "yet I can never play the part of a spy!"

"Nor did I ask you, wench," Carew answered grimly. "I would wring your neck with my own hand, thought I you were so mean a traitress. But remember that you owe allegiance to the king's grace and you cannot break it without as great dishonor. Let not soft words prevail with you. It is commonly reported that this poor lady is plotting mischief with the Emperor of Germany and the Bishop of Rome. Not that I greatly blame her, Heaven knows, but it is a damnable treason against this realm and is like to pull us all by the pates if it succeeds. Meddle not with it, bear no secret messages, open no barred doors, steal no keys, though the lack of them may lay a royal head upon the block.

Remember your allegiance, do your duty and leave the rest to wiser brains than yours."

"That will I promise to do right cheerfully," Betty answered, "but never could I betray a woman in so sad a case."

"It is well," Sir William said soberly; "do your duty and mind well your tongue, for it may be that there will be some who would right willingly set a snare for you to bring you to disaster and work my downfall. I know not how close an eye Cromwell hath upon me, nor how he means to try me withal. He is a cat who plays with many mice, and his trap is the Tower."

"Hast thou then so many enemies, uncle?" Betty asked, in some wonder.

"Enough and to spare, fair niece," he answered; "and there is much malice in a court: it crawleth, like the serpent, on its belly, and there is war between it and the seed of woman, for it ever stings the heel of him who would live honestly. It was such malice that pulled down my lord cardinal. But enough; you know your duty, and yonder is Kimbolton."

CHAPTER IV

THE QUEEN AT KIMBOLTON

THE shadows of evening were gathering fast when the little party halted at the gates of Kimbolton. There was much parley, and the royal warrant was produced before the visitors were admitted, the delay and formality impressing Betty with the feeling of entering a prison; and she followed her uncle reluctantly across the courtyard, where a few torches flared in the gloom. No womanish qualms, however, oppressed Carew, and he walked boldly forward, leaving Raby to attend upon his niece, an office which the younger man eagerly accepted; indeed, he had already won the good opinion of Mistress Betty by his courtly gallantry upon the road. Bred in the country and under unfortunate auspices, she was little accustomed to the attendance of a courtier, and she noted young Master Raby's courtesy and graceful tact with some secret admiration, though she held her head high and was, as usual, chary of her smiles, perhaps, because — like every beauty — she knew their value.

Unfavorably impressed both with the place and with the lack of state and hospitality, she shrank back a little, and so it was that she and her cavalier were late in entering the hall, and found Sir William already in deep converse with the castellan, Sir Edmund Bedingfield. Neither of these worthies heeded the young people, scarcely noting their entrance, but stood talking and perusing a letter, no doubt the instructions of my lord privy seal. Mistress Betty and Raby drew near to the fire in the great chimney, a pile of logs of such length that one end might burn while the other was cold, but giving little warmth, for the opening above was of such huge dimensions that gusts of cold air came down with greater alacrity than the sparks and smoke went up. There was a lack of due attendance, a cheerless and gloomy aspect that increased the young girl's unfavorable impression, and she shivered a little, bending over the fire and holding out her hands to the blaze.

"A dull place," said Simon Raby, in a low tone; "a dull place for an uncrowned queen."

"Poor lady!" murmured Betty, forgetful of her uncle's recent instructions, "'t is enough to break her heart."

"I never knew her," Raby answered. "I

was away in France with Sir John Wallop until the queen that now is was crowned, but they do tell me that this lady is too strong and resolute a woman to greatly mourn the loss of state or earthly glory; but 't is awful to consign a princess to so mean a case as this."

Betty, remembering now the commands that were laid upon her, turned the subject without an open expression of her own feeling on this point.

"You were in France?" she said; "'t is there my cousin Peter is; he ran away, you know, and coming to Paris, was taken into the household of Sir John Wallop."

"I know him," her companion answered, smiling; "a gay and fiery gallant, who is like to make a brave record for Mohun's Ottery."

At this moment they were interrupted by Bedingfield, who, turning from Sir William, for the first time cast a glance in Betty's direction.

"Is this the maid?" he asked.

"Come hither, niece," Carew said, "and make your curtsy to Sir Edmund; you are now committed to his charge to be introduced to the princess dowager."

"Who is little likely to be pleased thereat,"

remarked Bedingfield, with a frankness which yet farther chilled Betty's heart. "I bid you welcome, mistress," he added dryly; "it is a sorry place for a young maid at best, and of late her highness has been ailing and in no plight to crave gay attendance."

"Discourage her no more, Bedingfield," Sir William remarked; "the wench is sufficiently cast down at the prospect, without your croaking talk."

"It mends not a matter to dress it in gay colors," Bedingfield retorted briefly. "Come, young mistress, follow me to the princess; there is no place to bestow you until I know her wishes, and 't is best to cut a long matter short."

"I would make some changes in my garments," Mistress Betty said quietly, "before I go to — to her grace."

"There is no need," Sir Edmund replied, with evident impatience to have an unpleasant task accomplished; "you may lay aside your cloak in the antechamber while I learn her highness's wishes in the matter, and so end it."

Without more words, he turned to the staircase and began the ascent, and after one glance at her uncle to ascertain his wishes, Betty followed with a heavy heart. She was not with-

out a little thrill of excitement at the thought
of seeing this unhappy queen, and there was,
too, all a young girl's curiosity and eagerness
for adventure, but she dreaded a cold reception, knowing so well how unwelcome she was
likely to be, sent, as she was, by one whom
the poor woman must regard as her greatest
enemy. So in a tumult of contrary emotions
Mistress Betty walked down the gloomy, ill-
lighted corridor, behind the castellan, mentally
contrasting this dull place with Mohun's
Ottery. They were not to gain admittance
without some parley; the queen allowed no
intercourse with the royal officers stationed
about her by the king. She lived among her
own people, and Bedingfield had to crave permission to speak with her. Finally, a page
admitted them into a small anteroom, where
Betty was told to wait and lay aside her
mantle. There was a closed door opposite to
the one at which they had entered, and from
behind it came the sound of voices engaged in
conversation, which was hushed as Bedingfield
opened the door and passed through. Betty
knew that he was going into the presence of
the queen, and she stood listening with anxiety.
She heard a woman's voice address him at
once; the cold dignity of the tone and the

slightly foreign accent made her sure of the identity of the speaker.

"What tidings, Sir Edmund?" she asked; "my maids tell me there is a stir below, and truly we long for any change; ay, almost welcome evil rather than the dull monotony of suspense."

"No news, madam," replied Bedingfield; "only a messenger from my lord privy seal and —"

"Alack, alack!" cried Catherine, hastily, "I did not speak sooth; news from that quarter is ill news indeed. If it had been from the king's highness — but that comes no more to me."

"In a way it is, madam," Sir Edmund answered; "the king's grace hath sent another maid to attend upon your highness."

"Another maid!" the queen exclaimed, in a tone of irony; "you mock me, sir; 't is not possible that so great state is allowed the Queen of England? Four maids! Such a train will be a grievous charge upon you."

"Nay, madam, I do beseech you, lay not the blame of your poor attendance upon me," Bedingfield said, with some feeling; "I may not exceed my orders."

"Your orders," said the queen, bitterly;

"who gave them to you, man, but that tailor's son, mine enemy?"

"Nay, madam; you do wrong my lord privy seal," Bedingfield returned; "he is but the mouthpiece of the king's grace."

"It may be, and it should not be," Catherine said sadly; "yet the time may come when even Cromwell will regret it. I do remember that my lord cardinal wrought against me to his own downfall, and died loving me, as I believe, better than his creature, who still wears a paper crown."

There was a moment's pause, and then Bedingfield spoke abruptly.

"I would know your highness's pleasure in regard to the maid who waits without."

"The maid! — what maid?" exclaimed Catherine, as if awakened from a dream; "oh, ay, I do remember! Why, send her to me, sir; I fear her not, even though she be a spy of my lord privy seal. If she has a woman's heart, doubtless it will be moved to see her queen brought to so low estate; and if she has no heart, then will I rejoice that mine enemies may have a true report of how chastely and honorably the Queen of England bears herself under the deepest injury that a woman and a wife can suffer."

"Do I understand that your grace will see the maid to-night?" Bedingfield asked dryly.

"When it be your pleasure, sir," the queen answered coldly; "a prisoner hath no choice."

"Nay, madam," Bedingfield began haughtily, "I—"

"Send her, sir," exclaimed the queen, sharply; "I would see her now! I am weary, and words mend not my case; let us so end the matter."

"As you will, madam," the castellan replied; "I do but my duty."

"I doubt it not, good Bedingfield," she answered with sad courtesy, "but I have known duty more graciously done. Howbeit, send me the maid; I would see what sort of a creature my Lord Cromwell sends to watch his queen."

"Your grace mistakes the matter," Sir Edmund said awkwardly; "this is a well-bred maiden, the niece of a gallant gentleman of Devon, Sir William Carew."

"Carew?" repeated the queen, thoughtfully. "I should know the name, kindred of the master of horse, as I remember, and he is truly a noble soldier. Fate and Cromwell are propitious; I looked for worse. Let there be no more delay, sir; my heart fluttereth at the thought of four female attendants," she added, with a touch of irony.

Having overheard all this talk, so little calculated to allay her misgivings, Betty waited for Bedingfield's summons with increased agitation. When he came to the door and beckoned to her to advance, she did so with great reluctance; although never a timid girl, she felt deeply embarrassed as she entered the room beyond, and found herself in the presence of Catherine of Arragon. Her eyes dazzled by the greater illumination, she was, at first, only conscious that she stood in a large room where there was a bright fire burning on the hearth, and before it several figures. She made her curtsy almost mechanically, and it was a moment before she collected her thoughts, and then she found that the queen was addressing her.

"I bid you welcome, maiden," Catherine said not unkindly. "Sir Edmund tells me that you are sent by my lord privy seal, whereby I know you to be chosen rather to his liking than my own comfort; but God forbid that I should misjudge so young a heart as thine! What is your name?"

"Betty Carew," was the answer, in a low

tone, "the daughter of Sir Thomas Carew of Devon."

"Thomas Carew," repeated the queen, with sudden recollection. "Your mother was the daughter of Lord Penrith; I knew her well, and I do now recall that she commended her child to my care, when I was little able to care for any one; a falling tree doth crush the flower at its root. Blessed Virgin, how strange is destiny! That very child sent down to watch her royal mistress!"

Catherine spoke in a low tone, more to herself than to those about her, and sat for a few moments lost in revery. She was seated in a great chair before the hearth, and there was much calm dignity and sadness in her whole aspect, but she was both unlovely and unattractive; a stout woman with a pale, large-featured face which ill health and trouble had aged before her time. Her expression was austere, and there were traces of deep sorrow and anxiety in the furrows that already marked her brow and the deep purple shadows under her dark eyes. Her gown was of black velvet, with large, flowing sleeves over small, straight ones, which had lace ruffles over the hands. On her head was a high, crownlike, five-cornered cap edged with jewels, two pieces falling down from it over the ears, and at the back was fastened the Spanish mantilla, its graceful folds draping her shoulders and showing her face in strong relief against the black background. Behind her chair were grouped three ladies-in-waiting, and all bent curious glances on the young stranger. Mistress Betty's blooming youth and brilliantly colored beauty had never shown to a more dazzling advantage than it did by contrast now, and Catherine herself, looking up from her revery, observed it and smiled sadly.

"Alas!" she said, "poor maid, this place is like to be no better than a tomb to one so young, albeit safer for your soul's grace now than Greenwich. I have no entertainment, no masks, no dances to break the cold monotony. You may pray here, weep here, die here, but verily, you will have no revelry. If you but remember to be a woman, and bear a woman's heart in your breast, as did your mother, you will find me no unkind mistress to you, though, God knows, an impoverished one. Wilt serve me on such terms as these?"

"Madam, I will do my duty, and I can no more," Betty answered in a low tone, divided between her pity and her uncle's instructions.

The queen smiled ironically. "Well tutored

in her ' duty,' doubtless," she said, turning to her maids; "a cautious answer, aptly mouthed. But, pshaw! I grow a weak woman to be angered with a baby. The wench is tired, I know; these men take no thought for a woman's strength, and doubtless she has ridden long and far. Take her away and find some place to bestow her, and to-morrow we will give some employment to her. Can you sing, Mistress Carew?" she added to Betty.

"I can both sing and play upon the harp, madam," the young girl answered gravely, for Catherine's words offended her, even though she felt the justice of the queen's suspicions.

"A musician," said Catherine, more graciously; "now am I reconciled. Like Saul, my soul finds consolation in music; it seems my lord privy seal would send me a female David! Well, well, leave me, maiden; I am weary, and I would not have you think your queen a sour and uncharitable woman with no lenient word for youth. Go eat and sleep, and to-morrow we will be merry."

CHAPTER V

THE GENTLEMAN IN THE RUSSET CLOAK

Queen Catherine's prediction that life at Kimbolton would be gloomy for a young girl, seemed likely to be fulfilled. Happily, for Mistress Betty's comfort, she had already undergone such discipline in both poverty and solitude that she was better fitted to endure restraint and depressing surroundings than others of her years. Sir William Carew and Master Raby bade her farewell the morning after her arrival, and from that time she encountered no very friendly treatment, except from Sir Edmund Bedingfield. The queen was never unkind, but she looked upon Betty with suspicion, and a settled conviction existed in her mind that the young girl was a spy of my lord privy seal, while her three attendants, all women who were devoted to her person, resented still more intensely the presence of the new lady-in-waiting. At the same time, Betty's youth, beauty, and many attractions won upon them, in spite of themselves, and they could not be harsh or malicious to so charming a creature. After the first week or two they relaxed a little in their manner toward her, and gradually she won her own place in the little household, though she was never trusted in any confidential matter; and often, at her approach, conversation was hushed or writing materials put aside, and an artificial manner assumed, as before a stranger. Intensely as Betty resented the distrust and coldness, she was not without a feeling of thankfulness that her sympathies would never be appealed to, that they seemed to have no wish to work upon her for any of their secret purposes. That there was much scheming she could not doubt from many little indications, and from occasional passages in the conversation, she learned that Catherine was still industriously employed in appealing both to the Emperor Charles and to the new pope. To all these matters Betty tried to close her eyes and ears, and indeed it seemed to her that it could not last long; it required no very observant eye to see that the queen was suffering from some malady even more dangerous than grief and mortification. There were many days when the royal sufferer never left her bed, and at such times she seemed to find genuine consolation in Betty's harp and her clear, sweet voice. The young girl, moved by deep pity for the injured queen, was ever ready to give her the comfort of her music, and so, little by little, she gained a place in Catherine's regard, though herself chilled and sometimes repulsed by the coldness and suspicious austerity of the Castilian princess. Just, virtuous, and religious, Catherine did not also possess the attraction of sweet and gracious manners, and her natural austerity had been increased by the usage she had received in England. She was devout in the observance of her religion, rising at five o'clock in the morning for prayers, and fasting with rigid exactness. Beneath her robes she had always worn the habit of a nun of the order of Saint Francis, and she held the vanities of the world in contempt, even while she contended for her earthly honors. Heavily oppressed by her sorrows and deeply distressed for the future of her daughter, the unhappy queen had neither leisure nor inclination to win the affection of the young attendant so unceremoniously thrust upon her. So it was that Mistress Betty stood as one apart, and watched the sad little drama to its close without feeling herself one of the actors.

Catherine held a little court each day, unless her health prevented it, many visitors coming

and going at Kimbolton in spite of the surveil-
lance of the royal officers. Although he feared
her influence, the king had never isolated her;
he either respected her too much, or hesitated
because of the popular feeling in her favor,
and the attitude of the foreign princes. She
was in the hands of the officers of the crown,
but they dared not treat her as a prisoner, and
the sympathy of a large portion of the kingdom
showed itself, more or less openly, in many
ways. Yet life at Kimbolton was gloomy
enough, and the queen being almost constantly
indisposed, her maids had small opportunities
for out-of-door exercises and none for sports.
Their greatest entertainment was to embroider
in the evenings, gathered about the invalid's
chair, or to play cards, — a game in which the
queen sometimes joined, though it was whispered among her women that she had hated
the sight of a card since she had played with
Anne Boleyn at Greenwich. Although Betty
felt herself an object of indifference to the
little circle, she was more noticed and com-
mented upon than she was aware. The fresh
beauty of the young girl was often the subject
of conversation, when her back was turned;
even the queen observing it and speaking of
Betty's many charms.

"A fair face," she said to her attendants, "and a soft voice; 't is a pity if both are false."

"I cannot think so, madam," one of the older women replied; "the child has a candid eye and an upright conduct that denies all secret dealings."

"It should be so," Catherine remarked sadly. "I knew her mother, a very honest woman, but she is long dead, and how shall we know how they bring up our children? Alas! when I think of the Princess Mary, my heart bleeds. I, too, am led to think well of this little maid, yet I never knew my lord privy seal to send a lamb into my fold to comfort me withal."

"It may be he has mistaken his choice, madam," her woman answered; "there be more people for your grace than against you; yea, more than half this kingdom."

"It may be," the queen replied; "I will so believe it. Truly, I hate to look with suspicion on so fair a face, yet I know one fair face that hideth a false heart. But all women are not harlots, thanks be to the Virgin! This young girl tells me she has never been to court, never seen a joust, never joined the gay revellers at a mask. Doubtless her uncle will take her presently to curtsy to that woman whom they call the queen, the true queen being not dead, albeit like to die. Mistress Carew will make a fair figure at the court, fairer than many, say you not so, Patience?"

"Ay, gracious Queen," Patience answered, eagerly catching the drift of her royal mistress's thoughts, "I know none fairer; she is so tall and straight and withal so beautifully moulded. Not lean and long, but round and supple; and her skin is dazzling when the color comes, while those brown eyes of hers are two shining lights, and she has a mouth like Cupid's bow."

"Truly, you have drawn a picture that might delight a lover," Catherine said, smiling; "the court is a dangerous place to show such charms. What think you, my girls, is she not fairer than one Anne?"

"A hundred times," they answered gladly, ever willing to humor their unhappy mistress.

For a moment the queen did not reply; she sat looking before her with an ironical smile playing about her lips.

"'T is a pity to mew up such a beauty at Kimbolton," she said at last. "Ah, if we could but get my lord privy seal to take her to the court, then might we see if the star that shineth there is fixed, or but trembles to its fall. Alas!" she continued, after a moment, rousing herself from her mood, "how captivity and misfortune sour the temper! My thoughts were most unworthy and unqueenly. I may well let that poor creature rush to her certain doom unmolested by any ill-will of mine; a crown so ravished must press with thorns upon the wearer's brow."

Unconscious both of their admiration and their talk of her, Mistress Betty went her way among them, the gloomy experience telling in a manner upon her life and character, teaching her alike to repress her natural feelings and to endure suspicion without openly expressing her indignation. The last was no easy matter, for she had a high temper and a passionate resentment of injustice. Her only comfort was the privilege she enjoyed of long rides with Sir Edmund Bedingfield. Knowing her uncle, and trusting her where he would not have dared to trust the queen's older attendants, he gave her more license. Finding that she rode well and loved to be on a fine horse's back, having inherited her father's appreciation of a good animal, Bedingfield permitted her to accompany his party when he made excursions in the neighborhood. And so it was that, by a chance, Mistress Carew made the acquaintance of a person who was to play no unimportant part in her life. Accompanied by her woman and two stout grooms, she had been out with Sir Edmund upon an errand in the country near Kimbolton. Returning at noonday, they drew rein at the Inn of the Sign of the Blue Boar, where Bedingfield and his two male attendants dismounted and went into the tavern, Sir Edmund for some information, and the two men for liquor. Betty and her woman waited without, and as they were detained a little while, there was ample opportunity to look about them. It being noonday, the courtyard of the Blue Boar was full of horses, tied and awaiting their masters, who were eating and drinking within. A few idle grooms lounged near the stables, waiting to earn a guerdon from a new arrival, and in the window of the kitchen leaned two or three rosy-faced maids gazing out at the scene. Betty's horse, a restive creature, stood out upon the road at the gate, and being occupied with her own thoughts, she let the reins lie slack upon his neck, although she knew his spirit. Suddenly there was the sound of a horse's hoofs upon the road behind her, coming at a gallop, and she turned her head to observe the new arrival. As she did so, a piebald horse with a darkly cloaked rider on his back came dashing past her. She had no time for observation; her own animal plunged so wildly that she nearly lost her seat, and kept it only by virtue of her early training. So strange was the encounter that she was almost certain that the new-comer cut her horse with his whip as he passed. How it was, she could not tell, except that her gallant black was off at a gallop, and she could scarcely have curbed him but for the interference of the rider of the piebald steed. He dashed along the road, riding across her path, and with wonderful dexterity caught her bridle rein, halting the runaway. Coming thus to a standstill, some twenty yards from the inn, Betty found herself face to face with the stranger, while behind them there was a great commotion, all the visitors at the tavern having run out to witness what they expected would be an accident. Intensely angry and with scarlet cheeks, Mistress Betty gazed haughtily at the cause of her misadventure. The rider of the piebald was a man far below average size, thin and wiry, with a small, dark face, grizzled hair and mustaches, and eyes of such keenness and so intensely black that they startled the observer, saving their owner from any charge of insignificance. Insignificant he was not, in spite of his small stature and his plain garments, which were russet in color from his high riding-boots to his cloak, which he wore after the fashion of the Spaniards. Encountering now Mistress Carew's indignant gaze, he took off his hat with elaborate courtesy and congratulated her on her safety as if he were unconscious of having had any part in the matter.

"It was fortunate that I came at the moment, fair mistress," he said; and she noticed that he had a singular but not unpleasant voice. "You are riding too spirited an animal for a lady; let me recommend a gentler one to Sir Edmund."

Betty started at the mention of Bedingfield's name, but recollecting how well he was known in the neighborhood of Kimbolton, she thought it but folly to be surprised that the stranger knew to whose party she belonged.

"I thank you, sir," she said, a little curtly; "the horse has never acted so before unless switched, and, indeed, I do not think he would have run had you ridden at a more moderate pace."

"I grieve to think myself the cause of your discomfort, madam," the stranger replied, but

with an amused smile. "Jack Kotch and I
never go slow," he added, turning his horse,
and, to her annoyance, keeping at Betty's rein
as she went toward the inn.

"It is ill judged to run a horse so close to
one standing as mine was," she said, still too
angry to let the matter pass.

"It is, and I crave your pardon," the other
rejoined cheerfully; "another time I will bring
my horse to a walk, Mistress Carew."

Betty looked up amazed at hearing her own
name, and encountered the stranger's wonderful
eyes with a gleam of amusement in them.

Bedingfield, who had mounted in the interval,
now rode up, and the little adventure had to
be explained to him. He, seeing only ready
courage and dexterity in the conduct of the
new-comer, was cordial in his thanks, and even
permitted this strange person to ride back with
the party toward Kimbolton. This seemed to
be the opportunity that the little man desired,
and he was soon engaged in earnest conversation with Sir Edmund. So entertaining did
he make himself that Bedingfield, to Betty's
surprise, invited him to come in to rest when
they reached the castle. Usually, all visitors
underwent a severe scrutiny on account of the
presence of the queen, but this stranger seemed

to have overcome the castellan's scruples and the piebald horse was led to the stables, while the rider, smaller than ever now he was dismounted, followed Sir Edmund into the hall. Betty's mind still rankling with the belief that her horse had been cut with the whip of the piebald's master, and her curiosity piqued by the little man's appearance, she asked the woman with her if she had ever seen him before. They were going up the stairs from the hall, Sir Edmund and his guest standing by the table below, and at the question the woman, a servant at Kimbolton, drew nearer and plucked her dress with nervous fingers.

"Hist, mistress!" she exclaimed in a low tone, "his ears are long. I have seen him but once before, but I know him full well; it is the famous wizard."

"A wizard! that little bandy-legged man a wizard?" Betty cried, amazed.

"Hush!" said the woman, her dull face full of fear, "he reads your thoughts, he sees visions. 'T is said that he did see, in a dream, Richard Rouse put the poison in my lord of Rochester's bran meal at Lambeth Marsh, and that he had warned Richard, seven years before, that he would be boiled alive at Smithfield, as he was. I would not offend that little gentle-

man in the russet cloak for a kingdom; no, not
I! They do say that his piebald horse was a
good bay, until he waved a striped wand over
him, at which the horse sneezed three times
and eftsoons came out white with three bay
spots upon him.   'T is my belief that this same
wizard is allied with Satan, and so think many
honest folk.   Avoid him, mistress, and you
love your life!"

CHAPTER VI

THE WIZARD'S VISIT

IN their gloomy rooms Queen Catherine and her maids sat working when Mistress Betty entered, rosy from her ride and the excitement of her adventure, which promised now to be of some interest. The queen, glancing up at her entrance, caught the glow in the new-comer's face and smiled more pleasantly than usual.

"How wonderfully freedom and exercise affect young blood!" she said; "the wench is blooming as a Christmas rose. Come hither, my girl, and tell us of your ride; perchance it may seem like the recital of a chapter of wild adventures to us. Youth and hope see all things in a golden light; what knight rode at your bridle rein? what dragon was slain at your approach? Such faces as yours open new channels of chivalry in the hearts of men. Saw you not some marvel that may serve to cheer us in our solitude?"

"Nay, madam," Betty replied, smiling, "I met with no such wonders; but I did see a wizard riding on a piebald horse."

"A wizard on a piebald horse?" repeated Catherine; "'t is well, so you saw not Death riding on a white one, as they say my lord of Buckingham did once. How knew you the gentleman for a wizard? Did he carry the symbols of his trade displayed, or had he a terrible learned countenance that confounded all men at the view?"

"Your grace should see what a small, bandy-legged creature it is, much like a frog," said Mistress Carew, "only that he wears russet instead of green, and has a smooth tongue, so that even now he wins the regard of Sir Edmund."

"What, is he here?" exclaimed the queen, in surprise; "I knew not that Bedingfield would admit any one without the warrant of my lord privy seal; surely, Cromwell hath not sent a sorcerer to conjure me," she added with an ironical laugh.

"Rode he a piebald horse?" asked Patience, the queen's woman; "I think I cannot mistake the man."

"A piebald horse, surely," answered Betty Carew, "and he is clad in russet from top to toe; his cloak is of velvet, but his doublet, I think, was no more than sarsenet, and he wears one straight black feather in the front of his low hat. His eyes are bright — the brightest that I ever saw — and he has a pointed gray beard, after the fashion of the Spaniards. I noticed, too, that his eyebrows were arched up sharply, almost in a point, which gave him a strange look, like an owl."

" 'T is Zachary Sanders," exclaimed Patience. "Your highness does remember, surely; 't is he who made the wonderful ring for my lord cardinal and sent the scroll of her horoscope to the Princess Mary."

"I do seem to remember," the queen said musingly, "but it is strange I do. Like a great sea, raging and terrible, the waters of Marah have overwhelmed me, sweeping on every side in a mighty torrent, carrying away all my strong friends and steadfast helpers. As the ocean, overflowing its borders, sweeps high upon the land, and when its tide recedes, carries away all the habitations that man has built upon the sand, and there is no remnant left thereof to tell the tale of the disaster, so the tide of my sorrow hath carried all things from my memory, stripping the beach of my mind and leaving only wreckage where once were lovely mansions of thought and fancy. Yet, as the saints bear witness, I did build my hope upon rock and looked steadfastly for its fulfilment. Alas, alas!" she added, tears shining in her eyes, "the tides have beaten on it, and only the sure anchor of my hope in heaven doth endure."

"Nay, nay, madam," her woman cried, "speak not so disconsolately; the emperor bears up your just quarrel, and the new pope has declared for your cause. Look rather at the good hope you have in the love your people bear you and your fair daughter, the Princess Mary."

Catherine roused herself, her weakness had been but momentary, and she regained her composure almost as quickly as she had lost it.

"It is for the Princess Mary that I live," she said quietly; "in my good daughter I have an assured comfort."

"'T was the horoscope of the princess that this wizard cast, who is now below," her attendant said. "I should like to have your majesty see him; he would furnish much entertainment for an hour on such an evening as this." The good woman was eager to change the drift of Catherine's thoughts.

The queen smiled as she turned to Betty.

"What say you, maiden?" she asked; "would this marvellous little man divert my poor girls for an hour?"

"I cannot tell," Betty answered soberly, for she was touched at the queen's emotion — Catherine's habitual coldness was repulsive, but in such moments of sorrow she was more attractive; "'t is certain that he furnished me with ten minutes of sharp entertainment this noon," and she told them briefly of the wild gallop of the wizard and her own misadventure.

"We must see this fiery horseman, if Bedingfield will let us," said the queen when she had heard the story; "see, my maids, how obedient I grow from force of habit! If her jailer wills it, the Queen of England would see a travelling wizard for an hour of wild diversion. Forsooth, 't will cast in shadow the jousts at Greenwich in honor of the Marchioness of Pembroke! Go you, Mistress Carew, for you are in favor, and pray Sir Edmund to send this fortune-teller to us."

Thus admonished, Betty went upon the errand with alacrity, glad to escape from the sadness that the queen's mood had cast upon the scene, and moved, too, by a young girl's curiosity which had been awakened by the reports of the wizard. She found Bedingfield still entertaining the small stranger, and preferred Catherine's suit with some hesitation on account of his presence. Sir Edmund's face clouded a little at the proposition and he stood a few moments staring moodily at the floor. Betty, standing at a short distance, observed the two with interested eyes. The wizard had fastened his gaze on his companion's face as soon as Betty told her errand and watched him much as a cat watches a mouse, but there was no expression on his small and wizened countenance to indicate his feelings. He was sitting on a low settle, his short legs drawn under it and his chin resting in his hands; something in his gray hair and dull skin, his brown clothing and diminutive size, gave him the appearance of some hobgoblin of fairy lore. Bedingfield was manifestly puzzled; the queen's request was simple and natural enough, and there seemed no reasonable excuse for denying it, yet Sir Edmund was uneasy. There was something about the wizard which indicated a keen wit and no ordinary energy of purpose, and Bedingfield knew that there were dealings with Rome and Spain, — dealings that Cromwell and the king desired to break off, — and here was a stranger who might be bent on mischief, yet there was no reasonable excuse to refuse him admittance to the queen's presence. The fact that he had not petitioned for it was in his favor and Bedingfield knew well enough that the poor women in his charge were sadly in need of some small diversion. Catherine had done wisely to choose Betty Carew for her messenger; the wistful expression on the young girl's fresh face went far toward prevailing with Sir Edmund. After a few moments of hesitation, he despatched one of his own gentlemen with the wizard, to conduct him to the queen and remain in attendance during the interview, at the same time bidding Betty go before to warn the little court that the request was granted.

Mistress Carew sped on her errand with the swift feet of youth, and before the wizard and his escort had reached the top of the stair, she had entered the queen's room. As she lifted the curtain at the door, something in the scene within arrested her attention. Catherine sat more erect than usual, and her three maids were gathered about her talking in low tones; there was an animation in their looks so unusual that Betty thought in an instant that there was some new interest in the air, some scheme afoot. At the sight of her, however, the habitual expressions came back to their faces, and Catherine received her announcement with her usual manner.

"I have no royal robes to assume," she said, in a tone of bitterness, "but truly there must be some state with which to hold our levee. Come, my girls, stand around me, arrange the log upon the hearth, move yonder fire-screen; the Queen of England will receive the wizard Sanders!"

"Madam, the jest is bitter," replied Patience, sadly; "spare us — who so bemoan your case — the sharp edge of your wit, whereby the loss of your high estate is in no manner redeemed. You are still our gracious sovereign lady, and so would be were you an outcast from this realm which hath so uncharitably used you."

"I thank you, wench," Catherine replied, her face softening at the expression of her attendant's devotion; "you teach the queen to bear herself more worthily. Ah, good Patience, you know not how deep the wound corrodes my lonely heart. Albeit a queen, and the daughter of a king, I am yet a woman, and a woman's heart doth crave a little tenderness, — a little love, — a little shelter, or else, God wot, it starves!"

All her attendants drew nearer to her chair, and tears shone in their eyes; the touch of womanly weakness in the cold character of the injured princess appealed to them more sharply

because of its contrast with her habitual austerity.   Catherine pressed her handkerchief to her
own eyes, and there was a painful silence,
broken only by the sound of footsteps at the
door and the voice of the usher announcing the
entrance of the wizard.   At this interruption
the queen was herself in a moment, and
received the visitor with her usual cold
dignity.

The scene was a strange one; the fire was
burning low on the hearth, but a bright glow
shone from the bed of fiery embers in which
the fallen log lay smouldering.   The room, a
large and gloomy one, was hung with dark
tapestries, which increased the somber effect,
and it was only imperfectly lighted by the
narrow windows at the farther end.   In her
great chair by the chimney sat the queen clad
in black, and her hair entirely concealed by
her velvet cap.   Around her were grouped her
four ladies, Betty Carew alone blooming with
youth and beauty in this sad place.   Into this
little company of women came now the small,
strange figure of the man who called himself
Zachary Sanders, the most famous wizard in
the south of England.   He still wore his russet
cloak, fastened by a clasp and chain that had
been loosened so the mantle hung behind, only

kept from slipping off his shoulders by the chain. His jacket and doublet were of russet-colored sarsenet, and he wore no ornament but a curiously wrought silver serpent, which was secured below his collar and hung on his breast. Without his hat he was a far more notable person than with it, for he had a large and finely developed head, the sphere of the brain well arched and full and with no ugly slant of the forehead, and not too protuberant behind, but with a fine line from the nape of the neck to the crown. His owlish eyebrows and pointed gray beard and mustache gave a slightly sinister cast to his features, but his eyes were so remarkable, both for size and brilliancy, that all else sank into insignificance by contrast. He came forward with an ease that indicated a person accustomed to encountering people of all ranks in life, one who was as little likely to be amazed at magnificence as he would be touched by distress. He made a profound obeisance to the queen, and she held out her hand, prompted, perhaps, by the thought that she could not afford to lose a friend, however humble. He knelt on one knee and kissed it with an apparently sincere feeling of homage.

"I have heard of you many times, sir," said

Catherine, gravely, "and my women were eager to have some entertainment and instruction. Doubtless they would look curiously into the future, fancying great things in store. I pray you gratify their innocent desires, if you may; for my part, such prognostications are of little comfort. Having encountered so great disasters, I do dread to look beyond the hour; for me such dreams are done."

"Yet it should not be so, your grace," the wizard answered, regarding the queen earnestly; "your horoscope hath no such evil ending to it."

"You flatter me, good Sanders," she replied bitterly; "I am no longer young enough to be deceived by such follies. Here is a maid whose fortune should smile like her face," she added, pointing to Mistress Betty, who stood near her; "your arts should weave a tale of love and happiness for youth and beauty."

"I cast her horoscope this noon at the Blue Boar," the wizard said, with a queer smile. "Venus was in fortunate conjunction with Mars when Mistress Carew was born."

"Did you learn that by striking my horse, Master Sanders?" Betty retorted, with a mischievous glance from under her black lashes.

The astrologer looked at her with an immovable face.

"You are mistaken," he said calmly; "I touched not the beast. It sometimes happens that these dumb creatures recognize a power more than human, and are so thrown into a convulsion of terror."

"With your aid?" persisted the young girl, laughing incredulously, and even the queen smiled.

"My young mistress is inclined to jest," Sanders remarked grimly, "and to make light of my art, but this will not be so when she talks to her affianced husband."

"My affianced husband!" exclaimed Betty, with indignation; "you are much in error in good sooth, for I am not promised."

The wizard looked at her and laughed, his brilliant eyes almost fascinating the young girl's startled gaze.

"You were promised in your cradle, and a lovely mate you are like to get, Mistress Carew," he answered quietly, with such a tone of certainty that Betty experienced a sharp sensation of apprehension.

"'T is false!" she exclaimed passionately, her agitation so genuine that the queen interposed.

"Why fret the child, sir wizard?" Catherine said; "what warrant have you for this statement?"

Sanders turned to her with courteous respect, although his face showed a certain malicious enjoyment.

"We read these matters in the stars, madam," he said gravely, "and they cannot mislead us. Mistress Carew is promised to a tall, dark man with a sword-cut across his left eyebrow; one day she will find that the astrologer has not lied."

Seeing Betty's angry alarm, Catherine turned the matter aside; she had the tact to avoid a scene which was becoming unpleasant.

"You claim that all your knowledge is from the stars, sir?" she asked indifferently, "and there is no human agency in the affair?"

"None, madam," the wizard rejoined solemnly; "we read the destinies of men and women in the heavens, and the future even of this realm unrolls itself in that great scroll for the marvelling eye of the seer to read."

The queen leaned back in her chair and shaded her eyes with her hand.

"The future of this realm!" she said in a low voice; "I pray the saints for it! I, who have never done England any good, would be sorry indeed to do it harm."

"You need have no fear, madam," the sage rejoined, speaking as low as she, so that the usher sent by Bedingfield, who was posted at the door, could not catch their words.

Catherine looked up quickly.

"You speak confidently," she said; "why so?"

"Your grace does well to ask," he answered gravely. "I have seen a vision, such an one as no man sees but once or twice in a lifetime, even though he is born to read the stars."

"Speak on," said the queen, as he paused.

The little circle by the fire had drawn close, all eager attention except Mistress Betty, who stood apart, angry and secretly alarmed, although she fought stoutly against the dread which beset her. At the queen's admonition, the wizard drew nearer, and stood facing the hearth, the red glow of the embers casting a lurid light on his wizened figure and a fiery glint in his great eyes. He did not seem to see the others, but recited his tale like a man in a trance.

"'Twas night," he said, "and I was in my laboratory studying the heavens. Mars was red as blood. Suddenly, before me, there was a wide ray of white light which constantly expanded, until I saw in it a marvellous flower-garden, a vast place, full of bloom and with great gates, on which were emblazoned the arms of England. Within, there was a tall white rose upon a single stem, and it shone lustrous. No one was in the garden, and without were the pope, the Emperor of the Germans, and the Queen of Hungary, while, closer to the gate, stood your grace's champion, Reginald Pole. Presently I saw a woman walking through the garden dressed in cloth of gold, with a crown on her head, and on her robes the arms of England and Spain united. She came across the garden to the white rose, and it bowed down to her; she plucked it, holding it up and looking at Pole, and then I knew her. After that, she touched the gates with the white rose and they flew open, and those without came in and kissed her. When she kneeled to receive the pope's blessing, I saw her face plainly; it was the Princess Mary."

When he ceased speaking, Catherine covered her face with her hands; the superstition of the age and her blood stirred within a naturally strong woman. After a moment, she spoke almost in a whisper.

"And the king?" she said.

"Madam, you know the northern prophecy," the wizard replied; "the decorate rose shall be slain in his mother's womb, — which means the death of one who hath offended. And she" — the speaker lowered his voice so that it was scarcely more than a whisper — "she who hath wrought this woe, her horoscope doth show a sudden and a shameful death."

"I pray it may be so!" exclaimed one of the queen's women; "may a curse light on her — may —"

"Nay, curse her not," interrupted Catherine, coldly; "the time is not far off when ye shall have great reason to pity her, yea, to commiserate her estate."

"Ay," replied the wizard, "an agony awaits her — a blood-red axe is in her destiny."

This low-spoken conversation had irritated the attendant sent by Bedingfield, and conscious that to permit it to continue would be a transgression of his orders, he came forward now and reminded Sanders that he had exceeded the limit of his visit. The queen resented the interference, and turned as if to speak in anger; but, on second thought, repented her determination, only treating the matter with her accustomed scorn.

"Tell your master," she said to the usher, "that the queen was so wonderfully entertained that she forgot her usual obedience to his orders and craves his pardon. Master Sanders, I thank you for your diverting discourse," she added to the astrologer. "I am so poor I may not even reward my entertainment; but continue, sir, to read in the stars the salvation of this realm, and so find your reward."

The wizard made his obeisance and turned to withdraw; as he did so, a tiny packet fell from under his cloak, and Mistress Betty noted that Patience set her foot upon it, making no effort to restore it to its owner. When he reached the door, Sanders turned for the last time toward the queen, and making a strange sign with his hands, bowed and withdrew.

CHAPTER VII

MISTRESS CAREW'S ALLEGIANCE

IT was dusk; the shadows were folding thickly about the gloomy walls of Kimbolton. In the queen's drawing-room Betty Carew sat alone, a solitary taper burning on the table beside her, while she mechanically turned the leaves of the illuminated missal, her thoughts being far away. The queen had been ill for some days; she was able to sit up, but kept her own chamber. Below, in the apartments of Bedingfield, were two gentlemen from the privy council, and with them, as Betty knew, the Marquis of Exeter. Something had happened; what, the young girl scarcely divined. The three visitors had arrived almost at daybreak, and at noon there had been a stormy interview in Catherine's room, from which Mistress Carew was excluded. After it was over, the queen was in more distress than Betty had ever seen her; she even wept, and called passionately for her daughter,— an unusual outbreak, followed by a season of exhaustion. She was reported now to be asleep, her three favorite attendants watching her, while the youngest of all sat like an outcast and a spy in the outer room. There had been much secret dealing of late, Betty knew, and she felt that they were careful to shut her out, ever suspicious of her motives. That day, she had heard Exeter remonstrate with Bedingfield on the mean state of the household and on the queen's poor attendance; and Sir Edmund replied that he must even obey his orders, and that as for state, he had no money, and the council allowed none to support the princess dowager.

"Poor lady!" Exeter said, "there is little need of all this watch and ward; if I be not mistaken, there cometh soon a guest which no bars shall keep out and no privy council examine."

"Ay, so it looks," Bedingfield replied, "and yet I know not; she hath been ailing long, but seems to fight her malady as steadfastly as she did the divorce."

"A gallant heart," my lord of Exeter replied, "but she will die. Her eye looks it and her dull and yellowish hue betrays it. 'T is no place here either to stir the laggard blood in her veins; she is a Spaniard, and this sharp weather suits her as little as our northern temperaments. The end of a great sorrow draweth nigh."

So spoke the marquis, and Betty, hearing him, felt a chill at her heart. The gloomy life had weighed upon her, and she fell often into meditations which were full of dim foreboding. The wizard's tale had stolen into her brain and found a lodgment there, and she dreaded something, what she knew not. Youth is fanciful, and sees either a flood of sunshine on the path or a thick cloud. While the shadows without lengthened into night, Betty sat alone; and then there was a soft footfall behind her, and Patience came to summon her to the queen. Something in the woman's face betrayed that the call was unusual, and Mistress Carew was yet more surprised when she found herself alone with Catherine, who sat propped up in her chair, a rosary in her hands and her black mantilla shading her features even more than usual. The lights were so arranged that her face was in the gloom, and it was impossible to see her expression.

"My visitors are still below, as I hear, Mistress Betty," she said quietly, "and I would ask you to do an errand for me. Here is a little packet which, I pray you, give my lord of Exeter from the queen. These gentlemen will look askance at my own poor maids, but you, my child, are in favor with the powers that be."

Betty stood a moment irresolute, her heart beating high. The hour had come for her to show herself worthy of her uncle's confidence. She could not deceive herself about the packet; it was the same which the wizard had let fall a few weeks before. She was silent, her eyes downcast.

"What ails you, mistress?" cried the queen, sharply; "have you no tongue to answer me?"

"Madam," replied Betty, her tone faltering ever so slightly, "I may not disobey my instructions."

"Your instructions!" repeated Catherine, sternly; "from whom — and when?"

Mistress Betty's cheek was scarlet. How could she speak the truth to this injured woman, although the truth was not to her own discredit? Her embarrassment carried conviction to the queen's mind, and she was passionately incensed.

"So!" she said, in her coldest and most sarcastic tone, "the dove was but the serpent in disguise. For shame! How could one so young, so seeming innocent, become a tool in

the hands of villains? Had you no woman's
heart that you could spy upon and betray a
woman — and she your queen? My God! the
very babes and sucklings are utterly corrupted,
vile traitors and heretics!"

"Madam," Betty cried, with deep resentment, "you do me bitter wrong! I am no spy,
nor would my uncle have sent me to fill so foul
an office. I cannot — nay, I will not carry
secret missives against my instructions! That
would be as deep a treason to this realm as it
would be to you did I purpose to betray you."

"You say 'I will not' to your queen?"
exclaimed Catherine, harshly; "the saints bear
witness that the time was when so saucy a
tongue would have been treason. It is well to
make fine protests, wench, but 't will be long
ere you find one so foolish as to credit them."

"For that there is no help, madam," Betty
answered firmly. "I will even tell you the
whole truth; my uncle did forbid me to carry
any secret missives, or to meddle with these
matters, since he bade me remember that the
safety of this realm was a greater matter than
the sorrows of one woman, albeit she is a
queen."

"Is a queen!" cried Catherine, catching at
the words; "thine uncle is a worthy man — an

honest man. I am still a queen, it seems, despite the universities and Cranmer! Ah, well, something remains, albeit I can be insulted by a little wench like this one."

"I do assure your grace," Betty said, "that I am heartily sorry. I would gladly do any service for your pleasure, but I owe also much to my uncle; I would not lay his head in danger."

The queen looked at her a moment in silence; something in the sincerity of the young girl's tone touched her.

"Is it, then, so dangerous to serve the Queen of England?" she asked in a strange voice.

"Madam, the Act of the Succession," began Betty; but Catherine cut her short.

"Nay," she said sharply, "speak not of these things; they poison me. Go, wench! I have no need of you — such service is of little pleasure to me."

Angry, yet touched and wounded by the queen's reproaches, Betty moved to the door, but there she paused long enough to speak once more.

"I do beseech your grace to believe me," she said gently. "I would not harm a hair of your royal head — I do indeed think that you are despitefully used, the deepest sympathy for your wrongs is in my heart."

"I believe you, Mistress Carew," the queen replied, after a pause, "but those that be not with me are altogether against me. I am weary; I pray you leave me. Though uncrowned, I may claim so much obedience. When you are older, my girl, and broken in health and spirit, I pray no fairer face may steal your husband's heart. My fate is not so uncommon that it should isolate me; rather, think I, there be many women in England who should weep for me in very sympathy. A man's heart is like a ship which is ever prone to slip its moorings; look well, mistress, when you have one, that it is stoutly anchored."

Deeply disturbed and unhappy, Betty Carew left the queen's room, and going into the gallery beyond, walked to and fro. There was something so desolate in Catherine's situation, and so merciless were her enemies, that few women could have looked upon her with indifference, and Betty's heart was not so cold as to resist the appeal. She had often wavered in her allegiance to the king's party since her arrival at Kimbolton, and being young, was far more likely to be led by her sympathies than her reason. Had Catherine possessed in a greater degree the powers of attraction, she might have won the young girl wholly to her wishes; but the unhappy queen was not rich in nature's gifts and her austerity was repellent, while her proud reserve in some degree concealed the depth of her own suffering.

Moved though Betty was, she could not bear the packet to the marquis without deliberately violating her pledges to her uncle; and bred as she had been under the new influences of the changed times, she had, too, a horror of meddling with a matter which she knew involved the safety of the realm, threatened, as it was, with a multitude of dangers. While she walked in the gallery, with a heart full of varied emotions, she heard the trampling of horses below, and running to the casement, saw the three guests riding away, and knew that, unless the queen had speedily found another messenger, it was too late.

That night Catherine was very ill, or so her maids gave out, and for two days afterwards no one saw her but her physician and her three chosen attendants. Mistress Betty was not summoned, even to perform any small office, and it touched her sharply to feel how deeply she was distrusted; but after this, there was no time for reflections, for events hurried one upon another. The queen's condition could not be concealed, and reluctant as her personal attendants were to hold intercourse with the royal officers of the household, Bedingfield was notified of the danger in which she lay.

On New Year's Day, at about six o'clock, came the queen's Spanish maid of honor, Lady Willoughby, who had been Donna Maria de Salines. Bedingfield would have refused her admittance, since she had no warrant from the king, but she pleaded with such eloquence the cold and her fatigue that she finally gained her will. Once with Catherine, the Spanish woman never left her, but administered to her comfort to the end. The day after her arrival came also Capucius, the emperor's ambassador, bearing, however, the king's permission, though he was not allowed to see the dying queen save in the presence of the royal chamberlain. Bedingfield's vigilance was defeated, however, for Catherine and Capucius spoke to each other in Spanish, a language which the royal officer understood as little as Hebrew.

Like a gloomy pageant, scene followed scene in this sorrowful drama. The weeping maid of honor, the stately ambassador, the laments of the poor, whom Catherine had ever treated with sympathy and kindness, — all these things made a sad impression on the young girl, who was a reluctant witness of the gloomy closing of a tragic life, nor was she to escape without one more trial. It was after Lady Willoughby's arrival, and Catherine being very low, every member of the household shared in the service of attendance. Although she had been tacitly exiled from the queen's presence, Betty was now called upon to go to her apartment, and, Catherine's attention being attracted by her entrance, she called her to her bedside. The queen's voice was firm, although her face bore the unmistakable signs of approaching death.

"Come hither, Mistress Carew," she said; and as Betty obeyed her summons, she turned to Lady Willoughby, who stood on the other side.

"Maria," she said, "mark you this maid? She is likely to go to court; will she not outshine some stars at Windsor?"

Lady Willoughby glanced in surprise from the queen's face to Betty's, and doubtless thinking her royal mistress wandering in mind, replied gently that the maiden was fair enough surely to shine in any court.

"Hark you, my girl," Catherine said to Betty, a rigid sternness in her face, "I die the Queen of England, the true and lawful wife of the king's grace. Forget it not."

She paused, and there was no response.

Betty Carew, standing beside her with tears in her eyes, had no words to answer her, and, like Lady Willoughby, believed that her mind wandered.

"Kneel down," said the queen, solemnly; and both Betty and Donna Maria mechanically obeyed. The room was still, a dim light crept in at the windows, the tapers flared behind the dark canopy of the bed. The attendants stood back in the shadows. Catherine raised herself a little on her pillows and lifted her hands, clasping them before her; her eyes shone with a strange luster in the deadly whiteness of her face.

"His holiness the pope," she said in a clear voice, "hath declared my marriage valid. I am the wife of Henry, King of England. I do call upon you all to witness; this maid also, who is not of us, — I die the queen! And I do solemnly charge you, at the peril of your souls, to bear in mind that the king has one true and legitimate daughter, the Lady Mary, Princess Royal of England and heiress to the throne."

She remained a moment with her hands lifted, her face growing more rigid. There was the sound of suppressed sobbing in the room. The queen's arms fell heavily and she sank back in a deathlike swoon.

CHAPTER VIII

THE KING'S MESSENGERS

THE seventh of January had passed, the Queen of England had been carried to her last resting-place at Peterborough Abbey, and that other Queen of England rejoiced at Greenwich. The knot in the affairs of state, which had set emperor and king and pope at variance, was severed. The unhappy woman, whose troubles had shaken a throne, would henceforth seek only the crown immortal. She was gone, and the winter sunlight shone brightly on the walls of Kimbolton, as if to exorcise the phantoms of that sorrow which had broken a royal heart. Within, there was desolation in those rooms where the queen had held her little levees, and which now seemed peopled with ghosts. The long story of her passionate struggle to maintain her own and her daughter's claims seemed written upon the walls. Every footstep echoed sadly in the vacant galleries, every corner was full of shadows. Doors stood open, articles of wearing apparel, bits of unfinished embroidery lay on the floor, tapers that had burned low and sputtered in the sockets left a forlorn remnant of congealed wax upon the candlesticks; the great hearths were gray with ashes and the dead logs had fallen from the fire-dogs. The chill wind swept down the chimneys, roared and moaned at the casements, shrieking around the castle as if to tear its way within and sweep away the last vestige of the dead woman's presence. She had died like a queen, calmly and with unfaltering courage; even in death her claim to royalty remained, and here it was recognized; no man at Kimbolton thought of her save as the queen.

Her household was on the point of dissolution. The king's messengers had come down from London, — the crown lawyer, Dr. Rich, some gentlemen of the Privy Council, Sir William Carew and Master Simon Raby, — and there followed much stir and excitement. Catherine's effects were being examined, her maids separated, her servants discharged. The royal officers were busied with many matters and were peremptory and exacting; messengers ran to and fro, the courtyard was full of horses, the hall crowded with attendants. There was all the bustle attendant upon the final breaking up of such an establishment. On one side were the pale and sorrowful faces of the late queen's personal followers, who sincerely mourned the loss of a good and charitable mistress; on the other were the hard, shrewd countenances of the king's commissioners, intent only on fulfilling an unpleasant duty, and not a little relieved that the cause of so much dissension, and such a menace to the peace of the realm, was finally removed. It was a curious scene, and one to teach a lesson in the futility of all earthly ambitions, the fleeting pride of all worldly honors.

In a window recess of the hall stood Mistress Carew, cloaked and muffled for a journey, and at her side was Master Raby. The two stood looking down into the crowded court and talking in low tones. She was to ride with her uncle to Greenwich upon some errand, — what she knew not, but she had much curiosity to learn, nursing a hope that she was to have a glimpse of the court. However, she kept her own counsel, and listened with a serious face to the talk of her companion.

"This matter has been a grief to the king's grace," he said, speaking too low for any ears but those of his fair auditor; "I would not have believed that he could be so moved thereat.   'T is said that when he read her last letter, he wept and lamented her."

"Do men always weep so late?" asked Mistress Betty, coldly, her bright eyes turning scornfully upon the speaker; "forsooth, sir, I would rather be treated with more kindness while I lived than so lamented in death."

Master Raby was taken by surprise. The sudden sharpness of her tone, her expressive glance, came after a passive attitude of attention.

"And so would I," he said heartily; "yet surely, mistress, a late repentance is better than none."

"I would have none of it," retorted his companion, with disdain; "had I been treated like this queen, I would never have written so loving a letter to the king, no, not I! Poor lady! she was too meek, or, perhaps, too good a Christian. A little more spirit would have made him mend his ways in time. I do think that never was a woman who deserved more pity."

"There are some who would call your speech treasonable, Mistress Carew," Raby said, but his eyes were full of amusement as he looked at the flushed, angry face before him; "speak not too warmly in this lady's cause before other witnesses, I pray you."

"Sir, she was hardly used," declared Betty, stoutly; "I would say so if you were the king's highness."

"And if you said it with that tone and look, I do wager he would pardon you," exclaimed the other, smiling; "indeed, I believe the king has known some hours of regret. At least, he has ordered the court into deep mourning; but the queen — " Raby shrugged his shoulders and laughed.

"Queen Anne Boleyn? What of her?" asked the young girl, a certain scorn in her fresh voice.

"Queen Anne and all her ladies are wearing yellow," Raby said, "and a curious spectacle it is. They do say she has remarked that she only regretted that the Lady Catherine made so good an end."

"'T is a shame," cried Betty; "she is but a harlequin to dress so. This queen was a good woman, and so deserves all respect."

"It is reported that she plotted with the Spaniards against this realm," remarked her companion, watching her face.

Mistress Betty flushed rose-red; the thought of the hidden packet came to her mind. This charge she could neither parry nor deny, but her pity for the dead woman outlived her horror of treasonable practices. She lifted her head haughtily.

"And so would I, if I had been born a Spaniard and so suffered at the hands of the English," she declared; "it was only human."

At this Master Raby laughed outright. The dead queen's champion was irresistible in her youth and beauty and that fearlessness which was her birthright. He drew her out, delighted at the frankness and spirit of her speech; he was a courtier, sated, too, with the follies and the pleasures of that gilded life, a much admired gallant, a favorite with the ladies of Queen Anne, but here was a fresh experience and he found it irresistible. Meanwhile, Mistress Betty, whose nature was cast in a sharper outline, who saw things with the uncompromising eyes of youth, scarcely detected his enjoyment of the little dialogue.

"Truly, it would be dangerous to offend you, Mistress Carew," he said, still laughing softly; "but take you no thought of that other aspect of the affair? The peril to the state, the sharp necessity of loyalty when the kingdom is in peril, and the Bishop of Rome would bring us all to disaster if he could. Has he not caused his bulls to be nailed up on every church door in Flanders, and held us up as a legitimate prey for the faithful? Was it not wrong for this princess who had been a queen of England to desire the desolation of this realm?"

Betty stood a moment thinking, biting her lip and pressing her hands together. After a moment she looked up into Master Raby's amused eyes, and her cheeks burned.

"I believe that I should have done worse," she cried, "if any one had dared to so insult me."

"Happily, Mistress Carew, no man would ever attempt it," said her companion, softly; "your face is too fair to be so soon forgotten. This poor lady was older than the king and never handsome, nor did his grace ever love her."

"More shame to him!" said Betty, sharply; "she was his wife."

Master Raby laughed again. "Ah, Mistress Carew," he said, "you must talk with my lord of Canterbury! Must a man love a woman because she is his wife?"

Betty gave him a swift, sidelong glance. "Sir," she said demurely, "I know nothing of a man's heart, but I have heard that it is like a mirror and reflects every face that looks in it, only that, unlike a mirror, you may never break it."

"You are young to be so cruel," her companion cried, delighted, "and verily, mistress, you will find many hearts do break before you make one blest."

"You are a courtier, Master Raby," she replied, "and have a readier wit than mine, but you can never make me admire the woman who broke this good queen's heart."

"Nay," he answered softly, "it is you, fair Mistress Betty, who will make me do your bidding, not I you."

At this, she blushed the color of a fresh June rose, being as yet unused to fine speeches, and Master Raby stood looking at her, thinking her fairer than any beauty of the court, when Sir William Carew came up and cut the conversation short.

"Come, niece," he said briefly, "we ride at once. And you, Raby, will you bear us company or no?"

"I thank you, yes, Sir William," he replied with alacrity; "all is in readiness; the horses at the door, and my man, whom you admired so much, in attendance."

"The knave will hang," rejoined Carew, grimly. "Come, Betty, there is no time for fine speeches or farewells. I must set out for Greenwich without delay, and you go with me."

"Whither, uncle?" said Betty, quickly; "surely not to the court?"

"And wherefore surely not?" asked Sir William, testily.

"I know not what you will do with me there," his niece said softly.

"You go to the queen's grace, my girl," Carew replied grimly, "if she will have you."

Master Raby smiled and glanced at Betty.

"'T is come, Mistress Carew," he whispered, as he helped her to the saddle. "I pray thee tell the king thy mind."

"And so I will, if he asks me, Master Raby," declared Betty, with spirit, "and, mayhap, it will do him good. A bitter truth is ofttimes wholesome medicine."

CHAPTER IX

IT was a cold and dreary night in London, and through the mist the lights of the inn blinked like great yellow eyes. Within the public room there was much jovial entertainment. It was well filled with guests, some drinking, others playing at dice, and a few eating belated suppers. It was an establishment much patronized by men of fashion, and the assembly was of a less motley character than that of most public houses. Two or three young gentlemen in velvets and satins, with ruffs of fine lace and jewel-hilted weapons, threw dice at one table, while at another sat a stately personage in black velvet, perusing some parchments with the assistance of a shrewd-faced, deferential companion, the one having the appearance of an eminent jurist and the other being, no doubt, his clerk. At yet another table sat some travellers, whose fur-trimmed garments and full wallets suggested wealthy merchants. Mine host bustled about with a rubicund and smiling countenance, attended by several servants and a rosy-faced Hebe bearing the wine cups and glasses. The innkeeper had the air of one who felt his pockets filling and his reputation growing at the same moment; a state of bliss seldom attained except by those who minister to the inner man, the way to a man's purse, as well as to his heart, being through his stomach. There was a buzz of conversation, the rattle of dice, the click of glasses, but it was yet too early for the potations to take effect, and there was perfect decorum upon all sides.

Beyond this room, which was for public entertainment, there was a smaller one, opening into it by a low door, in one panel of which was a little window, a mere aperture, and through this the occupant of the private apartment might survey the outer room with slight risk of being discovered, — a convenient peephole, where mine host could spy upon his guests at pleasure. It was a small place and nearly filled by a table and two chairs. On opposite sides of this table were seated now two men engaged in earnest conversation. The tapers burning between them shed their light on the faces of both. To the right sat a little man clad in a russet cloak, the wizard Sanders; on the left, was quite a different person.   The stranger was tall and well made, fully forty years of age, and with a face that, while it was handsome in a coarse, bold fashion, was also rather sinister in expression, and with a sensual mouth and chin.   He was very dark, his hair, already touched with gray on the temples, accentuating the olive tint of his complexion, and his eyes being light gray, the effect was not altogether pleasing.   Yet his features were fine and only marred by the scar of a sword-cut, which almost obliterated his left eyebrow.   His dress was of the richest, his cloak covered with gold embroidery, and the green satin doublet slashed with white brocade, while his hands, white and soft as a woman's, were jewelled.   His embroidered gloves lay on the table beside his rapier, the hilt of which was beautiful in workmanship and glistened with precious stones.   He sat with his elbow on the table, leaning his head upon his hand and listening to the wizard, who was speaking in low tones, though no ear could hear him but his companion's.

"The trump card is gone," he said calmly, his keen eyes watching the other narrowly, "but we have yet the Lady Mary."

"Tush!" ejaculated his friend, "what of that?   'T is said the king may have a boy."

The wizard shook his head with a slow smile.

"Never," he said composedly. "Henry has ill luck with his men children. This gay lady is falling out of favor, too; another star riseth yonder."

"Ay, so they say," retorted the other, gloomily; "but the change is like to bring us small comfort, if it comes. We shall have no merry time until we get the base blood out of the council; yonder hell-hound tracks us by the scent. I would he were begging again at the door of Master Friskyball."

"Look you, Sir Barton," rejoined the wizard, "my lord privy seal is more like to pull you by the pate than you him;" and Sanders laughed with wicked amusement as he eyed his listener. "Bear in mind the fate of Ap Ryce, and be not too forward. Cromwell is beating the bush for traitors, and if he finds you," again the little man laughed unpleasantly, "a short shrift and your head would grin on London Bridge."

"And if it does, why, curse you, so shall yours, you evil spirit!" Sir Barton cried with a fierce outbreak of temper, the mocking tone of Sanders having struck him like a goad.

"Pshaw!" retorted the wizard, coolly, "why

fall out so swiftly? I do not fear you, man, or any one. Think you I am so great a fool as to play this game and lose? Who was it that dealt secretly with the Nun of Kent?"

He was watching the other with malicious enjoyment; noting the start of amazement and fear, he leaned back and laughed with a fiendish delight that enraged the dark man still more.

"You are a fiend!" Sir Barton said between his set teeth. "I tell you, Sanders, if you betray me, I will send you to the devil before you can grin that hellish grin of yours twice."

Undaunted 'either by the threats or the furious aspect of the man, the little wizard laughed with apparently intense amusement.

"Come, come, Sir Barton," he said mockingly, "sit, man; 't is not in your horoscope that you should murder me. I find you useful," he added in a changed tone, "and you, I believe, have found me so. Waste no more threats upon me; I fear you as little as the snake that I keep in my chamber, and whose fangs I drew long since, although he is still excellent to scare women and children. Save your excessive fury until such time as the Spaniards and the Irish come to set my Lady Mary on the throne, when we shall live right merrily again and this same king shall die as did the man-queller Richard."

"If we die not first and rot for our part in it," retorted his companion, sullenly, having recovered his composure.

"You are not wont to be so downcast, Sir Barton," the astrologer remarked, "nor need be. Cromwell's new notion of parish registers is working for us among the vulgar; they believe it but a design to find the means of taxing them, and that they shall no longer eat white meat or fowls without paying dues to the king's grace. More than half this realm is with us; and of the peers, from his grace of Norfolk down, I think they love not the new order of things, nor do they like the rule of the cloth-shearer's son."

"Ay," replied his companion, "we are like to have Lord Hussey and Darcy, besides the Nevilles and the faction of the White Rose. 'T is certain we can raise the northern counties when the time is ripe, and then, the devil take me if I be not the first to thrust a sword in Cromwell's belly!" He rose as he spoke and took up his weapon, handling it as if he loved the thought of the use for which he intended it.

"The devil is very like to have thee, friend," retorted the wizard, smiling; "but hark! what stir is that without?   Some new-comers are in the courtyard."

Sir Barton walked to the door, and pushing back the slide which had closed the window in the panel, he looked into the public room.

"It is a party of travellers," he said carelessly; and then changing his tone, "'t is Sir William Carew of Mohun's Ottery, that young coxcomb Raby, and a woman — a handsome one at that," he added with an oath.

The wizard, who was watching him as a cat watches a mouse, smiled maliciously.

"Is it a young maid?" he asked, "tall and fine-shaped as Diana, with red cheeks and great brown eyes that sparkle and change at every glance, and with hair like the raven's wing?"

"You have made a fair description," the tall man replied, "but, by heaven, you cannot do her justice! She is muffled up, but I saw her face as she came in, and she's a beauty."

The wizard laughed again so wickedly that Sir Barton turned on him.

"Thou grinning devil!" he said; "what is sticking in thy gullet?"

"'T is retribution, sir," Sanders said coolly; "you discarded a penniless betrothed. Penniless she is, but marvellous fair."

An expression of amazement tinged with superstitious dread came over his companion's face.

"How in the fiend's name do you track men out?" he asked.

The wizard pointed upward. "The stars, noble sir," he answered meekly; "my poor art."

"Who is this beauty?" Sir Barton demanded sharply; "you know well enough."

"Ay, I know," replied Sanders, calmly; "no velvet-tempered kitten, either. 'T is Sir William's niece, the daughter of that rake, Sir Thomas."

Sir Barton, uttering an exclamation of profane surprise, opened the door and walked into the public room, leaving the wizard alone in the little closet.

Sir William Carew was talking with the host, while in a retired corner, near the entrance, stood Mistress Betty, and beside her, Master Raby. The young girl's mantle was muffled about her shoulders, but her hood had fallen back a little, revealing enough of the face beneath to draw the attention of many of the guests. But she was so busily engaged in talking to her companion that she was unconscious of the admiring glances cast in her direction. A servant had brought some hot drinks for the party and would have set a table for them, but this Sir William refused, saying that he was pressed for time. Sir Barton walked up to him, to be received in no very friendly fashion, Carew's greeting indicating plainly that he desired no company upon the road. After an ineffectual attempt at conversation, the other drew back haughtily, but stood watching Mistress Betty, until the persistency of his gaze attracted the attention of her cavalier, who moved between, giving the offender a hard glance that was intended to teach him better manners. It was returned in kind, the two men looking defiance at each other over the heads of those who sat at the tables. In a few moments, however, Sir William led his party out again to resume their journey. As Raby helped Betty into the saddle, he saw the tall man standing on the threshold of the inn.

"Your uncle's friend must needs follow still, Mistress Carew," he remarked; "the impudent knave never took his eyes from your face; he deserves chastisement."

Betty laughed softly. "Nay, sir," she said in an amused tone, "surely the curiosity of a stranger is no great offence."

"I should be the happier for laying my sword across his shoulders, for all that," retorted her companion.

The young girl glanced at the dark figure on the threshold with new interest; she was not without enjoyment of the admiration that she was beginning to receive. One of the stable-boys came running with a lighted torch to help Sir William to adjust his saddle. Master Raby bent forward and took Betty's bridle-rein.

"Let me guide thy beast, Mistress Carew," he said.

But she heard him not. The light of the torch flared full on the figure in the door. Even through the mist, which hung between like a thin veil, she saw the glittering dress, the dark face, and the scar across the left eye-brow.

A moment afterwards, Carew's party rode out of the yard.

"Uncle, uncle," cried Mistress Betty, in a strange voice, "who was yonder dark man that spoke with you?"

"'T was Henge, Sir Barton Henge," said Carew; "but what is that to thee, wench?"

CHAPTER X

It was an hour before noon and the gates of Greenwich palace stood open. A crowd of attendants and gentlemen ushers were assembled in the anterooms, and the royal guards lined the halls. The king and queen were holding a levee, and, as usual, there was a great concourse of people, and the river was dotted with barges, wherries and all sorts of water-craft.

Sir William Carew had just landed at the water-stairs, opposite the main entrance, and was helping his niece to alight from the boat. They were accompanied by Simon Raby, and all three were dressed in the elaborate fashion of the court. Sir William's suit was of richer hue and finer velvet than that which he had worn upon the road; his cloak was shorter and more gayly lined, while his ruffles were of the finest lace. The younger man was even more richly attired in maroon velvet, heavily embroidered, and slashed with gold-colored satin;

and he had a face and figure that would scarcely pass unnoticed in any garb. But neither he nor Sir William had fully realized the beauty of their young companion until they saw her, no longer clad in mourning, but wearing a rich gown that her uncle had provided for the occasion. It was of gray velvet, with a yoke of rose-colored satin edged with fur, the inner sleeves being of the same tint, as well as the facings of the flowing ones, which came to the elbow. The gray velvet skirt was looped up on one side, showing a farthingale of pink satin trimmed with lace. The colors and the richness of the costume suited well her glowing complexion and dark hair, and she made a charming picture. As they passed through the crowded anterooms, she attracted universal attention, but moved on unconscious of it. The painful contrast between the splendor of these lofty rooms and the dreary ones at Kimbolton struck her generous mind with its full force. Here she saw gay courtiers, beautiful women, and all the magnificence of a court, and she had just come from the presence of death. Young though she was, she had too strong a character to be moved to forgetfulness by the brilliance of the change. Catherine had not won her affection, but she had inspired her with a feeling of profound sympathy. There was another shadow also on the mood of Mistress Betty; the wizard's strange statement had haunted her secret thoughts ever since it was made, and the sight of the scarred stranger at the tavern disquieted her. Again and again she told herself it was but folly, yet she could not put it from her mind; and she was strangely depressed as she walked beside her uncle through the crowd of courtiers, who gave place only to gaze again at the lovely face and erect form of the young girl. Behind her came Master Raby, secretly admiring her and comparing her fresh beauty with the charms of the gay dames who smiled at him as he passed. At the entrance to the presence-chamber, they were halted by the usher; but only for a moment, a few words from Carew gaining them admittance. The room opened into the gallery with great folding-doors, and through these the little party passed and found themselves in a lofty apartment beyond. To Betty, the splendid gayety of the scene was almost bewildering, and she paused a moment on the threshold, looking about her with perfect unconsciousness of the attention that she immediately attracted. The appearance of so beautiful a young woman standing almost alone in the doorway created in a moment a little sensation.

The room was crowded with lords and gentlemen, peers and peeresses; the glitter of gold, the sheen of satin and brocade, the sparkle of jewels, made a scene of varied beauty. Here were handsome men and the loveliest of England's women; on one side stood the stately figure of a prelate, on the other some foreign ambassador; here was a gay court gallant, yonder a reverend sage. Not far from the door stood the king surrounded by his favored nobles. He was, at this time, growing very stout, but still retained much of the fine appearance of his earlier manhood. His dress of velvet and brocade was rich with gold embroidery and his breast sparkled with jewels. His great size and the natural majesty of his bearing made him an imposing figure, but he possessed a frank and cordial address which won him many friends, even in those days of treason and discontent. Beyond him, almost in the center of the room, was Queen Anne Boleyn.

Mistress Betty had but one thought, and that was of this queen; and as soon as she had made her curtsy to the king, she passed on to greet Anne, with feelings of mingled curiosity and resentment for the sake of the dead

Catherine. Anne Boleyn was standing in the midst of her ladies, and yellow was the prevailing color of their costumes. The queen, a young and beautiful woman, appeared as lovely as ever even in that hour of unwomanly triumph. The perfect oval of her face, the brilliance of her eyes and the beauty of her complexion had made her the star of Catherine's court, and she was still lovely, although it seemed to many that she looked both ill and disturbed. She was dressed in yellow brocade with a train of cloth of gold trimmed with ermine, a coronet of jewels resting on her flowing curls, for she wore her hair frequently falling loose over her shoulders. She knew that Betty Carew had been in attendance at Kimbolton, and received her coldly, although with courtesy, as if she was at once displeased at the thought of her late service, and willing to win her to her own cause.

The presentation was over in a few moments and Betty was led out of the royal circle by her uncle, who conducted her to the other side of the room. He took her to a group by one of the windows, and Betty found that he was introducing her to some stranger before she had yet put the queen from her thoughts.

"My Lady Crabtree," he said, "this is the

niece of whom I wrote you. Will you take so great a charge, albeit not an uncomely one ? "

"Thou art a fool, William," retorted a sharp voice, "to bring the wench hither."

Betty Carew looked up in amazement and saw an old woman standing by her uncle; a woman, but one with so manly an air that the young girl was not a little amused. Lady Crabtree was tall and broad-shouldered, with a large waist and a flat chest, being one of those women whose figures are flattened out, with a great width from side to side. She had a masculine face with a large, hooked nose and keen black eyes; the face of a woman who had inherited not only her father's traits of character, but his full set of features, even to the strong, broad teeth. Her snow-white hair was put back under a large and ugly headdress, and her garments, though rich, were neither stylish nor elegant; and though an old woman, it was apparent that she would have been more at ease in doublet and hose than in a farthingale. She was regarding Betty with a shrewd but not unkindly glance, which seemed to comprehend not only the girl's great beauty, but also her present frame of mind.

"What is thy name, child?" this singular

person asked; "Carew, I know, forsooth, but it must have a handle to it."

"My name is Betty Carew," the young girl answered, smiling, "and I trust I may not make my uncle sorry for bringing me to Greenwich."

"If you do not, Mistress Betty, it will not be the fault of your face," retorted Lady Crabtree, calmly. "What say you, Mistress Wyatt, is not my cousin Carew a fool to bring such wares to such a market?"

At this, Betty's face flushed crimson, and she raised her head haughtily, but before she could speak, a richly gowned gentlewoman, who stood beside her new acquaintance, replied.

"Nay, Lady Crabtree," she said, smiling, "Sir William has shown his usual discretion and kindness to bring his niece to see the world, and I am sure that so discreet a maid will take no harm from the contact."

"You are a liar, Wyatt," the old woman retorted, laughing; "that is why I love you. To know how to lie gracefully, and at the right moment, is one of the most charming accomplishments and one of the rarest, albeit lying is more frequent than dying. There is the substance of a couplet for one of the court singers; I was born a poet, but am like to die unknown for such. Well, William," she added, turning again to Carew, "this wench is to be my charge, then?"

"Ay, if you will have her, madam," he answered; "for a while, at least. They want her at court, and I can scarcely make her a charge of any one more fit to guard her than my Lady Crabtree."

"I am a dragon then, William," the old woman said, with her queer smile, which was not mirthful; "so be it. I will take care that no wolf shall chew up this lamb. She shall have good watching, though I think the wench is no fool."

"Madam," said Betty, coldly, "I come here only at my uncle's will; I would rather, and it pleased him, stay at Mohun's Ottery."

"It would please me well enough, fair niece," Carew answered gravely, "but there be others, and I would fain do my duty by you and them. Therefore you will stay with my good cousin, Lady Crabtree, until I see fit to take you home."

Mistress Betty bit her lip. This settled the matter for her, but it wounded her pride to be a dependent on her uncle's bounty and be tossed about at his will. Nor did her new guardian attract her. However, she could only submit to fate, and she was compelled to remain standing by Lady Crabtree while Sir William mingled with the company, where he found many acquaintances.

"Do not take it to heart, wench," the old woman remarked, her shrewd eyes detecting Betty's sensations; "you will love this place too well erelong to leave it. 'T is no spot for any girl to mope in, and you are not of the moping kind, I think. Dost know any of the great people here to-day?"

"None but the king and queen," Betty replied, turning her eyes upon the gay scene, which was almost bewildering to one who had lived the retired life that she had.

"Poor child! 't is dull to know so little of the great folk here," said Mrs. Wyatt, who still stood by Lady Crabtree; "yonder is my lord of Canterbury, and beside him, Master Latimer, whom the queen has made Bishop of Worcester. Ay, the queen," she repeated, in reply to Betty's questioning glance; "he was her grace's chaplain, and she so wrought upon the king that he is a bishop; and because he spoke hard truth to her. And that goodly youth to the left there is his grace of Richmond."

"Ay, and 't is a pity that the king can get no other son so fair," said Lady Crabtree, sharply; "'t is a punishment."

"How can you tell what may happen in a short while?" retorted Mrs. Wyatt, with emphasis.

"No boy," said the old woman, calmly; "if we have much more ill luck, 't will be the King of Scots."

"They will nab thee as a traitor yet, if thy tongue wags so free, my lady," said Mrs. Wyatt, with a startled glance about her; but her odd companion only laughed grimly.

"Look there, Mistress Betty," she added in a moment; "'t is our relative, the master of horse, Nicholas Carew, and yonder is his grace of Exeter and that pretty boy, Courtenay. What would you say, Mistress Wyatt, if I prophesied that he would be a king of England?"

"Hold your tongue, madam, or surely you will lose your ears," replied Mrs. Wyatt, but smiled at her companion's manner.

"They can but roast me at the best, as they did the poor folks from Holland who held such queer notions, which were doubtless no better or sounder for the cooking," returned Lady Crabtree, laughing harshly. "Look you, Wyatt, they would have treated Latimer as they did these Anabaptists, and now he is a bishop. Presently they will make me a duchess for my sound policy."

Mrs. Wyatt, however, did not heed her; she was looking eagerly at a group across the room.

"There is Jane Seymour," she said quickly, "and she is radiant to-day."

"And will be more so presently," remarked the old woman, calmly; "my lord of Canterbury can make this matter straight, and the Bishop of Rome will nail no bull upon the doors of Flemish churches."

"I pray you speak less idly, madam," Mrs. Wyatt said, offended; "I love the queen's grace, as you know."

"And so do I," exclaimed Lady Crabtree; and then aside to Betty, "Mistress Wyatt is a fool, my girl; yonder beauty, Jane Seymour, is like to be a queen, and I mistake not. Mercy on us! can you look for such faithfulness in the king's grace when other men be weather-cocks?"

As she spoke, there was a movement in the group near by; it separated, and the stranger of the inn came up to where Betty and her strange chaperon were standing. He bowed low over Lady Crabtree's hand, speaking a few words to her in an undertone.

"'T is my cousin's niece," the old woman replied in her outspoken way. "Mistress

Betty Carew, here is a gentleman who craves to be presented to you: Sir Barton Henge."

Although the tall stranger turned to her with a smile upon his handsome dark face, Betty felt an instinctive repulsion. As she made him a curtsy in response to his profound bow, she looked up, and saw behind him Simon Raby. In an instant relief and welcome leaped into her eyes, and Henge seeing it, turned sharply to confront the other man, and both looked defiance at each other.

"Sir, you jostled me," Henge said haughtily.

"You crowded in my way," replied Raby, with disdain; "give place, I am a friend of this lady's!"

"Find room as you may," retorted Henge, sharply; "I will not budge an inch."

"Until I make you," said Raby, coldly. "You choose a strange place for a brawl, sir, but 't is worthy of you."

"Upon my word, this is fine talk in the king's presence!" exclaimed old Lady Crabtree, laughing bitterly; "have done, I will have none of this! 'T is too soon to quarrel for a child's pretty face. Master Raby, conduct my ward out of this crowded spot; and you, Sir Barton, stay with me; I would speak with you."

Passing Henge with a cold look of contempt, Simon Raby took Betty away across the room, and then the strange old woman turned upon her companion, who stood scowling.

"Look you, Sir Barton," she said in her hard tone of command; "I know you well and I will have no sword-thrusts with yonder boy."

"That young rake — " began Henge, fiercely.

"And what are you, sir?" she exclaimed, and laughed so harshly that even he winced a little. "Listen to me, Henge; this beauty — this young Mistress Carew — is penniless, and will have none of my wealth either. You want no such lady love as this, and need make no wry faces about it. If you behave as becomes your birth and station, you may even come and go at pleasure in my house, where, I think, you would come if you could. But hark ye, Barton; if I catch you at any of your devil tricks, I 'll have your ears off. Nay, scowl not, man; an old woman like me has naught to fear from you, and I know too much for you to brave me. Ah, I thought I saw you wince. Farewell, sir; here comes his grace of Suffolk, and 't would kill me if I could not ask him to weep with me for the princess dowager; 't is evident his grief sets well upon his stomach;" and she turned to greet the nobleman with a grim smile of enjoyment in the prospect.

Meanwhile Sir Barton Henge stood discomfited, staring across the room at Betty and her cavalier with a face of fury. A man of violent temper, his first impulse was to engage in an open brawl, but his better judgment told him that an attempt to chastise Raby for his insolence would only end in his own arrest in the king's presence. So he was forced to content himself with the reflection that when a better opportunity presented itself, he would make good use of it.

Across the room Master Raby had forgotten him in looking at the fair face of Mistress Betty, for 't is love that makes the world go round.

CHAPTER XI

THUS a great change came into Betty Carew's life. After her introduction to the court at Greenwich, Sir William formally placed her in the charge of his eccentric relative and went back alone to Mohun's Ottery. The young girl, left thus among strangers, endeavored to adapt herself to their ways as she had before taken up existence at her uncle's house. Deep in her heart were hidden wounded pride and a feeling of desolation. She was poor and felt herself but a toy in the hands of her wealthier relations, and she was alone amidst a throng of strangers. She had not a nature which repines; the harder elements of resolution and reserve grew faster in her heart than impulses of love and happiness. She found her new life far more full of interest and event than any she had ever known. Her guardian was so strange and active an old woman that she alone furnished no little entertainment to an observer. My Lady Wildrick Crabtree, as she was called, was the daughter of Lord Wildrick of Wildrick Hall at Deptford; her Christian name was Zenobia, but she was rarely called by it. She married, late in life, Lord Crabtree, who promptly died, as the husbands of such women always do. He was poor, but from her father Lady Crabtree inherited a large property, as she was an only child. It had been said of her mother that, having borne Zenobia, she could do no more in this world or the next. Yet Lady Crabtree was a woman of strong intellect, keen wit, and an untiring energy, and was more sought after than any woman of her age in London. Every man's business was her business; she knew all the gossip of the court; she knew all the miseries of the poor, and she was quick to right a wrong and to take up the cause of the oppressed. She could be in the saddle all day and show no fatigue, although she had passed seventy-five; a litter was ever scorned by her, and she walked miles through the muddy roads to aid the sick or destitute. Time she counted as of great value; no hour could be wasted; and so as to be out early in the morning, it was no uncommon thing for her to have her tirewoman arrange her white hair, of which she had a quantity, over night. At such seasons, her ladyship slept with her head propped up, that the great superstructure might not be injured. Her boots were all made heavy and clumsy, after the fashion of those worn by men, and her feet being large, she had the tread of a man. The strength of her wrist and fist had been rated high, since she knocked down the largest man upon the street in a group that laughed at her mannish stride. A valiant protector she was for any young woman, and as she came to know Mistress Betty, she took a fancy to her, so that this strangely assorted couple lived very peacefully together.

In the early part of February, when Queen Anne's illness cast a gloom over the court, Lady Crabtree retired for a while to her house at Deptford, where she held a little court of her own. Wildrick Hall was a great house of stone, built by the Normans and prepared for defence, its battlements being heavy and its windows little more than arrow-headed slits in the thick walls. Within, the household was like that of Mohun's Ottery, upon a smaller scale, and many people were daily fed under the hospitable roof. The old gentlewoman ruling with a rod of iron, and knowing well every detail of the house, from the kitchen to the banquet hall, was something of a terror to her servants and attendants. In her own domain she was judge and jury, and no man dared gainsay her will; while she drove the women like a flock of startled chickens cackling as they fled pell-mell before my lady's tongue, a scourge which she was quick to supplement with a blow. She was full of great oaths as any man, and knew how to hurl them at the ears of an offender; yet she had, too, a large sympathy for the unfortunate and a keen judgment of men. In this household Mistress Carew, finding her place beside its mistress, was often diverted by her strange ways. Although there were always many guests, it often happened that these two ate together, while at the lower end of the large hall were long tables for the others.

One wintry day, early in February, Lady Crabtree and Betty sat at breakfast It was seven in the morning, my lady's hour for breaking her fast, and all the tables were set with tapers which flared in the gloom, only a little light creeping in through the narrow windows. Betty's fresh face and brilliant coloring made a sharp contrast to the hook-nosed, strong countenance of the old woman, whose white hair, dressed over night, was nearly concealed by a great coif of yellow velvet. She wore a gown of gay brocade, the tight body, full sleeves, and huge farthingale being in the style first introduced by Queen Catherine. At her waist, on one side, hung a heavy bunch of keys, and on the other she wore a dagger. A fur-lined mantle was thrown over her shoulders, and was needed, for the sharp wind poured in at many crevices and swept through the hall in gusts. She was a marvellous figure, her spreading skirts, full sleeves, and huge headdress making her seem twice her natural size, which was above that of woman. She performed her trencher duties like a man, and a hungry one. On the table was set a chine of beef, and with this, for the two women, a quart of ale and a pint of wine with a square loaf of bread. It was well known that the salting tubs were numerous at Wildrick Hall at Michaelmas, and the stores of beef and mutton as great as any in the land; for my lady was one who lived well and drank well, as her father had before her, and ever quarrelled with the statute of the third Edward, which regulated the diet of both rich and poor. No man should be served "with more than two courses," said the law, "and each mess of two sorts of victuals at the utmost, be it flesh or fish, with the common sorts of pottage, without sauce or any other sorts of victuals."

My Lady Crabtree had received a letter from Mrs. Wyatt the previous day, and she read from it to Betty as she ate her breakfast, making her own comments upon it in her usual fashion.

"The queen recovers slowly from her illness and is in sore distress of mind at the loss of her boy, so says Mistress Wyatt," remarked the old woman; "like enough, there be other causes for her sorrow and rumors be true."

"You mean the king's fancy is caught by another?" asked Betty, quietly.

"Ay, that is the talk," Lady Crabtree rejoined. "Wyatt is too close to the queen to speak of it, but I have my information from a sure hand. They do say that my Lady Anne surprised him making love to the little Seymour. The queen came suddenly upon them; Jane sat on the king's knee, looking as demure as ever. 'T is said this brought Anne to her present case; and that the king's grace is furious at the loss of a boy."

"I wonder if she — the queen — thinks now of Queen Catherine," remarked Betty, thoughtfully; "poor lady! she bore enough from this same Anne Boleyn."

"Yet the statesmen would have us believe that the king does all this because he would have a boy to leave to rule in this realm," said Lady Crabtree, cutting the beef with a free stroke of her knife. "'T is an excellent excuse to marry a young wife to cheat the King of Scots. There be others that would rejoice to find a King of Scots in a like case, I doubt not."

"Yet the succession is a serious matter," said Betty, smiling; "I have heard my uncle speak of it with deep concern."

"Serious enough," retorted the old woman, grimly. "My Lady Salisbury is busy hatching an egg of conspiracy, if I mistake not; and there is Lord Hussey, who but lately had charge of the Lady Mary, a man who knows not the color of his own shirt from morn till evening. As for Reginald Pole, he fancies himself a pope already, and has thrown filth enough upon the king and will endeavor to pull down his grace, albeit he owes him much. 'T is a lovely muddle, and my lord privy seal is as much hated as the devil. As for this queen, she has put away from her, by some misfortune, the Duke of Norfolk, her uncle, while his grace of Suffolk hates her. As for Percy, whom she loved, he is like to be of more harm than help to her. 'T is the devil's pot and he is here to brew it. Ah, what have we here, Bronson?" This to a servant who stood near her.

At the moment there was a hubbub at the other end of the great apartment. The members of the household who were eating at the lower tables rose and peered over each other's shoulders, while at the door was heard the sound of a dispute. Lady Crabtree stood up and struck the table with the handle of her knife, her whole manner changing at once to that of a ruler of the domain.

"Silence!" she called, in her loud voice. "What fools make such an uproar at the door?"

Instantly her guests and retainers sank abashed into their places, and thus a view was given of the entrance. There the steward, a small, shrewd-visaged man, and the porter were struggling to bring in a great-limbed, burly fellow who resisted with all his might though his hands were tied behind him.

"Who have you there, Sir Steward?" asked his mistress, her eagle eye upon them and her clenched fist resting on the table.

"Madam, 't is a vagrant caught in the third offence," panted the steward, as he and the porter pulled the prisoner forward by main force.

Old Madam, as she was so often called, looked searchingly at the prisoner, a stout, ill-favored man dressed in ragged clothing and hanging his head, as if ashamed of his plight.

"How can you prove the charge?" Lady Crabtree asked sharply.

"Look at his slit ear, my lady," said the steward; "his second offence of begging in this parish was here too, yet he hath the boldness to come here again, with his ear bored at that."

"A very valiant beggar certainly," she remarked, eying the vagrant with pitiless contempt. "You are a rogue," she added, addressing the captive; "but what have you to say?"

"I asked but for a herring," the man replied sullenly, looking up, and Betty saw that he was cross-eyed, with an evil cast of countenance.

"And will hang for a herring, fool!" said old Madam, harshly; "and it would be right, for with that body you should work or die. Take him to the justice," she added to her steward, "and tell him I will pay for the rope."

The two servants began to drag the prisoner

back, and he offered no great resistance, seeming to accept his fate with sullen indifference; but Betty Carew rose from her seat.

"Surely, madam," she cried, "you will not hang this poor man for asking for a herring?"

Lady Crabtree looked up with grim indifference.

"He is a valiant beggar, wench," she said coolly, "and you know King Henry's law?"

Betty looked at her with passionate scorn in her young face.

"By heaven, madam," she cried, "you are a brute!"

Now this honest expression of her own feelings so pleased the strange old woman that she burst into a hearty fit of laughter. Meanwhile the steward and the porter had paused in amazement, and the prisoner stood between them with a look of dogged wretchedness upon his face.

"Go talk to the king's grace, Mistress Betty," said old Madam, wiping the tears of laughter from her eyes; "this realm is full of these knaves, and we must hang them or they will cut our throats."

"Is life so cheap?" cried Betty, looking at her with shining eyes; "have we not all to answer for our doings? I pray you, madam, spare this fellow for shame of the herring!"

Lady Crabtree looked thoughtfully at the vagrant, and then some strange notion moved her again to laughter.

"You shall have your will, mistress," she said; "here, Bronson, go out and get a dozen —nay, twenty stout rods and distribute them."

The servant went to execute her order, while Betty remained standing, a puzzled expression on her face. In a few moments the company, to the number of sixteen or seventeen, were armed with stout hickory staffs, and Lady Crabtree directed that these men should form in two lines from the door, leaving a small aisle in the middle. This was done, while all the members of the household were on their feet, women and girls and gray-headed men all looking on curiously. The light of day, now much brighter, shone in the room, and many of the tapers were extinguished. When her orders were carried out, Lady Crabtree rose and stood by the table, pointing her finger at the culprit.

"Hark ye, villain," she said harshly, "this young lady has interceded for you, and though I am breaking law thereby, yet would I pleasure her. I give you this chance for your life.

Yonder is the door; make it, but take your fortune with a beating and the magistrate upon the other side. You, my servants, belabor him well as he runs through the passage; spare not the rogue, I charge ye. Now, Sir Steward, loose him and let him go."

The cords were cut from the man's arms and the two men stepped back to give him room. For a moment he stood as if bewildered, and then, turning, he started at a run down the long hall. As he reached the middle of the place, he came in contact with the staffs of the men servants, who obeyed the mistress's behests with good-will. The beggar dodged wildly, but only to receive two blows for one that he evaded. They fell on every side, and he was driven in a zigzag course by the force of the encounter. The dull sound of the blows which hit the mark was mingled with shrill laughter and shouts of approval, for it was an entertainment to the household. Lady Crabtree stood up and clapped her hands.

"Well hit there, Jacob!" she cried; "strike again, Andrew, but spare his skull; cheat not the hangman of an honest job."

There was a wild scuffle at the door, and then the vagrant, with a strong blow from his fist, sent a serving-man sprawling upon his back and effected his escape amid a great outcry.

"Well done, marvellously well done!" laughed Lady Crabtree; "he will beg here no more. Sit down, Betty; you have won, and may finish your breakfast."

But Betty remained standing, her face pale and her dark eyes full of fire.

"Madam," she said, "I have no appetite; I could not eat the herring that you saved."

"What ails you, wench?" the old woman asked grimly; "your stomach is too dainty. Know you not that the king would hang all such?"

"I care not," Mistress Carew cried; "that scene was one to turn a stouter heart than mine. The man was a knave, but I have no love of seeing misery made a sport of."

"Tush, mistress," retorted old Madam, coolly, "you are a fool, as young women often are. I have no pity for a man who would live dishonestly, if he could; a dirty, lazy lout, who begs and steals. Sit down, my girl, for here is a guest who comes to look at your fair face and hopes that I may die and leave you rich, which I shall not."

Betty looked up and saw Sir Barton Henge. He had just been ushered into the hall, and wore a rich riding-suit and carried his plumed hat in his hand. He advanced with an air of eager pleasure, his bold eyes fixed on Mistress Carew.

"I crave your pardon, Lady Crabtree," he said, with a graceful salutation, "for coming so early, but I knew the morning star shone ever at Wildrick Hall."

"A very pretty compliment to an old woman, Sir Barton," Lady Crabtree said. "You find us much upset; my young mistress here flies out at me because I will not coddle a valiant beggar."

Betty closed her lips tightly and drew further away; her instinctive dislike for Henge increased every time she saw him, though his passionate admiration for her was plain enough to flatter the vanity of one so young.

"Mistress Carew has a tender heart," said Henge, smiling blandly; "I can see that in her eyes."

At this, old Madam burst out with a harsh laugh.

"Mercy on your imagination, sir," she said in great amusement, "if you can fancy any tenderness in the glance that Mistress Betty casts at you! You are in no favor in that quarter."

Betty blushed furiously, but held her peace. She was not entirely displeased at Lady Crabtree's frankness, for Sir Barton had pushed his addresses with such violent warmth and haste that she dreaded his visits.

"You are gay this morning, madam," he said sharply, with a glance of ill-disguised anger at the old woman; "happily, you are not the interpreter of Mistress Carew's heart or eyes."

"You fool," retorted Lady Crabtree, laughing, "Betty's eyes need no interpreter —"

"Madam," interrupted the young girl, sharply, "I crave your permission to withdraw;" and without waiting for a reply, she turned and walked from the room, holding her head high and with crimson cheeks.

"There, Sir Barton," laughed the old woman, "see how welcome you are! The wench has sense, I tell you, and will none of you."

"I am not so confident of that as you, my Lady Crabtree," he retorted angrily; "I can find a way to bring this haughty young mistress to reason."

The old woman looked at him sharply.

"You have an air of mystery," she said coldly, "but look you, Barton Henge, I love this wench, and I swear that you shall not disturb her, nay, or trouble her one whit. Sit down and eat; you are hungry, doubtless; but nourish no dreams of conquest, unless the maid is willing, which she may be in time, for all girls are fools once, else there would be fewer marriages."

CHAPTER XII

MISTRESS CAREW, finding herself pursued
even to Wildrick Hall by the bold addresses
of Sir Barton Henge, and having a superstitious dread of his scarred face, withdrew from
the company assembled about Lady Crabtree.
She pleaded a slight indisposition and kept
her room for a few days, although even there
she was followed by flowery missives from her
persistent suitor. They were brought to her
by one of the women, and after the first two,
Betty returned them unopened. She would
have dreaded Henge less had she been more
independent, but her peculiar position made
her fearful of his persecutions. She did not
know how her uncle would view the matter,
and if Sir Barton's suit was seconded by Sir
William's commands, it might distress her yet
more deeply. As she sat alone, she had food
enough for sorrowful meditations; she was an
orphan and, unhappily as she thought, endowed
with a beauty which attracted the admiration

that she least desired. Had the suitor been Simon Raby, her reflections would have been of a totally different nature. But she was not yet certain of Raby's feeling for her; she was wise enough to know that the fine speeches of a courtier counted for little, and she was too proud to permit herself to believe in the tender words which Simon had spoken to her. But there was no room for doubt of Henge's bold suit, and she shrank with horror from the thought of such a lover, although his fine appearance and gallant bearing might have won the fancy of many a young woman placed in similar circumstances; but Mistress Betty had a temper and a will that matched with decided opinions.

Henge had been two days at Wildrick, when the household was surprised by the arrival of Sir William Carew. He had been to London on a business matter and came to Deptford to see his niece before returning home. It was difficult to feign illness while her uncle was there, and Betty was forced from her retirement at last. She came down to receive a kind greeting from Sir William, but to be annoyed by the addresses of her suitor. She saw, too, that Carew treated Henge with courtesy, and the fear beset her that her relatives might be glad to be free of a penniless girl, at any cost. She was likely to have little voice in the affair, not even her preference would be consulted; and it might be that she would be driven into a marriage that she despised, nor would it matter if her heart was elsewhere. And indeed there was something more than prejudice in her hatred of Henge, a handsome man and one usually much favored by women. Betty saw, instead, a vision of the manly form and fine face of Simon Raby, and she found nothing agreeable in her dark-browed wooer.

It was the day after her uncle's arrival that she sat alone in a little turret chamber which looked out over the river, and here Sir William found her. A glance at his face told her that his visit had some unusual import, and she was troubled, half divining the truth. Carew came in and sat down on a high oaken settle beside her and was a moment silent, as if in thought.

"There is some trouble, uncle?" Mistress Betty said, a quiver of excitement in her voice, and her dark eyes on his face.

"Yea, wench," he said, "a trouble I had not looked for; albeit I might have known Thomas well enough for that."

"You mean my father?" she said in a low tone; "then it doth concern me."

"It doth concern thee, truly," retorted Carew, gravely; "nor do I see the end on it. Did I not love thee, wench, it would not so disturb me."

"I pray thee, uncle, tell me all," Betty exclaimed, the trouble deepening on her face.

"There is but little to tell, my girl," he answered, with a glance at her in which admiration and pity were mingled. "I find you are troth plight to Sir Barton Henge."

Betty sprang from her seat, her face aflame.

"'T is a lie of his!" she cried, "a miserable and cowardly lie!"

Sir William shook his head. "Nay, fair niece," he said, "it is no lie. I saw the papers; duly signed they are, too. 'T was done when thy father had wealth and estate; and there it stands, and would have stood, I take it, had it not been for thy face."

"It does not matter, sir," Betty cried, "I will none of him. From the moment that I saw him in the inn, I dreaded him, and there is something in his face I cannot endure."

"Belike there is, Betty," Carew returned gravely; "yet Henge is handsome, and esteemed a brave man, albeit I never liked him, nor he me. He drinks hard and lives better than his purse allows; yet I do think that many women would believe themselves happy and he chose them. He loves thee, wench, madly too, I think, as such men do sometimes; and it is sure that he will never quit his claim, but cry 'precontract' if you dream of wedding elsewhere."

Sir William's tone was matter of fact and calm, impressing his niece with a painful sense of helplessness. To him this seemed doubtless no uncommon affair, and a young girl's preference was of small consequence. Mistress Betty stood looking at him with horror growing in her eyes.

"Alas!" she said sadly, "that evil wizard told me I should wed a man scarred as Henge is, on the brow."

At this Carew pricked up his ears.

"What say you, niece?" he asked; "a wizard? To what wizard did you go?"

"To none," she answered; "but one came to Kimbolton, — a little, bow-legged man, with a russet cloak."

"Ah, Sanders," said her uncle; "and he was at Kimbolton? A sure sign that some scheme was hatching. 'T is well that the poor lady died."

Betty told him briefly the story of the packet, and he nodded his head thoughtfully.

"You did well, my child," he said; "I knew that I could trust you. As for Sanders's prophecy, doubtless he knew something of this contract. It is the business of such men to pick up all the information that they can. But what will you say to Henge? Having heard the whole matter from him, I could but lay it before you. For my own part, I will not force you, my girl; but bear in mind that you are likely to have few suitors. You are portionless, and this man loves you; of that there is no doubt."

He was watching the fair face closely as he spoke, but he made no sign of any relenting toward the penniless orphan. He did not divine the struggle in the proud young heart. She did not hesitate a moment in her answer.

"I thank you, uncle," she said with spirit, "for sparing me your displeasure, for truly I could not obey you if you bade me wed this man. I would sooner have his hatred than his love, and both I hold as worthy only of my contempt."

"Remember, wench, that you are like to die unwed, a poor dependent in the house of some relative, picking up the crumbs that fall from another's table."

"Sir," she answered proudly, "I would rather starve than eat my bread as the wife of this man Henge."

Sir William smiled. "My girl," he said, "I rejoice to see the spirit of your blood, and I cannot blame you; yet this contract exists — made by your father — "

Betty interrupted him with a passionate gesture.

"Uncle, I would know the truth!" she cried; "they told me — the old servants whispered it in my childish ears, and it ran through my veins like poison. They said my father wagered my mother at the gaming-table the night that I was born — and lost. Is it so?"

Her face was white now, and her great eyes were set upon her uncle's with a look that made him wince. A deep red color stole over his bronzed cheeks, and he bent his head, shamefaced.

"'T is true," he said harshly; "and it was to this man Henge, then a roystering young gamester, and he held the debt. Thy father made this contract for thee in its room."

"And he would claim it?" Mistress Betty

spoke in a low voice, but her face was like the face of a corpse.

Sir William bowed his head without a word.

"By heaven!" she cried, "I would sooner be torn in pieces! Let him never dare to come to me, or I shall insult him — I cannot bear this agony of shame!"

"Nay, offend him not, fair niece," Carew said gravely; "he is an evil-tempered man and may yet work much evil for you. I will tell him that your mind is set against this union, and that I will in no wise permit you to be enforced. But let the man alone; your tongue is sharp and will not mend your case, and remember that he was in no way one whit worse than your father — nay, less culpable than he."

"Uncle," she said passionately, "I know what my father was — may God forgive him. From my babyhood it has been told me — that he was my shame. In my childhood it was rated in my ears, and in my girlhood it was forced upon me by the indifferent treatment of those who should have befriended me, the canting patronage that made a kindness to me a charity. 'T was not my fault, God knows, that he fathered me; had I had the choosing, it should have been otherwise, but yet I suffer for it. I am to be sold as chattel, it would seem, because, forsooth, I am my father's child; but I swear that the man who buys me shall find that I have enough of my father in me to make his purchase a thorn in his flesh and a curse to his peace!"

"That I warrant, wench," Carew said grimly, "and I think that he will scarcely break thy will unless he breaks thy neck. Surely, I will not try to force thee. Henge shall know that thou art so set against the marriage that it may not be. And now, my girl, make ready to go back to Greenwich, for in my pocket is thy appointment as maid of honor to the queen's grace."

A change came over Betty's face, and then she answered with more composure.

"I had no wish to serve Queen Anne," she said; "I cannot put the dead queen from my mind, but this one has been ill, too, and in trouble. 'T is well that I should be no longer a burden here; I will go right cheerfully, and I thank you for it, uncle."

Sir William laid his hand upon her shoulder.

"My wench," he said, not unkindly, "think not so ill of me that I begrudge my orphan niece her bread. I did but try you. I had no wish for you to wed this Henge, though there be many worse, for men are not the paragons of a young maid's dreams. But you will meet him at Greenwich, and mark me, Betty, bear yourself courteously toward him. 'T is said of him that he has the spite and venom of a spider, and he is mad with love of that fair face of yours; and truly he has the claim of a precontract, albeit he shall not have you against your will. But these are dangerous times, and I have heard that he has the ear of my lord privy seal, though I do suspect him of being a malcontent and hating Cromwell, while he fawns upon him. Make a friend of this young queen, and perchance she may do you a great service. They say that the king's highness is not well pleased with her, but I take this for idle rumor; for I remember when he used to ride to Hever Castle to court her, as ardent as a boy. 'T is but a passing cloud and her sun will burst forth again to scorch those who have endeavored to work mischief against her, as was the case of my lord cardinal. I esteem it a good fortune to get this appointment for you, which I did through Mrs. Wyatt, the queen's particular friend. We will leave Sir Barton to Zenobia, who torments him as a cat does a mouse; and haste you, for in an hour we go by the river to Greenwich."

CHAPTER XIII

THE QUEEN AT GREENWICH

WHEN Sir William's barge stopped at the water-stairs at Greenwich Palace, Master Raby came down to meet Mistress Betty and her uncle. It was an accident, yet his pleasure at the encounter was so evident that Carew smiled; the beauty of that face was doing mischief in more than one case, he thought, and was amused to note that here his high-tempered niece showed only gentle courtesy.

"Sets the wind in that quarter?" Sir William said to himself; "then, verily, Henge is like to have a very pretty quarrel on his hands, for here is a young sprig who can handle a sword as well as he."

Meanwhile, unconscious of the thoughts running through Carew's brain, Mistress Betty and her escort walked a little in advance, engaged in conversation. Half-way to the palace gates, some acquaintances stayed Sir William's progress, and the two, coming alone to the entrance, stood waiting for him. They were undisturbed; the king was at Whitehall, and but few loungers showed themselves about the palace. In spite of his pleasant greeting, there was some constraint in Raby's manner, and now that the opportunity presented itself, he turned abruptly to his companion, a flush mounting to his face as he addressed her.

"Mistress Carew," he said, with some hesitation, "'t is said that you are plighted to Sir Barton Henge."

Betty started, her face flushing more deeply than his.

"Who tells these tales?" she exclaimed.

"They are but idle tales, then?" he asked quickly. "I could scarce credit them, knowing that you knew him not that night at the inn."

She looked at him with perplexity in her eyes. What could she do, she thought, and how defend herself against her enemy? Truth alone could help her, even while it wounded her, and she was brave enough to see it.

"Master Raby," she said, with a soft falter in her voice that her uncle would not have recognized, "there is a contract, made when I was a baby; not even my uncle knew of it. Upon the strength of that, Sir Barton must have set these rumors afloat; there is naught else."

Her companion's face fell at her words.

"A contract?" he said slowly; "and Sir William wishes it fulfilled, doubtless, and you, Mistress Carew?"

"Sir, I will never wed him," she said firmly, holding her head proudly.

There was a joyful flash in Raby's eyes which brought a softer blush to Betty's cheek.

"'T would be a sacrifice to make angels weep!" he said in a low tone, his radiant glance making her eyes seek the ground; "the man is a knave to claim it against your will."

"'T is prophesied that I will wed a man so scarred," she said, in a troubled voice, for superstition had stirred in her heart ever since she first saw Sir Barton's brow.

Simon Raby laughed as he took her hand, which offered but a poor resistance.

"Mistress Carew," he whispered, "may not another man be so scarred? Truly, there are many who would bear a greater cut for thy sake."

A roguish smile curved Betty's lips, but she averted her face.

"But I like not the scar, sir," she said demurely.

"Then I swear that thou shalt not wed a scarred face," Raby answered; and he kissed the embroidered glove that she had left between his fingers, having slipped her hand out of it.

"My uncle says a dowerless maid is not soon wedded, sir," she retorted, with a flash of pride in her brown eyes; "the scarred and battered remnants are for the portionless, I take it."

This sudden outburst took Master Raby by surprise. Unconscious of the wound in the young girl's heart, he could not understand the bitterness of her tone. But he had a frank and generous nature, and it kindled in quick sympathy for the beautiful orphan.

"Mistress Carew," he said gently, "there are some who need no richer dower than the one which nature gave at birth, and which outshines all others."

Ashamed of her sudden outbreak, she turned away and looked to see her uncle coming toward them. Before he reached them, Raby spoke again.

"I know not your uncle's mind, fair mistress," he said gravely, "but if this man Henge in aught offend you, I pray you remember that one sword is ever at your service, and one arm ever ready to defend your cause."

The young girl looked up at the fine, frank

face and kindling eyes, and her heart throbbed in her breast.

"I thank you," she faltered, and the flush on his face shone in hers like the rising sun; "sir, I thank you with all my heart, and I am your debtor."

"Nay," he answered softly, "I shall be yours, and you let me serve you."

And Sir William, coming up, found them blushing like two children, and smiled to himself, wondering not a little how this tangled skein would unravel. But he made no sign, only carrying Mistress Betty away to install her in her new post before he went on to his home in Devon, where there was need of his presence at all times.

The royal household at Greenwich was under a cloud. The queen's illness had disturbed the tranquillity of the new year, and there were whispers that the king was estranged by the loss of his boy, born dead on the 29th of January. Anne had made a slow recovery and had withdrawn herself from the festivities of the court; she chose to be much alone, and wandered in secluded corners of Greenwich Park, often unattended, save by her little dogs. It was an inauspicious time for Mistress Betty to receive an appointment in the household, but she was kindly welcomed by the queen's other attendants, and took up her new duties with a lighter heart since she had talked with Simon Raby. The young girl, who had been a dependent in her uncle's house, now found herself a person of some consequence. Each maid of honor was permitted a tirewoman and a little spaniel to attend her, and Betty had a liberal breakfast-table, served with a chine of beef, a manchet and a chet loaf, besides a flagon of beer in which there were no hops. But all the maids of honor dined at mess, and chickens, pigeons, and rabbits were served, as well as beef and manchets and much wine, according to the custom of the time. Their hours of attendance on the queen were ordered by rule, and for the first few days Betty was unnoticed by Anne, and found opportunity to make acquaintance with those about her, and more than once saw Raby, who was at Greenwich as an equerry of the queen.

The freedom of her life at Mohun's Ottery and Wildrick made the more confining office of maid of honor irksome, and the young girl took every opportunity to walk out into the park. She loved best the early morning hours, when few were stirring outside the palace, and she found her best amusement in these solitary strolls. It was thus, one morning, that she came upon the queen, also alone. Mistress Carew was returning from her walk, and entered the quadrangle court, where the morning sunlight was shining with little power. She was startled by the sight of the queen, sitting on a stone bench a little way before her. Anne Boleyn was alone, and sat watching her little dogs, who were playing in front of her, tossing a ball between them, snapping and barking in the abandonment of canine joy. The queen was dressed in red damask, a deep cape of black velvet edged with fur hanging over her shoulders, and on her head a five-cornered black velvet hood trimmed with pearls. So absorbed was she in thought that she did not at first notice the presence of her maid of honor, and Betty had time to note the changes made by illness in her face, and she thought, too, that she had been weeping. Unwilling to disturb her revery, the young girl made an effort to pass her unnoticed; but Anne, hearing the rustle of her skirts, looked up. For a moment there was no recognition in her eyes, and then she remembered the beautiful face.

"'T is Mistress Carew," she said, in her soft

voice; "come hither, I would speak with thee."

Surprised, but pleased by the queen's gentle manner, Betty drew near and stood in an attitude of quiet attention. Anne sat looking at her sadly, and so long that she became embarrassed, and the color mantled richly in her cheeks.

"You are marvellously lovely," said the queen, at last; "yet I, who once so prized my own beauty, have begun to think it of little value, and that the price we pay for its exaltation is too great. Tread carefully, my maid, else it will bring you only misery."

"I have been taught to place small value on it, your grace," Betty answered soberly, "I was fortunate in my schooling."

"Alas!" said Anne, "I would it had been so with me; but I was bred in France and, save for good Master Latimer, there have been few to tell the truth to me."

She paused, and her eyes rested thoughtfully upon the ground, and Betty stood uncertain whether to withdraw or remain, and for a few moments there was an uneasy silence. Then the queen looked up again.

"Mistress Carew," she said abruptly, "you were at Kimbolton?"

Betty flushed with surprise.

"Only for a little while, madam," she said.

"Were you chosen by — " she hesitated and then added clearly, "by the late queen?"

"No," replied Betty, quietly, "I know not the manner of my selection. One winter night Master Raby came down to Mohun's Ottery with letters from my lord privy seal, and in the morning my uncle took me to Kimbolton."

"Ah, my lord privy seal was then over-zealous in my cause, albeit now he cools," said Anne, thoughtfully; "doubtless you were sent in the room of one she would have chosen, had she had any choice. Alack!" she added in a strange voice, "'t is little more than a month since I rejoiced at her passing away and believed myself at last the Queen of England; but now — great heaven! how like a quicksand is the heart of man, and swallows up all things that touch it! Maiden, I have heard the stories of Catherine's death — were they true?"

"Ay, madam," said Betty, firmly; "she died like a Christian, and royally — like a queen; albeit the first estate is higher than the last."

"And I was sorry that she made so good an end," said Anne Boleyn, musingly; "and yet she never harmed me, even when I held her high place against her. I knew her; she was an austere woman and unlovely, yet, as you said, a Christian. My girl," she added, turning suddenly to Betty, "which would you love, her or me?"

Mistress Carew stood blushing, tongue-tied, for in her heart she had ever condemned this fair woman; but now, under the spell of her glance and voice, her resolution faltered. Anne, accustomed to reading the faces of those about her, read at a glance the trouble in the young girl's heart.

"I see," she said, rising, and laying her hand on Betty's arm. "Give me your help, wench, to the house, for I am not strong in heart or body. You loved the virtue of that dead queen, and you have seen me rejoice at her fall. Yet bethink you, Mistress Carew, how mighty was my temptation; and I was young and had been bred in that gay court beyond the seas. Judge not too sharply, lest you be in like case; for you have a beauty as great as mine in my first youth. My heart is heavy; I would have some about me to love Queen Anne Boleyn. I charge you, mistress, to think less of the dead and more of the living queen, who bears in her breast a sorrow and alas, has failed to bring a prince to England!"

CHAPTER XIV

THE STRANGE HOUSE BY THE THAMES

IT was evening and it was strangely quiet at
Greenwich Palace. The king was again absent,
and the queen kept her state alone. The gay
rufflers of the court were gathered in other
quarters, however, for that day Anne had but
few of her own maids about her. Grooms and
lackeys crowded the outer corridors, but the
lofty apartments of the queen were well nigh
empty. It was reported that she was indisposed, but this was rather an excuse for the
seclusion she desired. She sat in a great room
hung with rich-hued tapestries, a fire blazing
on the hearth and a hundred tapers burning;
its brilliance, warmth, the delicate perfume in
the air being a strange contrast to those rooms
at Kimbolton where a queen had died. Anne
Boleyn herself was clad in white and silver
brocade, a cape of Flemish lace upon her
shoulders, strings of pearls about that slender
throat, and on her head a coif of crimson velvet
edged with pearls, a great diamond set in the

front and shining on her brow like a star. But for her pallor and the haggard look about her eyes, she was as beautiful as she was in her days of triumph as the Marchioness of Pembroke. She sat in the center of the room, and at her feet, upon a crimson cushion, was Mrs. Wyatt. About these two were gathered three other attendants, Lady Rochford, the queen's sister-in-law, Mistress Gaynsford, and Betty Carew; Betty herself as lovely as the queen, dressed in pale blue with a chain of dull gold about her neck, given her by Anne. There were no others, and the talk was free of all restraint, the queen's easy intercourse with her own people and her carelessness of speech afterwards feeding the fire when scandal was busy with her fair fame.

Her favorite, Mary Wyatt, was recounting her adventures in seeking some one to cast her horoscope, and Anne, diverted by the story, encouraged her with eager attention. It was a charming scene, these five handsome women in their gay apparel, in that lofty chamber where the flames of so many tapers made a luster that expelled all gloom, and only the pale face of the queen told the story of the secret trouble, the growing estrangement between her and the king. She let her jewelled hand rest caressingly on Mistress Wyatt's shoulder while she talked.

"How ended it, Mary?" she asked indulgently; "you make a long tale before you come to the pith of the matter, yet we know your horoscope was cast — and happily, as I think it should be, albeit you are a naughty rogue."

"Madam, I found a wizard truly," Mrs. Wyatt answered, soberly enough; "indeed, a king of wizards, though a little man."

At these words Betty started uneasily; she hated the mention of a wizard since the prophecy of the scar.

"Little in measure, sweetheart, but great in power, doubtless," said the queen.

"Your grace would find him a marvellous strange character," Mrs. Wyatt answered; "when I sat and looked at him and heard him tell me the most secret thoughts of mine own heart, verily, my blood ran cold."

"Were thy secret thoughts so evil, Mary?" asked Anne, archly.

"It mattered not what they were, my queen," Mary Wyatt said; "it was his manner of telling them, and his fearful eyes which burnt into my brain."

"The girl is frightened," said the queen,

laughing; "for shame.   I thought you a brave heart."

"Madam, I am no coward, as ye know," her attendant answered with spirit; "but the man is gruesome, and he has tales and prophecies that are marvellous to hear."

"What is he like?" asked Anne, curiously.

"He is short and bandy-legged, and has a countenance like a wolf's, with great black eyes that burn like fire."

"'T is Sanders," said Betty Carew; "Zachary Sanders, the great wizard."

The queen turned quickly toward her.

"Where didst thou see him?" she asked.

Mistress Betty hesitated, casting a doubtful glance at the others.

"Speak," said Anne, impatiently; "here all are friends."

"I saw him at Kimbolton, madam," Betty answered softly, blushing at Mrs. Wyatt's reproachful glance.

"Ah, a partisan of the princess dowager," exclaimed Lady Rochford, with contempt; "you chose poor company, Mistress Wyatt, and a poor adviser."

"A man does not carry his politics upon his face," said Mary Wyatt, indignantly, "any more than his heart upon his sleeve."

"Hush!" said the queen, "it does not matter. Mistress Carew, how came he to Kimbolton, and wherefore?"

Betty briefly related the accidental encounter at the Blue Boar and the exploit of the piebald horse.

"Saw he the queen — I mean, the princess?" Anne asked quickly.

"Ay, your grace," Betty replied; "I was sent to Sir Edmund to crave his attendance in our private rooms."

"A ruse!" exclaimed the queen at once; "the rogue lashed your horse to gain some notice from Bedingfield. How thick are some brains not to see such manœuvers! But it only interests me more in the man. Where does he live, Mary? what manner of house has he?"

Mrs. Wyatt, abashed at her unfortunate blunder in bringing up Queen Catherine's affairs, was more reluctant to answer.

"'T is a gloomy place in London," she said, "and would little interest your highness."

"But it does interest me, madam," Anne exclaimed, with a touch of imperious temper; "I will know all that you do."

"Having said so much, Wyatt, there is no hurt in saying all," remarked Lady Rochford, scornfully.

Mary Wyatt cast a glance of anger and dislike at the woman whom she deeply distrusted, believing her untrue to the queen, but she obeyed Anne's behest and told the rest without further demur.

"The house is in London," she said calmly, "and we came to it by the water-gate, over the which is set a great image of an owl. The building is very old; 't is said that William Rufus built it, but I know not; it is dark and tall and narrow, for there have been two stories added to the original two, and these upper ones are graduated, being like two blocks set on the house, the highest being the least, and the roof is pointed like the houses that I saw at Antwerp. From the outside, it seems as full of windows as a sieve is full of holes, and none are even, but within 't is dark as a sepulcher. The door we came to, which faces the river, is small and very strong, having three cross bars of iron to stay the wood, and on it are the signs of the zodiac, and above it the head of a serpent. The house, they say, hath five doors, albeit you may find but three with the naked eye; but verily there should be one opening downward for the convenience of Satan. When you are admitted there are stairs to climb up, up, to the third story, the

first of the two little ones. Here there are
three rooms all draped, and here he receives
you. Above only his favored clients go; that
upper story is his observatory, from whence he
says he reads the heavens and casts your horoscope. Many gruesome things he has there,
a treasury of horrors. But truly, madam, the
man is marvellous and reads the mind as he
doth an open scroll."

"I will see this marvel," said the queen,
with sudden animation; "I will go to this
house — unknown — and have my horoscope
cast."

"Oh, madam, I beseech you not!" cried
Mrs. Wyatt, her face paling with some apprehension which she dared not tell; "if you must
see him, have him here, as becomes you, but
not there — not there!"

"Tush, Mary!" cried the queen, her whim
taking possession of her, "you are a fool!
'T will be a mask worth playing. Right glad
should I be to be merry for one hour; we will
go now — at once!"

"Madam, madam, 't is too late!" exclaimed
Lady Rochford; "the king's grace will be ill
pleased."

Anne drew herself up with flashing eyes.

"Who gave you charge of me, my Lady

Rochford?" she said bitterly; "am I the queen or you?"

Her sister-in-law winced and drew back, but she bit her lip in passionate anger at the rebuke.

"Have your way, madam," she said coldly; "we are but your servants."

The queen turned her back upon her with a gesture of disdain.

"Mary," she said to Mrs. Wyatt, "go you and get me a mask and a sober mantle and hood; and you, Mistress Carew, call hither some gentlemen we can trust to escort us; we shall need but two stout serving men beside."

"Madam, who shall I summon?" Betty asked, and then added with a slight hesitation, "Master Simon Raby?"

The queen smiled archly, bringing a blush to Betty's cheek.

"Ay, my girl," she said; "Master Raby and my cousin, Sir Francis Bryan."

Despite the anger of Lady Rochford and the evident reluctance of Mrs. Wyatt, the little party was soon organized, Anne Boleyn directing all things with feverish gayety, as if she snatched at any prospect of entertainment in her hour of melancholy. She was masked and muffled until all her splendid dress was hidden and there seemed no possibility of recognition. Then she made each maid of honor assume an equal disguise, and escorted by Raby, Bryan and two of the palace yeomen, she set out in a private barge upon the river. It was yet early in the evening, and the moon was shining with a light that cast a whiteness on the landscape. The voyage up the river was swift and uneventful, although the queen pretended to anticipate an encounter with the royal barge, as the king might be on his way to Greenwich. However, they passed but few craft, and came at last to the water-gate of the strange house upon the Thames. As Mrs. Wyatt had described it, there it stood with its two upper stories in tiers, and its many windows like bandaged eyes, for every shutter was up and not a ray of light shone anywhere; the moon shining upon the opposite side made the face toward the river black as night. The little party found the wicket at the water-stairs unfastened and, after some curious glances at the imperfectly outlined owl above it, the visitors passed on across the garden, Mistress Wyatt showing them the door, which was hard to find in the niches of the wall. Raby struck a resounding summons on it with the hilt of his sword, waking echoes within the house, but there was no response.

The wind from the water was keen and the place so forbidding that the queen began to shiver under her mantle.

"'T is cold," she murmured; "I should have worn my partlet of sable skins and my muffy. Knock louder, Master Raby; the fleshy ears of wizards are ever deaf, I take it."

The summons was repeated with more clamor than before, but still no sound within.

"Mary, thy bandy-legged sage is dead, or gone to visit the black man," said the queen, impatiently. "The place smells like a grave; 't is an ill-favored house. Bryan, bring the two knaves from the water-gate and force the door; I will not have this rogue bar out the Queen of England."

As she spoke, the door opened suddenly and silently, revealing a dimly lighted, seemingly endless stairway, but there was no human being in sight.

CHAPTER XV

A CRY OF TREASON

THE little party at the wizard's door stood a moment confounded by this mysterious response to their summons. They looked anxiously up the narrow flight of stairs, expecting to see the strange master of the house, but there was neither sign nor sound of human occupation. The more superstitious of the party drew back in alarm.

"'T is magic," said Lady Rochford, with a shudder; "let us leave this evil place!"

Simon Raby laughed. "Have no fear," he said lightly; "'t is but an act of mummery to frighten the ignorant. Madam," he added, turning to the queen, "will your grace ascend?"

"Ay, surely," replied Anne, with forced gayety, for the aspect of the place disturbed her; "we did not come so far to turn back like frightened children. My Lady Rochford, if you are afraid, you may even stay without with my two grooms."

"I thank you, madam," her sister-in-law retorted tartly; "I appreciate the company to which you assign me, but I am brave enough to follow where my sovereign leads."

"Good lack!" said Anne, laughing bitterly; "how hapless should I be to lose so brave an attendant! Come, Francis," she added, turning to her cousin, "you and Master Raby lead the way and we five women will follow, and remember that here I am not a queen, but only Mistress Anne."

"Madam, your will is law," replied Bryan; but although he had smiled at the fears of the women, he loosened his sword in the scabbard before he led the way up the narrow stairs, followed closely by the queen, who was assisted by Master Raby, and behind these three came the four maids of honor, while the two yeomen remained at the door.

The tedious ascent of the long staircase was made slowly, the queen stopping once or twice to complain that she was short of breath, being really discouraged from her plan but too wilful to surrender her whim. The stairs went straight up between two blank walls, having no landings or doors opening upon them. The steps were imperfectly lighted with tapers set in iron brackets at intervals all the way up.

"I marvel if Jacob's ladder was any longer," said the queen, laughing, as they came at last to the top.

At the head of the stairs a heavy curtain of black velvet hung before them, shutting off the rooms beyond. Sir Francis Bryan, lifting it, held the folds aside that the queen's party might enter, and thus revealed a brightly lighted room decorated with dark tapestries and carpeted with ray-cloth. It was richly furnished, and on the table in the center stood a great crystal ball. From this room a short flight of stairs went up to the upper story, a narrow pointed door at the top cutting off the view.

"We must conjure the wizard, it seems," Simon Raby said, as they looked about them at the empty room; and taking a few steps up the narrow stair, he struck the little door with his fist, after trying in vain to open it.

It was instantly unfastened, and the wizard himself stood on the threshold. Taken by surprise, Raby recoiled a step at the startling vision. The little man was arrayed in blood red from head to foot, his velvet doublet heavily embroidered in black, and on his breast, sparkling like an evil eye, was a splendid opal. He viewed his uninvited guests calmly, his keen glance instantly singling out the queen, though she had drawn back behind the others. Sanders smiled, coming down the steps to meet them.

"Sir Francis Bryan and Master Raby, you are welcome," he said quietly; "these ladies, I see, would not be called by their names, but, even unknown, they are also welcome."

"We have come here for entertainment and instruction, Sir Wizard," Raby said, seeing the hesitation of his companions; "'t is for your art to furnish it."

"Ay," replied the wizard calmly, his brilliant black eyes still fixed upon Anne Boleyn, "I saw you when you came down to the water-stairs at Greenwich."

The queen started and drew her mantle closer, while both Lady Rochford and Mistress Gaynsford recoiled in superstitious dread. Anxious as they all were to conceal Anne's identity, this remark threw them into confusion. It was Betty who came boldly to the rescue.

"Good Master Wizard," she said, "I pray you tell us our fortunes."

"Yours I have already told, Mistress Carew," he replied with a smile.

At this Betty, too, drew back in amazement, but Simon Raby reassured her.

"He knew thy voice," he whispered; "'t is but child's play, have no fear."

Alarmed at the wizard's knowledge, Lady Rochford had laid her hand on the queen's arm, trying to draw her away, but Anne shook her off with impatience; possessing a naturally intrepid and wilful nature, she had no mind to be so easily balked in her purpose. She walked over to the table, and pointed her finger at some glass instruments and a scepter lying there.

"What are these, sir?" she said curiously, her natural taste for adventure overcoming her hesitation.

"They are used to conjure the four kings, madam," replied the wizard, courteously; "I will gladly show you more curious things."

The room was hung with every gruesome evidence of his trade, and as he spoke, he opened a curiously wrought box of silver to show Anne a serpent skin, but her mind was on other matters.

"Sir," she said abruptly, "are you the wizard who consorted so freely with my lord privy seal when he was in the house of the cardinal?"

Sanders was too keen to be caught in the snare that she had set for him.

"Nay, madam," he replied coolly, "great

men have come to me, but not my lord privy seal. Yonder is the cardinal's great book," he added, pointing to a tome upon a cabinet, "and this is a ring he wore. I foretold the day that he would sit upon a mule, with his legs bound under its belly, for his machinations against the queen's grace; but he heeded me not, and lo, the end was accomplished even as I said. Whose horoscope shall I first cast, fair ladies?" he added, bowing to the group, for the others had gathered eagerly about the queen.

"Mine," answered Anne, laughing; "'t is I who would discern the future, sir; one, at least, of these good dames is too affrighted to ask her fortune," she added, with a haughty glance at Lady Rochford.

"Madam, I pray you, think," protested Mary Wyatt, plucking at her mantle; but the queen withdrew it with an imperious gesture.

"I am happy to serve you," said the wizard, blandly; and he turned, and ascending the little stairway, opened the door above. "Madam will ascend," he said, "while I read the stars."

Without a moment's hesitation Anne went up the stairs, and her maids would have followed her, but Sanders barred the way.

"But one here," he said with his odd smile; "more would destroy the spell."

"I will go with her," cried Mrs. Wyatt, too alarmed and suspicious to consider her words.

"That you will not," said the queen, haughtily; "you shall not spoil my entertainment. Remain there, good friends," she added, recollecting her disguise; "we must propitiate the sage. Lead on, Sir Wizard; I will follow."

"Be assured, madam, that I feel the honor of the visit," he replied complaisantly, holding the door open for her to enter and then shutting it deliberately in the faces of her discomfited escorts.

"This is your fault, Mistress Wyatt," cried Lady Rochford, angrily; "and if harm comes to her, you will rue it!"

"Have patience, madam," said Raby, smiling; "what harm could come to her grace when we are here? and why should the little man design evil against her?"

"There be plenty who do design it," she replied coldly, "and would gladly compass it."

"Ay, those who are jealous of her beauty and her high estate," said Mary Wyatt, with a hard glance at Lady Rochford, who affected not to notice it.

" 'T was no place to bring her in her nervous state," remarked Mistress Gaynsford; " 't is enough to set a strong man's heart beating. How could you dream of it, Mistress Wyatt?"

"Alas!" said Mary, passionately, " 't is hard that I who greatly love the queen's grace should be held charged with this expedition. How could I know that she would plan it? It was as unlooked for by me as by any of you, and from my heart I do regret my careless tongue which tripped out the idle story."

"You are not to blame," said Betty, with generous warmth; " 't is a shame to charge it on you. The queen was bent upon some change, some diversion. I know this man Sanders, and truly I do not fear that he will offend her grace, for I believe he knows her."

"He hath the eye of a ferret," remarked Sir Francis, "and with you, Mistress Carew, I think he will be careful; he knows that it would cost little to split his gullet if he designed evil."

They stood grouped about the steps, too anxious to retire from them, yet each trying to put a good face on the matter. Having been recognized, Betty had removed her mask and stood farthest from the stairs. There was an uneasy pause as they waited, and in it they heard a step at the outer entrance; before they could decide how to receive a new-comer, the black curtain was lifted, and Sir Barton Henge entered the room.

"How did he pass the guard below?" whispered Bryan to Raby, and both looked askance at the intruder, Raby's face flushing with anger.

Recognizing at once that this was a party from the palace, Henge made a graceful obeisance to the women, and was greeted both by Lady Rochford and Mistress Gaynsford with some show of cordiality. Divining, doubtless, who was within the wizard's secret chamber, he took his place amongst them, but singled out Betty Carew as the object of his attention. Approaching the young girl, he began to whisper to her in spite of her indignant gesture of disdain. Her instinctive horror of him gaining control of her already agitated mind, she shrank farther into the corner, casting an appealing glance at Simon Raby, who instantly responded. He pushed roughly past Sir Barton and began to talk to Betty, turning his back squarely in the face of her less favored wooer. Henge paused a moment astounded, his face crimson with wrath, and then he plucked Raby by the sleeve. Simon turned upon him with an air that was in itself an insult.

"Sir," he said, "was it you, or the devil, that touched my sleeve?"

"It had better have been the devil for your sake, Master Raby," cried Henge, fiercely. "I was speaking to Mistress Carew; mayhap you are blind and deaf and knew it not."

"And I am speaking to her now," said Raby, with a mocking laugh; "therefore, sir, go to the devil!"

Henge laid his hand upon his sword.

"You will answer for this insult," he said. "I would have you know that Mistress Carew is my affianced wife."

At this, Betty came forward, her face white but her eyes on fire.

"I call you all to witness the baseness of this man," she said. "When I was yet unborn a dishonorable and wicked contract was made that he now claims against me. I utterly repudiate it, and my uncle, Sir William Carew, of Mohun's Ottery, doth uphold me. I swear, and Heaven is my witness, that I would rather mate with the veriest beggar at Saint Paul's Cross than wed with this man!"

"And none but a coward and a villain would pursue so base a claim!" said Raby; and drawing off his embroidered glove, he struck it full upon Sir Barton's face.

In an instant Henge's sword flew from the scabbard; but Sir Francis Bryan, springing on him as suddenly, snatched it away and snapped it asunder.

"Hell and damnation!" cried Sir Barton, "I will have satisfaction."

"Not here or now," exclaimed Bryan, in a tone of authority.

But even as he spoke, they were startled by a shriek so shrill, so agonized, that their hearts stood still.

"'T is the queen's voice," screamed Mary, forgetful of everything but her beloved mistress.

"Help!—treason, treason!" shrieked the queen, in a tone of anguish.

They dashed up the stairs, jostling each other in their eagerness; but Mistress Wyatt outstripped them all, and was the first to enter the mysterious chamber. Here a strange sight met their eyes. It was a large square room, the roof of glass and the walls hung with crimson. There was no furniture in it but a great mirror that was opposite the door. In the center of the place stood Queen Anne; she had dropped her mantle and mask, and was revealed in her splendid dress of white and silver; her long hair had escaped its bonds and hung wildly about her deathlike face. She looked more like a corpse than one alive, save for her eyes, which were dilated with the terror of a mad woman. Before her, calm and unruffled, stood the strange figure of the wizard, looking at her in mild surprise.

"Treason!" she cried again, as her attendants burst into the room; "he is a traitor! Seize him, gentlemen, bind him, in the king's name!"

Raby already had his hand on the wizard's collar and had drawn his sword, but Sanders was calm.

"Her grace is overwrought," he said coolly. "She asked to look into the future; I but obeyed her behest."

"God's death!" shrieked the queen, with a recurrence of her anguish, "he would have slain me, gentlemen!"

"Madam, I do beseech you, do me justice," protested the wizard. "I laid no finger on you, nor intended harm to a hair of your royal head. Your grace should believe that I can but reveal, and not alter destiny."

The queen stood a moment staring at him wildly, and then, despite Mistress Wyatt's supporting arm, she fell forward on her knees, pressing her hands over her face.

"Alas!" she said, "the sight will kill me."

"Call the Captain of the Guard," cried Lady Rochford; "the villain hath bewitched the queen; she faints, she dies!"

Both Mary Wyatt and Betty were supporting Anne's sinking form.

"Madam, I pray you remember that you are the Queen of England," whispered her favorite, looking in agony at the white face of her mistress.

"The traitor has poisoned her!" exclaimed Sir Francis; "he shall hang at Tyburn!"

"I swear I have not harmed her," retorted Sanders, casting an anxious glance at the stricken woman.

Aroused by Mary Wyatt's passionate entreaties, Anne opened her eyes, and seeing the wizard held by Raby and the furious faces of her attendants, she rallied her sinking powers.

"Loose him," she said faintly. "I was mad at a fearful vision; I would not have this matter bruited abroad; men shall not jeer at Anne Boleyn."

Making a great effort, she rose to her feet, and stood, supported by her maids.

"Sir Wizard," she said coldly, "has it availed to conjure hell to fright a feeble woman? I forgive you, but 't is my mercy shelters you from the wrath of my lord the king."

"He shall to jail, madam!" exclaimed Raby.

"Nay, I charge you, loose him and depart with me," she said, with sudden majesty of demeanor; "it was my folly to come here. Lend me your aid, Cousin Francis; my limbs tremble beneath me, but my heart is stout."

She took but two steps, however, before she tottered, so that Bryan almost carried her from the room, followed by her maids like a flock of startled pigeons. As they departed, Henge stepped in front of Raby.

"At what hour and place, sir?" he asked fiercely.

Raby laughed scornfully. "To-morrow at sunrise, at the tryst beyond the palace park," he answered lightly, and ran down the steps to overtake the royal party.

When he reached the water-gate, the almost unconscious queen had been already laid in the stern of the barge, her head resting in the lap of Mary Wyatt. And the slow journey back began in silence, the attendants all being too alarmed for conversation. The moonlight still shone upon the waters and fell full on the deathlike face of Anne Boleyn, but there was no sound save the soft dip of the oars in the river.

A few hours later, her three maids of honor, Lady Rochford, Mistress Gaynsford, and Betty, sat around the fire in the anteroom of the queen's chamber, anxiously awaiting tidings of her condition. Within, an old and skilled nurse and Mrs. Wyatt labored to still Anne's hysterics. For she had wept and laughed at intervals ever since she regained consciousness. They feared to call the court physician, lest the escapade should reach the ears of the king, and it was long before the royal patient sank into repose. Her cries and weird laughter had been hushed for half an hour, when the door opened silently, and Mary Wyatt came out with a look of horror on her face. So strange was her expression that it hushed the anxious inquiries upon the lips of the others. She came to the fire, and falling on her knees, gazed into it while she told her story in a strange voice, and the superstition of the age held her listeners in a spell of terror.

"She has told me all," she said; "that evil man — that prince of devils — cast her horoscope, and told her that her end would be as much in shame and misery as her present state was lofty. This, pretending that he knew not the queen, the lying jackal! Then he caused her to look into that mirror — you saw it opposite the door — he told her that it was enchanted and would show her her life. He chanted an incantation while the poor lady looked and saw, she says, every event of her life; and some, she swears, were known to none. She saw her childhood at Hever; her journey to France with Queen Mary; her sojourn there at court, with Mary and with Queen Claude. She saw her life in Catherine's court, the love of the gallant Percy, Wolsey's interference; the visits of the king's grace to Hever — she saith it was the king's very face and walk before he had the swelling in his legs. Then she beheld the glorious pageant of her coronation; saw herself, young and lovely, kneeling to Cranmer for Saint Edward's crown. After this a black veil hung over the mirror; the wizard knelt and mumbled, making passes, when of a sudden the veil lifted, and she saw — oh, heaven! why took I the queen to such a devil?" For a moment Mary Wyatt was choked by sobs, and then she whispered the rest, so low that the others knelt about her to hear, all their faces stricken with awe of the supernatural.

"She saw," continued the sorrowful woman, — "she saw the Tower green, and by the block were my lord privy seal, the Duke of Norfolk, his grace of Richmond, the king's son. From the Tower came Sir William Kingston leading — the queen herself. 'Twas her face, her form, her gait, her image, clad in black with a white cape upon her shoulders, and behind her came I and three others weeping. She saw herself speak, kneel down, and as the axe fell, she shrieked in mortal agony; and in a moment the mirror was blank, and no one with her but the conjurer."

CHAPTER XVI

In the gallery adjoining the apartments of
the queen, Simon Raby waited for tidings of
her condition, and also for a glimpse of Mistress Betty. Francis Bryan had been called
away to attend upon the king. Henry had
returned to Greenwich, but made no inquiry
for his consort, for of late they had met only
in public.

Raby walked alone in the lofty gallery, pacing to and fro, with his arms folded on his
breast and his head bent in thought. He
came of a brave race, and showed it in his gallant bearing and the fine expression of his face.
Trained from boyhood for a soldier, as every
English boy was in those days, he had seen
service both in France and Ireland, and was
esteemed a courageous and keen-witted officer,
if somewhat reckless. Reared in a worldly
school, he had led a gay and careless life; but
there were too fine elements of manhood in
him to be choked by the evil that in many

natures, under such influences, shoots up more rapidly than the good. None of his family were living except his father, and death was soon to sever that last tie. Among all the beauties of the court who had won his fancy and even touched his heart, none had ever seemed so charming as the penniless orphan whom fate had made an attendant upon Queen Anne. His admiration kindled by the beauty of Betty's face had swiftly grown into the proportions of a far deeper passion than he had ever known, and his generous nature, too, was touched by the peculiar hardships of her situation. For forgetting her lack of dower he deserved no great credit, since a man like Barton Henge could also be completely dazzled by the young girl's personal loveliness.

As Raby walked there in the gallery, he gave no thought to his appointment with Henge; a duel was a matter of too common occurrence in his adventurous life to be of any particular moment. He was an expert swordsman, and his contempt for his adversary's character was so great that he underrated his skill and regarded him as no very dangerous foe.

After the queen's return, her shrieks were audible even in the place where Raby walked;

but they were hushed at last, and in the stillness he heard the great clock of the palace striking twelve. He went to a casement, and throwing it open, looked out upon the night. The moon was setting and a few soft clouds drifted above it; below, the park was full of black shadows, and in the distance the hounds of the royal pack bayed in a melancholy monotone. The strange adventures of the evening might well have stirred hardier nerves, and Raby shared the superstitions of the times. The weird black and white outlines of the scene oppressed him; it seemed to him that a calamity hung over the palace, and the queen's wild cries still rang in his ears. He closed the casement sharply and turned just as the door opened, and Mistress Carew came in alone. A glance at her pale face told him that something unusually painful had occurred.

"How fares the queen?" he asked eagerly.

"She sleeps at last," Betty replied; "but she has been in a grievous state, crying and laughing like a mad woman, and would take no comfort. She told her fearful vision to Mistress Wyatt, and 't is no wonder that she is so distressed;" and with an awed face and agitated voice she went on to tell Raby of the mirror and its dark revelations.

"I remember," she said, in conclusion, "that he made this prophecy to Queen Catherine at Kimbolton, or something very like it; and when her maids would have upbraided this queen, she said that they would soon have cause to pity her and lament her case."

"Some estrangement there is between the king's grace and Queen Anne," Raby answered in a low tone; "but I take it for a lovers' quarrel, and no more. As for this vision, that wizard should be jailed for it. What need had he to so torment the unhappy lady? Doubtless he is of the party favoring the Lady Mary and would right gladly drive the queen to madness. Conspiracy is everywhere, and the death of Catherine has but discouraged it for a moment; the papists are openly discontent, and there is a great faction among the nobility, who hate my lord privy seal. We may be sure that this wizard is among the plotters, and had I any doubt of it, 't would be removed by the appearance there of Henge, who, I believe, is up to the elbows in these treasons, albeit he hath yet the ear of Cromwell."

A wave of color swept over Betty's face at the mention of the obnoxious name.

"Master Raby," she said, with embarrassment in her tone, "I have to thank you for coming to my aid this night, but I was most unhappy to provoke a quarrel between you and that man, who is unworthy of your notice."

"And did you dream that I would stand by to see you annoyed by the rogue?" he answered lightly; "I would sooner break his neck."

"And I would not grieve were. it broken, sir," she said, "though I would not rejoice to cause the death of any man, however vile. Master Raby, I pray you, let the matter go no further; there is no need for you to accept a challenge from a rogue."

Willing to conceal the true state of affairs, Raby smiled.

"We will not speak of that which pains you, Mistress Carew," he said cheerfully. "A flogging at Saint Paul's Cross would better serve the knave than to meet a gentleman, albeit Henge is of noble blood."

Mistress Betty gave him a searching glance. Accustomed to the clash of swords and to many a wild scene in Devon, she had but few feminine fears, yet her heart throbbed at the thought of a sword-thrust in the breast of this brave gentleman.

"You are going to fight him," she said in a low voice, "and for me. Alas! I was both

foolish and wicked to provoke the quarrel; sir,
I pray you to forbear."

Their eyes met, and she saw a light shining
in Raby's that a duller woman could have read.
A sweet confusion made her stand blushing
like a timid child.

"And if I draw not my sword in your quarrel,
for whom shall I draw it?" he said in a softer
tone. "Fear not, Mistress Carew, the rogue
shall have a just chastisement; 't is not worthy
of a thought of yours, yet I rejoice to think
that what I do is not a matter of indifference
to you."

Betty looked up bravely. "Sir," she murmured, "I shall never forgive myself if you
take hurt in my cause. I pray you let him go;
't was you who were the aggressor, and there
can be no dishonor in counting the matter too
unworthy for your notice. For my sake, since
I made the offence, I do beseech you leave the
quarrel to oblivion."

Raby took her hand and kissed it passionately. "For thy sake, mistress, I would do
all save lose my honor," he whispered tenderly.

Betty drew away her hand with a crimson
face just as Mary Wyatt and Lady Rochford
came from the queen's room, and so interrupted
the tender little scene.

"Master Raby, I pray you do me the courtesy to bear this missive to Sir Francis," Mrs. Wyatt said in a weary voice; "and then I trust that we may all sleep sound till morning dawns, and so try to forget this agony."

"Has the king come?" asked Lady Rochford; "they told me that his grace came late last night."

"And so he did, madam," Raby replied, as he took Mary Wyatt's missive and, with a salutation which included all, although his eyes sought Betty's, he left the gallery to do his errand.

"To bed, to bed!" said Lady Rochford, when the three women were alone; "I am well nigh faint for lack of sleep."

As they walked together to their chambers, Betty turned thoughtfully to Mrs. Wyatt.

"Where was the king's grace to-day?" she asked in a low voice.

"I know not," retorted Mary Wyatt, in a bitter tone, "but doubtless with that trollop Seymour!"

Betty asked no more questions, but went to her own room and said a prayer for the protection of Simon Raby from the man she hated; and after tossing for a while upon her pillow, fell asleep at last, as the first light of the winter morning dawned in a gray sky.

A little later, when the sun was rising, its rays shining but faintly through the heavy mist that was hanging over the scene, making the tall trees of Greenwich Park loom like spectral giants through the folds of vapor, Simon Raby set out alone to keep his engagement with Sir Barton Henge. Armed only with his rapier and muffled in a heavy cloak, he walked leisurely away from the palace, and proceeded through the more lonely portions of the park toward the river. His depression of the night before had passed with the darkness; Queen Anne's vision concerned him too little to disturb his thoughts longer. As he passed beyond the immediate vicinity of the palace, he quickened his steps. Even at that early hour there was the stir of a great establishment awakening; he met a company of cooks and scullions running toward the royal kitchens, and several messengers rode out post-haste, for the day's errands began early.

The spot appointed for the meeting was on the outskirts of the park near the river, and took Raby through the loneliest places. The morning fog cut off his vision beyond a short circuit as he advanced under the trees, and after a while all sounds from the palace ceased to reach his ears. His path grew narrow as he came in sight of the river and was surrounded by a low thicket where the underbrush had not been cleared away. The beautiful face and dark eyes of Mistress Betty filled his mental vision, and he walked on, careless of possible danger from a treacherous foe; it was not in his nature to take any precaution for his own safety. He was scarce twenty yards from the trysting-place when there was a crackling of dead branches on either side of him, and two masked men sprang out upon him. Unprepared as he was for the onslaught, he was too bold a soldier to be disconcerted, and his sword flew from the scabbard. Being swift of foot and agile, he evaded the heavier of his two assailants, and getting his back against a tree, made a fair defence. But it was two to one, and he had small chance to escape, and saw it. In the desperate struggle which ensued, he had no time save to parry the blows which were aimed at his throat. Then, remembering that he was near the river and boats might be passing even then, he shouted twice for help even while he fought with the courage of despair. The black masks with holes, through which shone the eyes of his assailants, their silence and their determination began to work upon him, and the cold perspiration stood out on his face. But with marvellous firmness he beat back their swords, the gleaming points of which began to dazzle his eyes. Once more, though sore spent, he shouted, and now there was an answer, a cry from the direction of the river. At the sound of it the stouter of the two villains turned and fled into the thicket, evidently having no mind to encounter a reinforcement; but the other engaged Raby the more fiercely. However, it was now an equal struggle, and Simon was giving thrust for thrust when a party of strangers broke through the thicket from the river side and the mask received so sharp a blow on the back of his head that he fell prostrate. Looking across the body of his stricken assailant, Raby recognized with amazement the manly figure of Lady Crabtree, her farthingale looped high and displaying her huge boots, while a stout staff was clasped in the great fist that had dealt the blow. Behind her were a group of her attendants and some watermen, all gaping at the scene in wide-mouthed curiosity.

"What gear is this, Raby?" she demanded, and stirred the unconscious man with her foot.

"A small matter, madam," responded Simon; "two villains would have murdered me."

At this, the fallen man began to move; and Lady Crabtree, bending down, tore the mask from the handsome dark face.

"Henge!" she exclaimed; "a pretty business and a pretty rogue! Now have we a chance to deliver him to the provost. Here, fellows, lend your hands and put this gentleman murderer in the barge."

"Stay, madam," said Raby, "this is my quarrel; let the villain go. He hath forfeited all right to meet a gentleman upon equal terms, and if you drag him into court, he will but blow abroad a matter which concerns a noble lady. Let the brute run to his kennel. He comes to himself. Is this your way to fight, Sir Barton?"

Henge staggered to his feet with a muttered curse, and groped about for his sword.

Old Madam pointed to the path that led from the palace.

"Look you, Barton Henge," she said; "here be men enough to lay you by the heels, and if you stir a finger, your throat will be slit, despite this gentleman who spares you. Go! — and swiftly, for my fingers itch to rap your pate again, you villain!"

"A curse upon you!" answered Henge, as he prepared to obey, having no alternative; "for once you have outwitted me, but the devil take me if you do it again!"

My lady laughed a shrill, discordant laugh.

"He hath you, friend," she said; "go to the wizard's house upon the Thames and worship him!"

Henge gave her a strange look and walked sullenly away without a reply.

"'T was a chance thrust," said Lady Crabtree, "but it hit — some deviltry is brewing in that hole, and I be not mistaken."

CHAPTER XVII

RABY would gladly have parted with old
Madam at once and made his way on foot to
the palace, for he did not wish to be seen in
his disordered dress, and there was blood, too,
on his face, from a slight cut upon his forehead.   But she was not of the same mind; she
would not let him go back alone after his
encounter, but scolded and badgered him in
her own fashion, until she forced him into her
barge.   And there she questioned him sharply,
trying to draw from him the cause of the
attack which Henge had made; but she failed.
Simon kept his own counsel; he was as determined to keep Betty's name out of the matter
as the old woman was resolved to trace it back
to her, for she had suspected at once the true
state of affairs.   It was an encounter of wits,
for old Madam was as keen as a needle, and
Raby was no fool.   Back and forth the subject
went, thrust and parry, until the boat stopped
at the water-stairs, and there Simon lost no

time in making his escape. Lady Crabtree
was bound for London, intending to return at
noon to Greenwich; so he evaded her, at least
for a season. Waving his adieu, he turned
from the river and made his way swiftly toward
a side entrance of the palace. The morning
was now well advanced, and avoiding a group
of courtiers, he came at last to the quadrangle
court; and here, to his surprise, he met Mistress Carew. She had just come out, roused
from her slumbers by her anxieties, and a glance
at Raby told her the story of his morning journey. Her quick eye detected the blood that
he had failed to wipe away entirely, and she
stopped him with an imperious gesture.

"You are wounded!" she cried, her tone as
full of emotion as he could desire; "what have
you done?"

"'T is but a scratch," he answered lightly;
"a little water will soon remove the traces
of it."

But she was not to be put off so easily.

"You have been fighting with Henge!" she
exclaimed. "I felt it, and I am thankful that
it is no worse."

"You do not inquire into his fate," Raby
rejoined, smiling, "yet you know not what
it is."

"Nor care," she answered, her eyes sparkling with anger; "sir, he was unworthy of your steel."

"That I know now, Mistress Carew," Simon said heartily; "until a few hours ago I believed him, after his own fashion, a gentleman, save for his pursuit of you, and for that — except the manner of it — there is an excuse."

"He is too base a man to be aught but a coward," said Betty, scornfully. "But that cut upon your forehead," she added in a changed tone, "I grieve to see it; you must call a leech."

Raby looked at her with a smile, and his expression brought the color to her cheeks.

"Mistress Carew," he said softly, "you told me the prophecy, and was it not natural I should strive for a scar?"

"But I told you also that I liked it not," she answered archly.

"Ay, but, then, what if the prophecy held?" he said, still smiling. "I thought it safe to be on the winning side."

"Alas, sir!" she exclaimed, "I fear that your heart has already too many scars; add not one only to your face."

She had stepped back a little and was laughing and blushing, her face framed with the

furs that muffled it. He thought her charming, and her wayward mood pleased his fancy.

"Ah, mistress!" he replied, "my heart has
left my keeping, therefore I have only my face
to scar, unless you give me back the other."

Betty looked down demurely.

"Master Raby," she said, "I have been with
two queens, and both have warned me about
the hearts of men. One called them ships
that rode uneasy at their moorings, and the
other, quicksands. After such goodly advice
and wise discourse, verily, sir, I have my
doubts about the matter also."

"Then there is greater reason for you to
listen to a truthful argument," he answered,
smiling; "these poor ladies manifestly have
not found a faithful heart."

"That is the very point of the matter," Betty
answered quickly; "are any faithful?"

"Ay, surely," he answered more earnestly;
"and mine—"

"Hush!" exclaimed Betty, softly, "look yonder, sir, and judge a man's heart by the king's."

Raby turned quickly, following the direction
of her glance. A door on the opposite side
had opened, and Henry was coming out, followed by two of his attendants. The king was
cloaked, but his figure could not be mistaken;

and when Simon turned, he had paused upon the threshold and was looking up at a window above him.   At the casement was the figure of a woman, and she waved her hand to the king as he looked up.   Henry threw her a kiss and walked on, followed by his equerries.

"'T is not the queen," remarked Betty softly, as the party passed around and out of the quadrangle.

"Nay," replied Raby, gravely, "it was Mistress Seymour."

For a moment neither spoke; both were thinking of Queen Anne in the wizard's house, both heard again her shriek of terror.

"Alas!" said Raby; "poor lady! I fear there is some truth in the whispers of the court."

Betty looked at him with a sparkle of mischief in her dark eyes.

"Sir," she said, "I fear that you have no very true witness for a man's loyalty; you will need a better proof."

And she made him a little curtsy as she turned to go back into the palace.

"Stay!" cried Raby, eagerly; "I said not that a king should be the standard. Why, mistress, a royal heart cannot be measured with that of a plain, honest man."

Betty laughed archly, still retreating.

"Is a king, then, the only knave?" she asked.

"There is one heart that waits for you to test it, Mistress Carew," Simon answered, following her, his face flushed and his eyes upon her laughing ones; it was no longer jest with him, but she evaded him.

They had reached the door which opened into the private way to the apartments of the maids of honor, and here he was forced to halt. She, too, paused an instant, with her hand upon the latch, and looked up with serious eyes, her whole manner changing in a moment.

"Master Raby," she said gently, "I thank you from my heart for the part you have taken this morning in my quarrel. Believe me, sir, the orphan is not ungrateful to her gallant champion."

Before he could reply, she was gone, and he stood looking at the door with a glowing face. She had bewitched him and he believed that she was not indifferent to him, but she could sustain her manner of gay pleasantry, and was as skilful as he in the trifling talk which made even a serious matter seem of little weight.

He turned, at last, to find his way to his own apartment, determined to bring Mistress

Betty to consider the question at a more propitious moment; but he was destined to wait many days for the opportunity. When he reached his room, he found a messenger with a summons for him to come without delay to see his dying father. There was no time for leave-takings; he had to secure the king's permission to depart, and when that was obtained, was forced to set out with no better satisfaction than a note of farewell to Mistress Betty. Not knowing how carefully she kept that missive, he went with but poor comfort upon his sad errand.

CHAPTER XVIII

A ROYAL LOVE TOKEN

THAT strange house upon the Thames, with its receding upper stories and its many windows, had strange visitors. Not in the daytime; then its numerous eyes were often blinded with iron shutters, and only the owl's head above the door, which opened on the street, indicated the office of its master, as did the owl upon the water-gate. At nightfall came the never-ending stream of visitors, and usually by the river entrance, though there were other doors; one, indeed, opening through a labyrinth of cellars into a subterranean passage which had its outlet somewhere by the water's edge, and whose key was hidden in the wizard's breast. The master of the house quite naturally was much sought, being, by repute, the greatest necromancer in England and shrewd enough to work upon the fancies of the common people, dealing out philters and horoscopes with a liberal hand; but his real business was of a deeper and darker nature. Men of all conditions came by night to that silent house, and often one party dreamed not of the presence of the other, although the strange, small man held intercourse with both. In the lower portion of the building, with no communication with the stairs by which the queen had entered, was a large plain room, furnished with a long table and many chairs; and the ceiling was dark blue, set with gilded stars, so it was called the wizard's Star Chamber. Here were frequently assembled a large company, and here the dealings were free from sorcery; they savored of a deeper and more subtle matter. Here, sometimes, were peers of the realm, the vacillating Lord Hussey, Darcy, and, less frequently, my lord of Exeter, and, once or twice, the master of horse, Sir Nicholas Carew. On one occasion, too, appeared the pale, fanatical face of a poorer gentleman, Robert Aske, who was to lead in the Pilgrimage of Grace. In this secret chamber of the secret house festered conspiracy, undiscovered even by the falcon eye of Cromwell. Here were represented the remnant of the party of the White Rose, the infatuated followers of the Nun of Kent and the papists, who flocked to the secret meetings where Pole's book against the king was known, before the king saw it, and was eagerly devoured; where the pope's bulls were quoted, while the name of Mary Tudor was coupled first with the dauphin and then with Charles V. The possibilities of resistance to the crown, the downfall of Cromwell and the Archbishop of Canterbury, the king's increasing corpulence and the sores upon his legs, — all these matters were fruitful of discussion, and in the midst of the malcontents, the dwarfish figure of the master of the house flitted about with fiendish activity. It was in his nature to love the brewing of so evil a caldron, and he was happiest when he could count the greatest number of the peers caught in his net. Yet, if he was sincere in anything, he was in his devotion to the hope of a revival of the old régime. Through the length and breadth of the kingdom spread the tendrils of conspiracy, while the strong hand of the king was on the helm of the ship of state, guiding it through troubled waters to a liberty of which he, despot that he was, had no conception.

Through the months of that short winter, the procession to the wizard's Star Chamber continued and waxed nightly larger, while at Greenwich the king and queen lived estranged, and the gossips of the court were busy with a matter that they whispered only on the back-stairs or in the chimney-corners, while the beauty of the queen waned under the frown of fortune. A cloud hung over the gayeties of the court, while she was nervous, anxious, ever suspicious of those about her, and time passed heavily with the young maids and court rufflers, and there was much secret grumbling. Master Raby was still in Sussex; his father was dead, but the new Lord Raby could not leave the estates unsettled, and he had not yet returned. My Lady Crabtree, however, had published such an account of the affair in the park that Henge was forced to keep in retirement, and for a while, at least, Betty was free from annoyance.

April came, and Latimer, the Bishop of Worcester, was at Greenwich for a time, and in the chapel preached a mighty sermon to the unhappy queen. The king was absent, and the suite of Anne Boleyn filled the space around the pulpit. The great bishop spoke in a clear voice, bearing fearless witness to the queen of the errors and the sins of a worldly life and the penitence by which alone she might hope to enter the Kingdom of Heaven, where her earthly majesty would be a shackle to her immortal soul. The preacher lifted his voice courageously to call an erring woman to re-pentance. Latimer saw the truth too plainly, and was too honest to bear false witness, — a great man whom the great cardinal plucked from the burning, seeing those qualities of soul which a strong mind recognizes even in a foe, and Wolsey saved him to be the martyr of bloody Mary.

Queen Anne left the chapel weeping, and going to her apartments, bade Mary Wyatt bring her Tyndale's translation of the Bible, the book that her intercession with the king had saved from the fagots. About her stood her maids of honor, and while she sat thus with the open Testament before her, tears in her eyes and her whole manner full of agitation, the door opened to admit a young and beautiful woman. In contrast to the pale face of the queen, the luxuriant beauty of the new-comer seemed dazzling; her features were perfectly regular, while her eyes have been called "starry" in their luster. At the sight of her, Anne's face changed instantly; she rose, and advancing to the center of the room, looked at her haughtily. The young woman was splen-didly dressed, and wore a girdle of pearls at her waist, and on her neck a great jewel, which attracted the eye of the queen.

"What have you there, Mistress Seymour?" she exclaimed sharply, indicating the gem.

Jane Seymour drew back with a flush of mingled embarrassment and indignation.

"'T is but a gift, madam," she said, faltering under Anne's searching glance; "'t is naught of importance. I —"

The blush, the stammering tone were alike fatal to an attempt at evasion; the queen snatched at the jewel and tore it from her rival's throat with such vehemence that she cut her hand upon the clasp and the blood dropped on her dress. She took the ornament, and looking on the reverse side, found a curiously contrived spring, which opened to reveal a beautifully painted portrait of the king. For one moment she stood transfixed, such an expression on her haggard face that her attendants shrank back and the fair Seymour was covered with confusion. Then the furious nature of Anne Boleyn roused her from her womanly dismay; she turned upon the maid of honor like a lioness at bay, her wrath bringing a terrible beauty to her face and her eyes blazing with fury. She hurled the bauble at Jane Seymour with such force that it fell shattered at her feet.

"Go!" cried the queen, pointing to the

door, "get from my sight, you accursed traitress, and take the image of your paramour away with you!"

"Madam, I pray you —" began Jane.

"Begone!" said Anne, her impassioned voice ringing through the room; "doubtless the king awaits thee. Lie not to me! let me not see thy face again!"

In her resistless fury the queen towered like an avenging spirit, and Jane Seymour could only gather up the fragments of her sovereign's love token and retreat in deep confusion. Anne Boleyn watched her until the door closed behind her, her own pose full of queenly dignity and injured womanhood; but when the rival beauty had withdrawn, a great change swept over Anne's features; she turned, and seeing her favorite friend near her with a face full of sympathy and indignation, she fell weeping on her neck.

"Oh, Mary, I have sinned!" she cried in a voice of anguish; "oh, my God! is my punishment to be administered in like measure with my sin?"

CHAPTER XIX

IT was the first of May; the trees in Greenwich Park were budding with the tender tints of spring, and the short turf was studded with the little daisies, pink and white, and the hawthorns were in bloom, while from the hedgerows came the music of the birds. In the lists at Greenwich the silver trumpets blew. The heralds proclaimed the names of the challengers and challenged in the tournament. The royal gallery was hung with cloth of gold, and the king and queen sat there together, in apparent concord; yet there were dark whispers in the palace, there had been a secret session of the privy council at Whitehall a few days before, and a gentleman of the king's household had been committed to the Tower. But outwardly all was gay for the great festival of May Day. Banners floated over the lists, pennants of dyes as varied as the rainbow, while from the galleries hung rich tapestries and wreaths of flowers. Garlands decorated the canopy above the head of Anne Boleyn, garlands lay on the gallery balustrade before her, and she was robed in all the splendor of a queen. Her surcoat was of scarlet and gold brocade, and her mantle of cloth of gold was lined with ermine, while on her coif was a circlet of rubies, the same which she had worn on that Whitsunday when she received the crown. Unusually pale, but beautiful, the queen leaned forward in her chair to watch the tilting, while beside her sat the king, seeming to share her interest in the games. He also was arrayed in a regal fashion, his dress of purple velvet slashed with white satin and his breast covered with jewels, which sparkled also in his low-crowned velvet hat, in which were set white ostrich plumes. The strong face of the king was slightly clouded, though he smiled, and his tawny eyes flashed with the fiery spirit of his race. About the queen stood her maids of honor, Mistress Wyatt, Mistress Gaynsford, Betty Carew, and many more; and in the rear was the tall, square-shouldered Lady Crabtree, who had that day asked Anne's leave to take Betty away to Wildrick, pleading some excuse in response to the queen's inquiries. Permission had been given, and when the festivities were ended, Mistress Carew would depart for a while from court.

With the braying of trumpets and the sound of music, challenger and challenged rode into the lists,— the queen's brother, Lord Rochford, and Sir Henry Norris, who had been one of the witnesses of Henry's secret marriage with the Marchioness of Pembroke in the attic turret of Whitehall. Both the contestants were fine riders, and expert with sword and lance; the first encounter called forth a burst of applause. Men shouted, women waved their handkerchiefs, and the queen let hers fall from her hand into the lists. Before the eager host of sycophants could reach it, Norris had it, and pressing it to his face, presented it on the point of his lance to Anne. There was a moment of silence; the king rose with a dark frown and, followed by a few of his confidential attendants, left the gallery without a word or a glance at his consort. At the barrier of the lists, the royal officers arrested Lord Rochford and Sir Henry Norris upon the charge of high treason. In an instant the bright scene was changed; the trumpets ceased to sound, men flocked together, speaking low, the jousts were stayed, the women stared affrighted at the queen.

"The king! the king!" was whispered; "what doth ail the king? Something has happened, some mischief is ripe! The Northern Counties must have risen! My lord privy seal is murdered! These gentlemen have poisoned the Princess Elizabeth!"

Almost a panic reigned below, while in the gallery the queen rose with a white face and withdrew, followed by her women. In half an hour the lists were vacant, the garlands hung wilting in the sunshine, the idle crowd trailing off full cry after some new scandal. The news had spread that the king was gone to Whitehall and with him the prisoner Norris. Tales that had been whispered began now to be told aloud; fingers were pointed at the windows of the queen's rooms; idle gossips watched upon the water-stairs for possible arrivals from London, and the superstitious remembered signs and sounds. A step had been heard upon the palace stair at midnight, yet no one ascended, though the heavy tread came through the gallery before the door of Anne Boleyn; it had so walked at that of Catherine, and at the threshold of the hapless Anne of Warwick, queen of Richard III. One old wife had seen Death riding on a tall white horse through the park in the full light of noonday. Another, who had heard the Bishop of Worcester's great sermon at Paul's Cross, had been in terror ever since, lest England should fall away to the Bishop of Rome, so valiantly had his lordship preached against friars and abbots, and the like.

Meanwhile the queen was in her own apartments. Although deeply disturbed by the king's anger and abrupt departure, she bore herself with composure, talking quietly with her women, speaking not at all of the arrest of her brother. Her maids flocked about her startled, dismayed, and each suspicious of the other's fidelity, except the few who were close to the person of the queen. Never was a May Day so full of trouble since the Ill May Day when the poor apprentices of London rose in Queen Catherine's time to be butchered by the Duke of Norfolk.

Night came at last, but sleep visited but few in the palace, and the morning found many haggard faces about the queen. Yet the suspense continued; the daily life at Greenwich moved on as usual, men and women tried to smile and made ghastly jests. The king came not again, and noonday brought no tidings. Dinner was spread in the royal apartments, and Anne sat down, attended by her maids of honor and the servants of her own household. The customary greeting from the king, "Much good may it do you," came not, and the queen's face paled as she glanced at the sorrowful women about her. More than one had tearful eyes, and all failed to respond to her attempted pleasantry.

"Mary," she said, turning to Mistress Wyatt, "what ails thee? One would think that a death's head grinned upon the board. 'T is a dull hour and my maids are red-eyed; truly, it seems that they might make some jest to entertain the queen."

"Oh, madam!" exclaimed Mary Wyatt, bursting into tears, "I cannot — I am ill."

"Ill?" repeated the queen, sadly; "nay, my girl, not ill, but fearful. I knew not that thy blood was so weak. When Anne Boleyn sees danger approaching, her heart beats with a bolder pulse; she feels that she is sprung of a warlike race which is not so ill a match for the Tudors. Come, come, Mary, dry thy tears; the May sun is shining; it is almost as fair a day as that first of June on which I made my progress through London."

"I pray that it may shine on you with greater blessing, madam," replied Mistress Wyatt, drying her eyes.

The queen looked down the long table; at

the end one of her old servants stood weeping; on either hand were pale faces, even Betty Carew had lost her splendid coloring.

"Mistress Carew," said Anne, "why is your face so long? I do not think you love me, yet your cheek is wan. Is my case, then, like the queen's at Kimbolton?"

There was a rustle, a stir of amazement, but the words were spoken.

"Madam," said Betty, in a low voice, "between the ill and suffering lady who died yonder and your grace's youth and health there can be no comparison."

"My Lady Crabtree takes you to Deptford," said Anne, quietly; "'t is well. I would not bring disaster upon one so young, and who has no cause to love me."

"I pray your grace to let me remain," Betty cried, her generous spirit stirred; "I would not leave you in the hour of trouble."

"Trouble!" the queen laughed hysterically, "who speaks of it? 'T is gay, a festival at Greenwich. Hark!" she cried suddenly, "what is that?"

The stir of an arrival in the antechamber, the great doors thrown open, the voice of the usher announcing his grace of Norfolk and the lords of the Privy Council.

Anne rose from her seat with a low cry.

"'T is a message from the king's grace," she cried joyfully; "my lord hath sent to comfort me for the arrest of my sweet brother."

She stood with a white face, her splendid dress disordered, her beautiful hair unbound. Her ladies clustered about her, but leaving a space in which she stood alone; behind were her frightened servants. Toward this group came with slow steps, as if their errand was a heavy one, her uncle, the Duke of Norfolk, Cromwell, the Chancellor Audley, and others of the Council. The queen looked at them with dilated eyes, her breast heaving, and her expression changing from expectation to terror as her glance fell on Sir William Kingston, the Lieutenant of the Tower.

"My God!" she cried in a low voice, "there is death in their looks!"

Then she added aloud, "My lords, why come ye here?"

"Madam," replied Cromwell, sadly, "we come at the king's command to conduct you to the Tower, there to abide his highness's pleasure."

Mary Wyatt with a scream clutched at the queen's robe, but in this supreme moment Anne regained her self-command. She put her devoted maid aside and stood alone.

"My lords, if it be the king's pleasure," she said, "I am willing to obey."

The Duke of Norfolk ordered her attendants from the room that she might be examined privately by the Council.

"Uncle," said the queen, sadly, "from thy hands I might look for more tender usage."

Before she left the room, Betty Carew approached the unhappy woman; the young girl's generous heart beat high and her dark eyes sparkled with anger. She saw here only a repetition of the blow that had smitten Catherine of Arragon.

"Madam," she said in a low voice, "if it be your wish, I will go with you to the Tower; I would not leave you now!"

The queen was deeply touched; she took a ring from her finger and placed it in Betty's hand.

"Nay, Mistress Carew," she said gently, "I also can be generous; thou art young, go in peace. Mary Wyatt and my other maids may presently come to me; now I am the king's prisoner. Farewell, fair girl, I pray thy beauty may not bring thee to so evil a case."

CHAPTER XX

My Lady Crabtree hurried Mistress Betty from Greenwich. At sunset of that fateful day, the two went by water to Deptford. The barge glided gently along the placid river; the soft spring air was full of fragrance and the banks of the Thames on either hand were clad in a mantle of varied green, while above the blue sky was flecked with rosy clouds. Betty and old Madam sat in the center of the boat, and the young girl was silent and manifestly unhappy. After casting one or two of her eagle glances at the beautiful, downcast face, Lady Crabtree accosted her with her accustomed frankness.

"What ails you, wench?" she asked sharply; "you had no love for this queen when you were sent to her, and now you pull as long a face as ever you did for the Lady Catherine."

"I had only condemnation for her when I went first to Greenwich," Betty answered, "nor do I love her as does poor Mary Wyatt, and a few of the others also; but it seems a cowardly thing to leave her now — it hurts me to seem a time-server."

"Tush!" retorted the old woman, calmly, "the queen cares naught for you. Nor would they let you go if you would. They took her to the Tower without even giving her time to change her farthingale, — like men it is to do it so, — and I hear that the king's grace will have her aunt, Lady Boleyn, and Mrs. Cousins, whom she hates, attend her. Doubtless they will strive to wring some confession from her, poor thing!"

"She is charged with high treason, so Mary Wyatt told me, weeping," Betty said; "but the whole matter has been conducted so secretly that the unhappy lady knows not the charges."

Lady Crabtree's stern face stiffened.

"That may and may not be," she retorted dryly; "Anne Boleyn has been more foolish than ever she was wise. The greatest fool was she to think that the man whom she had made unfaithful to his wife would be faithful to her. Poor shallow pate! she but taught him the door by which he should slip out. Well, well, there will be a great trial, and what will my lord of Wiltshire do?"

"The queen's father?" Betty said; "alas, poor gentleman!"

"Alas, poor ass!" retorted Lady Crabtree; "yet was he clever enough to wring a promise from the king's grace to marry Mistress Anne before Queen Catherine was put away. They tell a tale of his visit to the Bishop of Rome," she added, laughing. "The king sent him upon this business of the divorce, and he, getting there, refused to kiss the pope's toe. 'T is added that his dog bit it, in which case it is no great wonder that his highness's cause suffered at Rome."

"My Lady Rochford does not love the queen," Betty remarked thoughtfully, "nor does the queen love her."

"There is gossip about her as a witness against Anne," old Madam replied, "but there is scandal enough now to raise the stones of the palace. 'T was the rumor of this matter that reached your uncle through his kinsman, the master of horse. Whereat I get a letter, writ in haste, to tell me to propound some excuse to get you to Deptford. William Carew must take me for a liar; that I never was, because I could not cover one without a thousand, and it is a weariness to the flesh."

There was a pause between them; they were approaching Deptford, and Betty's mind was full of those last melancholy hours with the unhappy queen.

"Hast seen thy lover, Henge, of late?" Lady Crabtree asked, as they reached the landing.

Betty raised her head haughtily. "I pray you call him by some other name," she said coldly; "I am happy that I have not seen him."

"And did Master Raby — I beg his pardon — Lord Raby not tell thee of the game in Greenwich Park?"

A deep blush came into Betty's face.

"I saw Lord Raby but once before he went away," she answered, "and he told me but little, albeit I have heard much since."

Taking a grim pleasure in the recital, Lady Crabtree told the story of the ambush and the rescue, and her sharp eyes did not lose a blush or quiver of the face beside her.

"'T is a mercy that the matter is so ended," Betty said in a low voice; "now I think he will scarcely dare to show his face again."

Old Madam laughed harshly. "Little you know of Barton Henge," she said; "he will remember the injury and the disgrace until he has avenged it. Lay no such unction to your soul; he is a devil and he will do a devil's work."

With these threatening words still ringing in her ears, Betty went with a heavy heart to take up her life again with this strange woman.

For a while, however, all hearts were absorbed in the terrible tidings that came from London. The indictment and the trial of a Queen of England, the pitiful spectacle of a woman who had sacrificed all to obtain a crown now forced to such a shameful ignominy. The minds of honest Englishmen were stunned; the sadness of the fate of Catherine was as nothing compared with this.

Moved by pity for the wretched queen, awed by the recognition of the fearful workings of retribution, Betty Carew was filled with amazement, sympathy, unbelief. Finding small matter in common with old Madam, the young girl was much alone. Sitting in her own room, which overlooked the river, or walking through the garden and orchards of the manor house, her mind found plenty of food for reflection. In a few short months she had attended two queens, each doomed to misery, — one a sternly virtuous woman, dying as a Christian should; the other — she could not think of Anne's great beauty, the attraction of her manner, without commiseration. She had seen her in a brief hour of triumph at Catherine's death; she knew that it was commonly reported that her malice had pulled down the great cardinal, but she could only think of her in her distress; she heard still her shrieks in the wizard's house, her anguish at the sight of the king's gift to Jane Seymour.

Betty had been ten days at Deptford, and one morning walked alone in the apple orchard. Beneath her feet the soft green turf was broken here and there by the gnarled root of an apple tree; overhead the low boughs made a network, white and pink with bloom, and through the beauty of the fragrant blossoms she saw the soft blue sky, and before her, through the trees, was the river. The birds sang with the joy of the spring. She went on down to the river bank, and watched the wherries going to London; then, as she came slowly back, she looked up and saw, coming through the avenue of trees, a stalwart figure, and a face she knew. She had not seen Simon Raby since that morning in the quadrangle court, and she blushed a little as she saw the glad look on his face. But she had profited by her lessons in the world, and she met him with an air of demure dignity.

"You are welcome, my Lord Raby," she said gravely; "you have been long in Sussex, and I was sorry that you went on so sad an errand. Sir, I am an orphan too, and do commiserate your case."

Despite his black garments, Simon Raby was wearing a cheerful countenance, having been long separated from his father, a close-fisted man, whose only love was gold, which had made his son run to the opposite extreme. Having little in common, Raby had not felt his loss too deeply; but at this speech from Mistress Betty, he pulled down his face and tried to make a proper answer, although all the while he was thinking how radiant was her dark beauty in the white gown she wore, and what a picture she made with the apple-blooms overhead and in her hands. And she knew his thoughts well enough, but chose to turn the talk away.

"How long have you been back in London?" she asked, arranging her flowers; "we have been ten days here, but at this dreadful time it seems much longer."

"Alas, poor queen of a day!" Raby said compassionately; "'t is a great misfortune for this realm, nor do we see the end of it. I came back but yesterday, and heard the tidings at an inn. They stunned me; I could not believe it until I made inquiries of the matter.

'T is said that my lord privy seal sent for Sir Francis Bryan, but he is quit of it. And Archbishop Cranmer wept; he hath a gentle heart. I thought of the wizard's house, Mistress Carew, and of the shrieks of the queen. 'T is a marvellous thing, and makes an honest man shun the bandy-legged creature. I passed that house as I came on the river; the shutters were open and the windows — verily, they shone like evil eyes in the sunlight."

Betty shuddered. "'T was a fearful place," she said, and added: "I owe you a debt, Lord Raby. My Lady Crabtree told me more of that encounter with Henge than ever you did."

Raby's face flushed as he laughed.

"It was a petticoat rescue," he said, "of which I have little cause to be vainglorious. Hath the villain troubled you again?"

"Nay," Betty answered, "though my lady tells me that he will avenge his grief. I pray you, beware of this dangerous foe."

"I would right cheerfully encounter more such in your cause, Mistress Carew," he answered softly, and then added after a brief pause, "I was not only in Sussex; I have been down to Mohun's Ottery."

"To my uncle?" asked Betty, in surprise. "How fared they all?"

"Well, and sent loving greetings to you," he replied. "Can you not divine my errand, Mistress Carew, down there in Devon?"

Betty looked up archly, but meeting the ardent glance of his brown eyes, looked down again and colored like a rose.

"Nay, sir," she said, "I never yet could read a riddle."

A soft breeze shaking the bough overhead, some apple blossoms dropped upon her like a fragrant snowfall.

"I saw your uncle, Mistress Carew," Simon said softly, "and I pleaded my cause with him and won it; 't is for you to condemn me now, or bless me."

They stood near the high wall of the orchard; it was very still, and Mistress Betty kept her eyes upon the ground.

He put out his hand and took hers gently; his manner was tender as to a child; her stately beauty did not make her a great lady in his eyes, he saw beyond it the tender heart.

"Mistress Carew, Betty," he said softly, "I have no scar upon my brow."

At this, a smile stole over Betty's rosy face and she gave him an arch glance.

"You might have had one, sir, but for my Lady Crabtree," she said roguishly.

He kissed her hands. "I love you," he whispered tenderly; "will you make me happy, or must I go hence with a heavy heart?"

"My Lord Raby," Betty said quietly, "I see my uncle and my Lady Crabtree coming through the orchard; did my uncle come with you?"

"I must have my answer," he exclaimed, between hope and doubt, still detaining her hand though he heard the others coming.

"Bethink you," she said proudly, "I should be but a portionless bride."

"To me the noblest and the richest in the kingdom," he exclaimed.

She looked at him with radiant eyes.

"Sir," she said roguishly, "my uncle calleth thee!"

CHAPTER XXI

In the strange house upon the Thames, the wizard entertained a guest in a small, dark room upon the lower floor. There was a low chimney in the corner, and on the hearth some logs were burning; over it was swung a kettle, the steam issuing from its iron lips proclaiming, by its unsavory odor, some tea of herbs. On the table in the center of the room were two sealed packets, one large, the other small, and near this table sat the wizard and his friend, Sir Barton Henge. The outer shutters being closed, there was no light in the place except the red glare of the fire which flickered on the faces of these two, and cast their shadows magnified upon the wall behind. A strange couple, strangely fitted for mischief.

"Anne Boleyn is sentenced," Henge said moodily; "my lord of Northumberland was carried fainting from the court."

"Let the drab die!" retorted the wizard, with indifference; "as for Percy, he is a

fool. In-spite of all, he is firm for the king
and Cromwell; there are others whom we will
get. Yet this woman's death will go far to
heal the differences between this realm and
Rome; the pope but fears the emperor, and
the emperor's aunt is now avenged. Happily,
however, the visitation of the monasteries sets
ill on the stomachs of the common folk."

"How like a spider you are!" said Henge,
watching him. "Sitting here, you weave and
weave until one fly and then another is caught
in the meshes of your web, and then you gloat
over the victim's struggles."

"As you will gloat," remarked the astrologer, "when your victim is caught in the snare
that you are setting."

His dark companion started and looked at
him uneasily. Even in his bold heart there
lurked a secret dread of this dwarfish creature's
power; the shining eyes, the keen, fox-like
face were full of cunning, wit, relentless purpose, and Henge knew it.

"What hints are these?" he said roughly.
"I am not a man to plot as you do; I am no
schemer, but an open foe."

The wizard laughed unpleasantly, lifting his
brows with a look of incredulity.

"An open foe?" he remarked placidly; "so,

so, 't was open in the park that morning, but wherefore the masks, Sir Barton?"

Henge sprang up with a curse.

"You spying devil!" he cried; "how came you there?"

At this the little man laughed long and loud, rocking to and fro on his stool, tears of merriment gathering in his eyes, while his fellow conspirator stood staring at him like a wild beast at bay.

"I was not there," he said at last, wiping his eyes, but shaking still with laughter, — "I was not there, or I might have engaged my Lady Crabtree; an equal match we would have made. Sit down, my son, 't is no time for such quarrels; I know too much, too much!"

Henge stared at him, his hand fondly fingering his sword.

"Ay, curse you!" he said, between his teeth; "you know too much, but so do I, Sir Wizard!"

"Only that which would cost you your head long before it harmed a hair of mine," the little man replied calmly, while he rose and stirred the beverage in the kettle.

"What devil's broth is that?" Henge cried, turning away in disgust; "it stinks like some filthy gruel brewed for death."

"Nay," said the wizard, smiling, "'t is not poison; thought you to see me boiled like Richard Rouse? When this is thoroughly compounded, the smell of it stealing in a man's brain will make him forgetful for a space; 't will be useful to you, and the cost is trifling for the purpose, a hundred guineas."

Henge shuddered. "I have no use for it," he said hoarsely, "while I have a sword or a knife. Keep your devil messes for your richer clients."

Suddenly there was a deep boom, and the house shook, the windows rattled.

The wizard took from the table a wine-glass which stood filled, and raised it in the air.

"My Lady Anne, once Queen of England, your health!" he said, and drank it.

Henge watched him with a look of dread.

"'T is the signal that she is beheaded," he said with a ghastly face; "why drink the health of a dead woman?"

The little man grinned. "Why not?" he asked. "I may the sooner conjure her to speak to thee."

"The fiend take thy conjuring and thy visions!" exclaimed Henge, uneasily; "keep them to frighten petticoats."

Sanders chuckled maliciously. "You have

a great scorn of petticoats since a woman
rapped your pate," he said.

"Curse you!" cried Sir Barton; "because
you have me in your power, would you insult
me? Did you send for me to-day for this sole
purpose, your amusement?"

"Nay," retorted the wizard, calmly, "you
came for your instructions. Yonder lie the
packets, — one to carry to our friends in York-
shire, where, my lord privy seal having so
roughly handled the jury, they are ripe for us;
the other packet, being on your person, may be
found, if need be, 't is but a bluff."

"A likely errand," said Henge, bitterly,
"when Cromwell's spies are thick as harvest
gnats. Verily, I thank you, Sir Wizard, but I
made no such bargain."

Sanders put out his hands with a deprecating
gesture.

"As you will," he said grimly; "there are
others, and doubtless if your visit to the Lady
Mary was known — "

Henge sat staring at the packets; in his
mind had flashed a scheme so devilish that he
was fascinated. For the moment, even the
wizard's covert threats fell on deaf ears; suddenly the possibility of vengeance, on a larger
scale than he had dreamed, intoxicated his

brain. The scheme was born full grown; he had but to execute it.

"I will take the packets," he said, wetting his dry lips with his tongue; "I did but jest."

The wizard regarded him uneasily; something in the sudden change of manner displeased him, yet he knew the man to be too deeply committed for retreat.

"You have a pleasant way of jesting," he remarked dryly, "a gentle playfulness. What is your haste?"

Sir Barton had risen and gathered up the packets.

"The fumes of your vile drug intoxicate me," Henge said curtly; "I must breathe in the open air or choke."

The wizard smiled and gazed fondly at his kettle.

"'T is useful stuff," he replied, "most useful."

Sir Barton took up his cloak and sword, eager to be off.

"Some day you will fall into your own caldron," he remarked; "but I tell you, Sanders, that I will not be there too."

The little man rubbed his hands, laughing wickedly.

"How can you know? 'T would be a warm

meeting," he said, and stood still laughing when Henge closed the door upon him.

At Deptford, on that fair nineteenth of May, the household at Wildrick waited for tidings. In the warm sunshine they stood upon the terrace facing the river, — old Madam, Sir William Carew, Betty, and Lord Raby.

"There was some confession to my lord of Canterbury," Carew said, walking to and fro and looking curiously at the river; "'t is hoped that a bill of divorcement may save the sentence."

"If she be guilty, she deserves the sentence," remarked Lady Crabtree, sternly; "if she be innocent, she should stand acquitted. She was tried by her peers."

"I would it were not a woman," Sir William said uneasily. "I like not the death on the block of a woman and a queen."

"Would you rather burn her?" asked old Madam, coolly. "I know not why a woman, being wrong, should be less punished than a man, or more so. Men are quick enough to break a woman's heart, but over-squeamish about breaking her neck."

"Yonder comes your messenger," Lord Raby said, pointing to the river, where a wherry had stopped at the water-gate and a manservant in Lady Crabtree's livery was seen disembarking.

The messenger came up the terrace, and pausing in front of the group who waited so eagerly for tidings, he lifted his cap.

"The Lady Anne Boleyn died on the Tower green at noon to-day," he said in a monotonous tone; "the king's grace will wed to-morrow the worshipful lady, Jane Seymour. Parliament will meet to pass a new Act of Succession."

There was a silence; Betty turned and went weeping into the house. Simon Raby played nervously with his sword. Sir William looked about him with a stern face.

"He is the King of England," he said with stubborn loyalty, raising his hat. "God save the king's grace and give the realm a prince!"

"Ay," retorted my Lady Crabtree, bitterly, "and God pity his wives!"

CHAPTER XXII

Lord Raby and Mistress Carew walked up and down the terrace before Wildrick Hall, while at the water-stairs a barge waited to take him to Whitehall. Her white gown fluttered in the soft breeze as she walked, and in her eyes shone the light of the spring sunshine.

"I go to arrange my affairs," he said, "so that I may ride with you and your uncle to Mohun's Ottery to-morrow. Happily, there is naught to detain me else, dear heart. I fear I should forget my duty for your sake."

Betty smiled. "You will need to be prompt," she said lightly; "my uncle waits for no man and is ever beforehand with time."

"'T would be a shame on me to be a laggard at such a time," he answered. "Ah, Betty, how different the world looks when love touches it with golden fingers! I do think that I bear no man malice or ill will, but rather would be friends even with mine enemies, but never with thine."

A cloud passed over her face. "I pray you," she said slowly "remember to avoid Barton Henge. My Lady Crabtree predicts that he will yet endeavor to do us some great mischief, and it makes me uneasy for you."

"Fear not for me, my love," he replied tenderly; "and as for you, surely the love that enfolds you shall ward off this snake. But I will be mindful of your fears, albeit I think he will avoid me as he would a pestilence."

"I know not," she said, shaking her head; "my heart is full of misgivings when I think of how he set upon you like a cut-throat."

"And I cannot but rejoice that you are anxious," he said softly, "since it shows that my safety concerns you."

She looked at him with a tender light in her eyes.

"'T is more to me than my own," she said very low.

He kissed her hand passionately, although Sir William Carew was coming down the walk toward them.

"Your love," he said, "has made a new life for me. I swore when I left Raby Castle that I would not return until I brought it the fairest mistress in all England."

"Alas, sir," she answered, smiling, "'t was a foolish oath, and not likely to be fulfilled."

Without regarding their feelings, Sir William Carew cut short their talk, which might have continued long; for they were lovers, and knew how to make much of a little matter. He held a package of papers in his hand, sealed with red seals, and gave it to Raby.

"I would have that sent by a sure hand to Cromwell," he said; "it pertains to some matters of the county of Devon and claims his eye, yet is not so important that I need take it in person."

"It shall be delivered directly," Raby replied, putting it in his breast; "'t is time I went, doubtless you came to remind me."

"Ay," Carew answered, smiling; "I remember the days when I lingered so. It is nearly noon, however, and you were to have gone an hour since."

"My excuse is so admirable that I deserve forgiveness," Simon said, laughing; but he hastened his farewells, and in a few moments he and Sir William were walking to the water-stairs together, while Betty waved her handkerchief from the terrace.

"You have your rogue yet with you, I see,"

Carew remarked, his eye lighting on Raby's groom.

"Shaxter?" Simon replied, smiling; "ay, I had forgotten your prejudice. He is a useful fellow."

"He looks it!" said Carew, with a shrug; "farewell, and forget not the packet."

Looking back as the barge swept away, Raby saw the tall white figure on the terrace and the fluttering of her handkerchief. The picture of the great stone house, the green slope of the terrace, and the beautiful girl waving him farewell, framed itself in his mind and was a solace to him in the months which followed.

He was so light-hearted that he whistled to himself as the boat went on to London. The river was full of water-craft, and the scene was gay. The same river that had borne the unhappy Anne Boleyn to the Tower smiled in the sunshine and rippled gleefully from the strong strokes of the oars. Life was full of sweetness to Simon Raby, and he sat in the boat with a smiling face and a ready greeting for any chance acquaintance. In the afternoon he would go to my lord privy seal in person, now he had matters of his own to attend to. He must go to his haberdasher's and his barber's; he had a dozen errands, and presently found dust upon his clothes and went to his old lodgings to change them. Shaxter was with him as usual and helped him to make the change; he put on a rich suit of satin with a short cape of velvet, and bidding his attendant remain in his apartments until his return, made his way down the stairs alone and opened the street door. Looking out into the road, he saw no one, and came out humming a new song, popular at court. He had taken but two or three steps when three men stepped out from under an adjacent arched doorway. They barred his progress, and he looked in surprise to recognize the captain of the watch.

"What now, Ludlow?" he said; "I need a little leeway to pass your company."

"My Lord Raby, you are arrested!" was the reply, as the officer laid a heavy hand upon his shoulder.

Raby drew his sword. "You villain!" he said, "this will be a sorry jest for you."

"I arrest you in the king's name," repeated the captain, sharply; but so angry was Simon that for a moment they grappled, and the officer's assistants were forced to take part in disarming the furious nobleman.

"Of what avail is this resistance, my lord?" cried Ludlow. "I tell you, as your friend, you had best submit. I was ordered to take you and must, sorely against my will."

"Upon what charge?" demanded Raby, fiercely; "'t is an evil time if an innocent man may not walk safe upon the streets of London."

The captain shrugged his shoulders. He was a kindly, honest man, but he could only discharge his office.

"I have the warrant for your arrest, my lord," he answered soberly, "from my lord privy seal; but the reason of it?" he raised his brows, "you must ask the man who set the trap, not him who merely springs it. Verily, Lord Raby, I trust it may be no great matter, for your own sake. Mayhap you know well what folly brought it."

"Not I," said Simon, angrily; "'t is an insult. Where are you taking me, Sir Captain?"

"To my lord privy seal," he answered, glancing with some compassion at the prisoner's indignant face; "belike he has some questions to ask. But come, here I linger talking like a featherpate, and Cromwell waits. I would have left you your sword, my lord, but that you were so thirsty for blood."

"I will go quietly," Raby said, in great

perplexity and wrath; "it was foolish to fly at thy throat for nothing, but it makes my blood boil."

"For that I do not blame thee," the officer replied, "though it doth usually make a man's blood run cold."

"You speak for a guilty man," said Raby, sharply; "no honest man would shiver at an insult."

There were but few more words exchanged, the little company closed up about the prisoner, and the walk through the streets was a rapid one. Many stared, and some insulting jests were made. It was no uncommon sight; disloyalty was rife enough to make the arrest of a nobleman a matter of usual occurrence. They passed some of the gay young gentlemen of the court, who looked aside on seeing their acquaintance in such company. He was taken to Cromwell's house, and waited but a little while at the door before he was brought before him.

Cromwell was in his private room sitting at a table by the window, and a large mass of papers lay before him. It was his custom to apply himself closely to business, and much of it was transacted by his own hand. Here was a man who held the threads of many conspiracies, whose falcon eye was peering into every secret lurking-place from Land's End to the Tweed, whose relentless grip closed on the traitor like a vise. His back was to the light where he.sat, so that his strong face was in the shadow, but his penetrating eyes were bent on Raby at his entrance with a not unkindly look.

"Master Raby, I had it in my mind to send you some advertisement of my regret at your father's death," he said gravely, "when this charge was lodged against you, to my infinite surprise."

"Sir, I am ignorant of the cause of my arrest," Raby replied, "nor can I imagine what accusation has been made against me."

"You are charged with high treason," Cromwell said, turning over some papers before him, "having conspired with certain persons against the safety of the realm, and the life of the king's grace."

The expression of amazement deepened on the prisoner's face.

"My lord," he said, "I am dumbfounded; I have been absent more than two months in Sussex, busy with the settlement of my father's estate, which, as I think you know, was much in need of my administration. As for consorting with conspirators — you, who have known me from my boyhood, should know the folly of the charge.   I thought my loyalty to the king's highness was established by faithful service. This accusation is but the baseless falsehood of mine enemies."

"My Lord Raby, my heart inclines to believe you; I have ever held a good opinion of your family," Cromwell rejoined, "but the nature of this charge doth not allow it to be overlooked. But ye shall have an ample hearing.   Sir, there is a strange house here upon the Thames, I think you know it, — I see you do, — the house of the wizard, Zachary Sanders.   You were there one night this winter, and upon what business?"

Raby's face had changed at the mention of the wizard's house; the shrieks of Anne Boleyn had a strange trick of haunting him.

"I was there indeed," he said frankly, knowing no harm could come now of the truth, "with Queen Anne and her ladies.   It was an unhappy whim of the queen's, and the wizard caused her to see so evil a vision that I was near seizing him as a traitor; would, indeed, have delivered him to the guard but for her grace, who would not have the matter known, fearing the king's displeasure at her folly."

Cromwell's face clouded at the mention of

Anne. He had seen her die, sent to perform that duty by the king, and the man who had been faithful to Wolsey, in the misery of Esher house, was not without compassion.

"What was the queen's vision?" he asked moodily.

"She saw her life, and her death upon the block," Simon replied; "and the poor lady was thrown into such terror that she would by no means be quieted, and for hours her shrieks were heard at Greenwich. By Saint Thomas! they ring yet in my ears."

Cromwell was silent for a while; evidently the frankness and sincerity of Raby, together with his previous knowledge of him, made it difficult to reconcile the man with the accusation.

"I will be frank with you, sir," my lord privy seal said, at last; "I make no effort to conceal the perils of this realm, you know them. My Lady Mary Tudor, by her stiff-necked attitude toward the king's grace and the Act of Succession, hath made herself a stumbling-block, and a point round which the malcontents may gather. Then there are the papists, ever stirring in the cause of the Bishop of Rome, and with these the country gentle-men, who detest the breaking up of the monasteries and the abbeys, with no profit to themselves, and the travelling friars, and, God wot, I know not who, to stir up mischief which would bring us swift to civil war. At such times, my Lord Raby, I may not be lenient. The charge against you is so grave that I would have you make a clean breast of the matter. You came to town this morning from Deptford; what was your errand?"

Raby thought at the instant of Sir William's packet and put his hand in his doublet and drew it out.

"My lord, I came to attend to some matters of my own, of a petty nature, but mainly to attend the king's grace and also to give you these papers."

Cromwell stretched out his hand for the packet and broke the seals without waiting for further explanation from Lord Raby. He unfolded the wrappers and began to go through the papers without making any comment. Simon, watching his grave face, read nothing after the first quick flash of surprise. Of the nature of Carew's communication, Raby was ignorant, but believing it to refer wholly to affairs in Devon, he did not greatly concern himself about it. His mind was but too actively engaged with the state of his own fortune. His arrest had been so sudden, so entirely without reason, that he found no immediate solution of his difficulty. He noticed that Cromwell, with all his apparent frankness, held back the full substance of the charge against him, and the names and condition of his accusers. Secure in his own innocence, Raby did not doubt his ultimate exculpation, but he knew not what course to pursue, whose name to mention, fearing to drag others into his misfortune. While these thoughts passed rapidly through his mind, Cromwell was deeply engaged in the perusal of Sir William's packet; every paper was carefully examined and some were read twice over. Simon began to think that Carew's business would indefinitely prolong his own suspense, when the king's minister looked up. However, he did not address Raby; his face was inscrutable; he touched a bell upon the table and immediately an attendant replied to the summons.

"Call Captain Ludlow," he said calmly; then turning to Raby, he looked at him with cold eyes. "Sir," he said, "you gave me the wrong packet."

Simon returned the look with surprise.

"I had but the one, my lord," he said.

The officers had entered at Cromwell's orders.

"If you had but one, you did a strange thing to give it to me," said my lord privy seal; then to the captain of the watch, "Ludlow, remove Lord Raby under strong guard to the Tower to await his examination."

Taken by surprise at the entire change in Cromwell's manner, Simon was about to say that the papers were from Carew, when a second thought made him hesitate. If Sir William's name was not upon them it would be strange indeed, and he did not wish to bring him under greater displeasure.

"My lord," he cried, "I pray you to remember that I was but the bearer of those papers; I am ignorant of their purport."

Cromwell's face was both incredulous and unrelenting.

"You are not the man to bear such papers ignorantly, Raby," he said harshly; "who gave them to you?"

Simon started; then Sir William's name did not appear. A horrible doubt assailed him, but he was a man of stubborn loyalty to his friends. He closed his lips; if his silence could shelter Carew it was well, especially since he was groping in the dark.

Cromwell, who had waited one impatient moment for his answer, smiled grimly. He had seen too many men turn traitors to feel amazement at the aspect of one.

"You are tongue-tied," he said sternly, "It may be we must enforce the matter from you," he added, touching the papers; "never saw I a greater batch of treason in so little space."

"My lord, I am innocent!" exclaimed Raby; "I —"

"Remove the prisoner," Cromwell interrupted coldly, making a sign to his officers, and returning to his work without another word or glance at the nobleman.

A short while afterwards, Simon Raby entered at the water-gate of the Tower, and its gloomy doors closed upon him, shutting out the beauty and the fragrance of the summer world and separating him from the woman he loved. The king's prisoner, charged with high treason, had little cause to rejoice in his lot.

CHAPTER XXIII

TIDINGS of an arrest for high treason travelled
but slowly. The movements of the government were swift and secret. A man might be
pounced upon, examined, committed to prison,
and his own family be unconscious of his situation. It was a golden opportunity for the false
witness; for the public gratification of private
malice. The marvellous stories told at the
trials showed the luxuriance ·of the popular
imagination.

No intimation of Lord Raby's fate reached
the household at Deptford. He had been
expected to return almost immediately, but he
came not, and his absence was attributed to
some unlooked-for business. At first, Sir
William threatened to set out for Devon without him, but seeing his niece's disappointment
and remembering that Raby had accepted a
commission from him, he decided to wait,
although he chafed under the delay.

The third day after Raby's departure, Mistress Betty was riding through the fields behind Lady Crabtree's house. She had been out with her uncle and was returning alone by a short cut, leaving Sir William some distance behind, engaged in conversation with an acquaintance. The meadow through which Betty rode lay behind the orchards and was skirted on the right by a copse of beech-trees. She was walking her horse and had come nearly to the middle of the field, when a man stepped out from the shadow of the trees. At first, taking him for one of old Madam's household, she did not notice him, and it was not until he had fairly placed himself before her horse that she recognized Sir Barton Henge. Her animal stopping of its own accord, Henge caught the bridle and for the moment held her prisoner. She was not naturally fearful and her only feeling was one of indignation.

"Let go the bridle, sir!" she said angrily; "what right have you to stop me?"

"I have tidings for you, fair mistress," Sir Barton replied, with an evil smile upon his handsome face; "tidings of my Lord Raby, which are for your ear alone."

"Sir, loose my horse!" she cried, vainly endeavoring to drive the animal forward or to one side, but Henge was too strong for her and held the creature's head.

"You seem not over-anxious to hear tidings of your lover," he said mockingly; "yet it may be that you will presently find it difficult to get any more."

Something in his manner, more than his words, drove the blood to her heart. What had this wretch done? Where was Simon Raby? Yet so little was she like other women that she forbore to cry out or ask a question. She sat her horse like a statue, her face white and her great dark eyes fixed on her tormentor. She scorned him, scorned even his power to injure her, and he saw it and hated her the more; for between this wild passion, that such men call love, and hatred there is but a single step. Her beauty set his blood on fire, her scorn of him awoke every evil impulse in his breast and made him long to humble her.

"So," he said, with keen anticipation of the pain he had in store for her, "you have no questions to ask, and Simon Raby's fate is a matter of indifference to you? 'T is well; it would be a shame to spoil those bright eyes with tears — even for a lover."

She set her teeth and struck her horse upon the flank; the animal plunged, but Henge held him yet. She looked back wildly for aid, but she could not see her uncle. What folly had made her ride on alone?

"Well, well, I must tell you," Henge said, smiling in evil triumph, "since you are too shy to ask. Lord Raby is in the Tower."

She knew the man to be a villain, yet something in his manner convinced her that he spoke the truth. Raby's long absence was explained, and a chill of horror crept over her, but her pride sustained her resolution.

"He was taken the day he left you here," continued Henge, a little baffled by her manner and her silence; "he is charged with high treason and is like to suffer for his sins. All these years he has but fawned upon the king's grace to betray him. A traitor and a pretty rogue, this lover of yours, Mistress Carew!"

Wrath overcame Mistress Betty's womanly fears; in her right hand she held a stout whip, and she sat upright in her saddle, looking like a beautiful young fury.

"You knave!" she cried; "you lying knave!" and she struck him full across the face, below the eyes, with such sudden violence that he relaxed his hold, and her horse plunging, set her free, and dashed away across the field, while Sir Barton Henge stood staring after her, a curse upon his lips and on his face the great red welt that followed her lash. And she, riding to the house, dismounted, and running into the hall, fell on her knees before old Madam, and hiding her face in her lap, cried out that Simon Raby was in the Tower.

"Yea, I know," said my lady, calmly, "and they have taken the wizard, Zachary Sanders; 't is a pretty mess. Come, my wench, tears will not mend the matter nor unlock the jail."

As she spoke, Sir William came in, fresh from a gallop across the fields, and smiling; but at the sight of Betty's white face and the frown between old Madam's brows, he stopped.

"What means this?" he asked; "you look as if you had seen a corpse-light."

"There be tidings from London," Lady Crabtree answered; "Lord Raby hath gone to the Tower accused of high treason."

Amazement tied Sir William's tongue; he seated himself opposite his cousin and waited for an explanation, his honest face much clouded. Lady Crabtree spread out a letter on her knee and prepared to read the news.

"This comes from Mistress Gaynsford, Queen Anne's maid," she said, her open hand resting on the long roll of parchment; "she is a gossip, but I doubt not the truth of the matter."

"Let us hear it, Zenobia," Carew returned impatiently.

"She says of the arrest," began my lady, reading, "'Lord Raby was taken on a charge, secretly preferred to my lord privy seal, and on examination, a packet was found on his person, filled with treasonable papers, and exposing the network of a huge conspiracy. Many names were on a list therein; whose we know not, but Cromwell and the king's grace have the papers, and doubtless many tremble in the fear of apprehension. No one knows where the lightning hath struck or who is spared, but 't is said the gentlemen in the northern counties are many of them singed. The strangest part of the matter is that there runs a story that Raby gave this budget to my lord privy seal himself with every show of innocence, and when it was thought that he did it through an error, having two upon his person, he was searched, but none other was found; and what madness made him give this to Cromwell, no man can devise.'"

"'T is passing strange," remarked Sir William; "where was my packet?"

"'These papers,'" continued old Madam,

reading, "'contained such full betrayal of the wizard Sanders, who so frightened the late queen, that the order for his arrest was given. The fashion in which he was taken will furnish you with entertainment withal. The man who played the informer, in the first instance, before Raby's arrest, had mastered almost every secret of the strange house upon the river. He told the officers of the guard who went to take the astrologer that there was a tunnel from the cellar of the house, and that they must guard first the outlet of that before they strove to force the upper part. The entrance in the house he had never found, but the outlet by the river he knew. They said 't was scarce larger than a mole-hill and cleverly concealed. Well, here sat down three of the king's men, while others went and searched the house. There they were transfixed by terror, for when each one looked in that magic mirror, he saw the devil, horns and hoofs and tail, but when they all looked, it was blank. A young page with them had a fit from fright. 'T is said by some that it is only too faithful a glass. They found not the wizard, nor was there a bit of writing there. But the trio by the hole in the ground had better luck. Out of it the magician appeared so suddenly, and was so near the color of the earth in his russet cloak, that he frightened them so much that two fell sprawling in the river mud, and had not the third been a big man and valiant, my lord wizard would have escaped. They have him now safe in the Tower, though 't is said he rides out of it each night upon a moonbeam and returns when the cocks are crowing.

"' How came my Lord Raby to conspire with this man? I remember that he and Francis Bryan were ready to slit his throat the night the queen took her fright. Yet 't is said that the case is clear enough, and there is some wonder when the trial will come off.

"' The court is dull; Queen Jane is not yet crowned, though there is constant talk of it. She will have no maids save those who wear a girdle of over a hundred and twenty-five pearls. Anne Basset had one from her mother, Lady Lisle, of a hundred and twenty, and she could not appear in it. The king's leg is said to be worse than reported; he is fond of the queen, whom some think fairer than Anne; she can, at least, wear more fine clothes at once and look better, while Queen Anne was more beautiful in simple robes. This queen is very gracious to the Lady Mary

Tudor and 't is thought will win upon the papists. She is — ' "

"Oh, hush!" ejaculated Carew; "the woman's pen is worse than her tongue. I must to London to see what can be done for Raby; 't is a bad business, and I understand it not."

All the while, Mistress Betty had listened with a pale face, resolution growing in it as the matter unfolded itself. She did not speak of Barton Henge; his part in it sank into insignificance now.

"Uncle," she said firmly, "I will go with you."

"What, wench?" he said in surprise; "of what use would you be?"

"Nevertheless, deny me not," Betty said; "I would go and, at least, I will not hinder you."

"Let her have her way, William," Lady Crabtree said; "the girl's face will help you, and she is in a mood to fret out her heart here."

CHAPTER XXIV

Sir William Carew and Mistress Betty were both kindly received by Cromwell. He gave them a private audience, and Betty sat in the window recess in silent suspense, while her uncle talked with the king's minister. Cromwell's face was calm and inscrutable; Carew's deeply furrowed with anxiety. The one was master of the situation, the other exceedingly perplexed and doubtful of a way in which to help his friend.

"My lord," he said gravely, "I come to inquire into the arrest of Simon Raby, and to know the fate of certain papers that he bore of mine."

"He was arrested upon the charge of high treason," Cromwell replied, "and I regret to say that, upon examination, the evidence against him was materially strengthened. I regret it exceedingly, for I knew his father and have ever held a good opinion of the son. But unhappily, Sir William, in these times a man knows not where to look for backsliding; 't is on every side, and the younger men are brought into temptation more easily."

"I find it hard to believe so much ill of my Lord Raby," Carew said stoutly; "he hath ever borne the character of an honest man. I pray you, sir, to allow him full opportunity to clear himself of this foul charge."

"Sir," answered Cromwell, "every subject of the king hath justice. Look you, Carew, I have no wish to cut off this man's liberty. It is my unpleasant duty to stand for the king in these matters, and the odium of it lies on me. No man grieved more deeply than I for the loss of More, yet More's death is charged to me. 'T is like the outcry against the king's lawyer, Dr. Rich, because he went to Kimbolton in the matter of the will of the princess dowager. The papists claim that her property was not respected. Yet the truth is plain as daylight. The Lady Catherine claimed to be the king's wife and left no will save in the form of a petition to his grace; and dying as she did, in law, a sole woman, the administration of her estate lapsed to the next of kin, the emperor. But for the work of the attorney-general, the king could not have fulfilled her bequests. Yet Rich and I were pilloried for the matter, which was but a woman's obstinacy and the plain course of the law. Every rogue who goes to prison, every gentleman who is sent to the Tower, raises the hue and cry against me as the root of evil. 'T would pleasure me far more to set them all free, but, unhappily, the safety of the realm forces me to a different course. As for Raby, I found upon his person papers more full of treason than an egg of meat. A lamb he may be, but, verily, he seemeth a wolf."

"He is innocent!" cried Betty, unable to keep silence longer; "give him but the opportunity to prove it."

Cromwell glanced in surprise at the animated and beautiful face as she stood before him, one hand pressed against her heart and the other outstretched, as if imploring mercy.

"What wench have you here, Carew?" he asked; "such eyes should plead a cause if there were not such lips to enforce it."

"My niece, my lord," said Carew, hastily laying a restraining hand on Betty; "a silly fool, who knows not enough to hold her tongue before her betters."

"I cannot sit by and hear an innocent man accused and not defend him!" exclaimed Betty, with all her natural impatience.

Cromwell smiled grimly. "This nobleman hath truly won an advocate," he remarked; "I take it that the young lady hath more than a common interest in him."

"They were but lately affianced," said Sir William shortly, his cheek flushing, "but that will be soon broken if he proves the traitor."

"I am sorry, fair mistress, to lose you a lover," Cromwell said, looking with some admiration and much kindness at the passionate distress on Betty's face, "but the service of the king's grace should be nearer your heart than this young nobleman."

"My lord," said Betty bravely, her face flushed and her eyes shining, "you have been misled by circumstances; you do Lord Raby an injustice. I know that he is guiltless; I pledge my faith upon it!"

"I doubt not your faith in him, my mistress," Cromwell answered dryly, "but, unhappily, he gave me the packet which revealed the most damnable plot that it hath been my misfortune to behold."

"Would he have given it, my lord, had he been guilty?" exclaimed Raby's defender, valiantly; "surely that alone declares his innocence."

My lord privy seal shook his head.

"'T was but a mistake," he said; "doubtless he meant to give me another. What was it you said of papers, Carew?"

"I had intrusted some documents full of reports of matters in Devon, which you had requested, to Lord Raby's keeping," Sir William answered; "he was to deliver them to you, but I fear they went astray."

Cromwell looked thoughtfully from the window.

"'T is strange," he said; "there were no such matters on his person. If I told you what he bore, 't would amaze you. I fear that there is no clear excuse; though, in the interest of this young lady, I would rejoice could one be found."

"My lord, it shall be!" said Betty, firmly. "I pray you only give me time; let me see my Lord Raby in the Tower, and I will unravel this mystery."

Cromwell glanced from her impassioned face to Sir William's. Woman's devotion was an old story to him, from the faithful love of Margaret Roper to the loyalty of Mary Wyatt. There was something in the spectacle that depressed him.

"The charge against Raby is of the most serious nature, mistress," he said, "but I will give him all the time I can, albeit the king's service must not suffer therefrom. Nor will I refuse to let you carry him what comfort you may, but 't is a sorry errand for one so young, so beautiful, and so brave. I wish your heart were more happily placed."

"My lord," said Betty, gravely, "love is nothing worth that may not bear misfortune."

Cromwell gave her an earnest look. It may be that his own thoughts went back to the dying Wolsey, and he knew that he had not failed to fight the last gallant fight for the fallen cardinal.

"That is true enough, fair mistress," he said kindly; "I do think that Raby hath at least a greater happiness in the Tower than some true men who go free. Carew, I will give a warrant for you and this brave wench to visit the prisoner, and I speak sooth when I say that I would gladly see the matter righted."

As he spoke, he wrote a formal warrant addressed to the Lieutenant of the Tower, admitting Sir William and his niece to visit a state prisoner. He handed it to Betty.

"There, mistress," he said, "I had not the heart to refuse thee;" and then, after another look at her, "I know that face surely; thou hast been at court?"

"'T is the wench you sent to Kimbolton, my lord," Carew said, "and lately she attended Queen Anne Boleyn."

Cromwell leaned back in his chair, shading his face with his hand.

"I meant not to give the wench two such sad appointments," he said gravely. "I do not care to think of the past in either case. Happily, the king is well married and if there be but a boy!"

"Ay," assented Carew, heartily, "'t is the wish of all true Englishmen."

"Sir," said Cromwell, solemnly, "God only knows what it would mean to this realm. Parliament hath happily placed the crown at the disposal of the king's grace, but to have the succession established would mean England's salvation; and all these conspiracies which bring us such misery would be harmless as a still-born babe."

He paused; his face deeply overcast. Then recollecting himself, as he encountered Betty's inquiring gaze, he summoned an attendant.

"This man will go with you," he said to Sir William, "and will secure you immediate admittance at the Tower."

Carew thanked him heartily, although he half suspected the attendant of being a spy, but he had no choice but to accept him.   After a few more words, Cromwell dismissed them and they set out without delay for the Tower.

Sir William was not altogether pleased at being pushed forward upon the errand, but he was too kind-hearted to blame his niece, who was so deeply distressed already.   So he made the best of an unpleasant business and walked briskly to the wharf, where Cromwell's servant obtained a wherry with a readiness that increased Sir William's uneasiness.   However, it seemed but an ordinary river craft, manned by four stout oarsmen, who haggled, as usual, over the fare.   But Carew was so liberally inclined that in a few moments the bargain was completed and the three set out on their voyage.   Betty's face was muffled, and she sat quietly by her uncle as the boat travelled swiftly over the waters.   They crossed that part of the river which was most thickly crowded with shipping, but the young girl had no eyes save for the low dark walls of the Tower, which presently came in sight.   She shuddered when the boatmen, obeying the directions of Cromwell's servant, turned under the dusky bastion to the Traitor's Gate.   The tide was rising and bore the wherry under the low arch to the stone steps, where the water lapped gently as it rose.

Above them the arch was closed by a wicket of heavy wooden cross-bars, and behind this rose the causeway leading to the prison. On the other side of the wicket could be seen the sentries on guard. This was the view before them; behind, looking back through the arch, was the sunshine on the river, the gay life of the world. Here, but a short while before, had entered More and Fisher, the Charterhouse monks, and the unhappy Queen of England — a strange company!

Sir William and Mistress Betty alighted on the stone steps, and the wicket was promptly opened at the warrant of the privy seal, which also ensured the visitors a respectful welcome. Without more delay than naturally accompanied the formalities of a military prison, they were shown into the presence of Sir William Kingston, who received Carew with every mark of kindness, as an old acquaintance.

"I am well pleased to see you," he said, "and better pleased that you come not as a permanent guest."

"God forbid!" said Sir William Carew, bluntly; "but I come to see one of your guests, Kingston; my friend, Simon Raby."

The officer's face became grave at once.

"I am sorry for his case," he said; "he was

the last I looked for. He will be glad to welcome you, for he takes not kindly to confinement."

As he spoke, he led the way to the rooms near the chapel, and having a warder with him, soon caused a door to be unbolted and signed to Carew to enter.

"You have the privy seal's warrant," he said, "and yonder you will find the prisoner."

After an instant's hesitation, Sir William pushed his niece forward and then followed her across the threshold. Kingston, closing the door, left them alone with the imprisoned nobleman. It was a low, dark room, so insufficiently lighted that at first they could not plainly see Lord Raby's face as he rose at their entrance. A small fire took off a little of the chill of the place, but the atmosphere was unwholesomely damp. The unwonted captivity and the anxiety had driven all the color from the prisoner's cheeks, and his expression was stern and sad. For an instant he did not recognize Carew, and then he uttered an exclamation of joy.

"This is kind of you indeed!" he exclaimed, advancing, and as he did so, his eyes lighted on the cloaked figure beside Sir William. In an instant he recognized her, and regardless of her uncle, he sprang forward and caught her in his arms.

Mistress Betty's high spirit would at other times have resisted her lover's fashion of taking possession of her, but his situation made a sad difference, and she clung to him a moment, tears shining in her eyes, while he caressed her and blessed her for coming. It was Carew who interrupted this little drama.

"Come, come," he said with gruff kindness, "our time is short; and if we are to serve you, we must inquire into your case."

"'T is so," said Betty, withdrawing from Raby's embrace; "you must tell us all."

Her lover drew forward the only two chairs the room afforded for his guests, and seating himself on a low stool at her feet, listened patiently to Sir William's harangue.

"My Lord Raby," he said gravely, "but yesterday we received the tidings of your arrest, and came post haste to London to my lord privy seal to learn what we could of the matter. Nor can I say that we were comforted thereby; the information is so strange that it perplexeth me marvellously. We were granted permit to come to the Tower by Cromwell, and here we be, but how we may serve you is not so plain to me. Doubtless, though, you can make some clean statement of the matter, albeit it seems so bewildering to others."

Sir William's frame of mind was not easily mistaken and Raby's cheek flushed at the doubt implied, even though he saw only faith and trust in the eyes of Betty Carew.

"Unhappily, sir," he said stiffly, "I can make no explanation; could I do so, doubtless I should not be in the Tower."

Carew bent his brows. "My lord privy seal tells me that you were chiefly condemned by the packet you gave him," he said slowly; "therefore it would seem that you must hold some key to the matter. What was this packet? Wherefore did you give it to Cromwell?"

"The packet was yours, Sir William," Raby replied sharply, "therefore 't is you who should unfold the story."

Carew's face flushed red with indignation.

"My Lord Raby," he said coldly, "that is a child's tale, but not for the ears of men. My papers were innocent of any offence to king or council; they pertained entirely to affairs in Devon, and were writ at Cromwell's request."

"Sir," replied the prisoner, sternly, "it hath been a mystery to me, and, albeit I would not have spoken of it, for fear of offence to you, now I will even speak my mind. The packet that you gave me was cherished with care, and when I was apprehended, was yet in the breast of my doublet. My lord privy seal had received me kindly, and used me with the justice I had a right to expect. Being willing to serve you, even in my own misfortune, I handed your packet to him. Scarce had he opened it before his face changed, and after reading half its contents, he sent me to the Tower. Had I been minded to think ill of you, Sir William, surely I had cause enough, but I strove to judge the matter with charity. In return, you cast suspicion on my motives and charge me with falsehood in regard to this same evil packet. Sir, it tries my patience to its limit."

"'T is sheer nonsense to lay the matter to my papers," retorted Carew, irritably; "know I not what was writ there? Am I a fool? If all your conduct was as innocent, there is little doubt you would be a freeman."

"I am a prisoner," Raby replied proudly, "and mayhap it pleasures you to cast aspersions on a man who may not defend himself, but 't is unworthy of you."

At this, Betty interfered.

"I pray you both to forbear," she said, looking from one face to the other imploringly;

"surely there is some terrible mistake, and do not make it worse by a quarrel."

Raby, seeing her distress, pressed her hand affectionately.

"Dear heart," he said, "I would not quarrel with thy uncle, but no man can endure such insinuations with patience. I am innocent, and I have no such meek spirit that I love to be suspected by my friends."

"I am an old man, my lord," said Carew, impatiently, "and I am not over-smooth-tongued; I have no wish to offend your nice feelings, but I see a plain matter and you give me a foolish excuse. My packet! Why, Lord Raby, I would have sent this child Betty with it and taken no thought."

"Sir, I never accused you of malice," Simon replied more calmly, "but I had the packet of you, I gave it to Cromwell, and I am here."

"Tush!" exclaimed Sir William, testily, "am I a fool? Do I look a dullard? Can you think to pass this dream off on a sane man? Raby, it was not my packet!"

"Sir!" exclaimed the younger man, springing to his feet, "do you accuse me of falsehood?"

Mistress Betty rose and ran to her uncle,

who was standing, his strong face working with anger.

"Uncle," she said, pushing him toward the door, her rosy palms pressed against his broad breast, and using all her young strength, "go — go to the door and wait for me. I would speak with him. You will only quarrel. Hush! hush!" she added, as she saw the angry words trembling on Sir William's lips; "he is a prisoner; 't is unworthy of you."

Sir William looked at the beautiful young face so close to his, and his heart relented.

"Thou art a witch, Betty," he said; "have thy will, but make the man talk sense to thee."

She had pushed him to the door, and would have thrust him out if the warder had not fastened it from without. Having disposed of one, she ran back to the other disputant, who stood leaning on his chair with a gloomy face.

"Have you also so poor an opinion of me?" he asked, looking searchingly at the fair face.

"Would I be here?" she answered simply. "Ah, my lord, a woman comes not lightly to such a place!"

"Forgive me!" he exclaimed, kissing her hands passionately; "Sir William's suspicions of me struck a sore heart. My darling, while

I have your confidence, no man shall dare to doubt me."

"Think, think!" she cried, pressing her hand on his arm earnestly; "how did it happen? What can we do to explain it away?"

Lord Raby shook his head; he knew too well the secret nature of such charges, the slow course of the law, the difficulty of defence.

"I know not," he answered, looking fondly into her troubled eyes; "we must even let the law find its own way. The attack on me is of a nature which I can least easily defeat. I trust most in mine innocence. Let it not so distress you, happy as it makes me to feel you care. Ah, Betty, I had no thought of such a fate when I asked you to be my wife; will you keep faith? Forgive me; I ought not to ask you to remain plighted to a prisoner."

He was looking sadly at the beautiful, animated face. She raised her head proudly; her eyes shone.

"Sir," she said sweetly, "I will wed you or none!"

"God bless you!" he cried, catching her in his arms and kissing her; "I have no right to ask such a pledge of you!"

"You asked not," she said archly; "I gave

it.   Hark! there comes the warder; doubtless our time is expired.   I pray you think better of my uncle; I love him.   He is a blunt man and too free-spoken, but he is true as steel."

"Dear Betty," the prisoner whispered fondly, "if he were a monster, I would try to love him for your sake."

"Come, niece!" called Sir William, impatiently, "we must be gone; the warder is here."

"I must go," Betty said, tearing herself away from her lover's detaining arms; "I must go, but surely will I work for your deliverance with all my might, and so shall my uncle. Farewell — oh, farewell till we meet again!"

Her eyes were shining now with tears, and there was a third summons from Sir William before she parted from the prisoner, and ran from the room, drawing her mantle over her face.

When they sat again in the boat, Carew turned to her with a grim face, but there was a kind light in his eyes.

"My wench," he said bluntly, "thou art a fool, but I love thee."

CHAPTER XXV

Lord Raby was arrested in June, and at
the time there seemed to be an immediate
prospect of a trial, and he looked forward to it
with the earnest hope of establishing his innocence.   But he was doomed to a far different
fate; he and his fellow prisoner, the wizard,
were held while Cromwell slowly unravelled
the threads of a great conspiracy, which had
been only partially indicated by the papers
in the mysterious packet.   It was not good
policy to seize at once upon men whose names
figured in the documents, some of them the
foremost in the land, and the privy seal
played the waiting game, in which he was
an adept.   The slow months of the summer
passed, and with Michaelmas came the rising in the northern counties, ostensibly pro-
voked by the visitation of the monasteries, but
really the outgrowth of many grievances, and
the full fruit of a long-planned conspiracy.
The Pilgrimage of Grace doomed Lord Raby

to a long confinement. With this example of
the result of treasonable machinations before
his eyes, Cromwell had less mercy for those
accused of direct complicity in it. As the
rebels, under Robert Aske, advanced to Don-
caster, threatening to overwhelm the king's
small army, the prisoners in the Tower were
subjected to closer confinement. One of the
avowed purposes of the insurgents was the fall
of Cromwell, and it was not probable that he
would be lenient to such offenders as were
within his reach. It was, however, an incon-
venient time for trial of the prisoners, and Raby
and Sanders remained in suspense.

Sir William Carew could not forgive the
doubt of his packet expressed by Simon, and
he turned a deaf ear to Betty's entreaties. He
would not move a finger in the cause. In fact,
the stout-hearted gentleman doubted Lord
Raby. The evidence was so plain, as Cromwell unfolded it, Simon's accusation of Sir
William's documents so childish, the outbreak
of the insurrection so convincing, that Carew
felt certain that the nobleman had been led
into dabbling with conspiracy and had committed himself to the cause of Mary Tudor and
the papists.

Mistress Betty, indignant at her uncle, distressed for Lord Raby, and helpless to combat the course of events, remained with Lady Crabtree. She was unable even to see the king in regard to the matter. Having been one of Anne Boleyn's maids, she was unacceptable to Queen Jane, and her petitions to the king remained unanswered. She lived in seclusion at Wildrick, having no heart for the festivities at Hampton Court, where Jane held her court, and being unwelcome, she stayed away. She could not even obtain leave to see her lover; after the outbreak of the rebellion, she was denied access to him; he was kept in solitary confinement and under rigorous military discipline. The suspense told on the young girl's nerves, and before winter was over she was pale and thin; but her eyes gained in beauty as her color faded, and her striking face drew many a glance of admiration when she went upon her pilgrimages to Cromwell's house. Lady Crabtree, though sharing some of Carew's doubts of Raby's innocence, had a warm regard for him, and was ever Mistress Betty's companion, her untiring energy accomplishing as much as the young girl's devotion. The two figures, so strangely contrasted, — the gaunt old woman, with her long stride, and the graceful girl, —

were familiar in Cromwell's anterooms, but their efforts to win better treatment or an open trial for Lord Raby were alike in vain. The privy seal, conscious that in the magician he had a master traitor, saw in Raby a probable accomplice. There was one also, always about Cromwell, whose offices boded ill for Simon. Sir Barton Henge was active in working for the government, tireless upon the scent of traitors, a conspicuously zealous loyalist. Yet, though he and the two women, old Madam and Betty, travelled often upon the same errand, they never met. The sting of Mistress Carew's whip was still upon his face although the mark had faded, and he watched his opportunity with that feline patience which belongs to the panther tribe, whether walking on two legs or four, for the kinship to the beast is strong in some human beings.

There were many anxious hearts in England through that long year of trouble, and the enemies of the king rejoiced. On Christmas Eve, at the great mass at St. Peter's, the darkness of the church was illumined by a thousand tapers, while the marvellous cap and sword were laid upon the altar, consecrated for James of Scotland to unite the enemies of the faith. And in Flanders, Cardinal Pole looked eagerly for the opportunity to overthrow Henry VIII., and for the return of the supremacy of Rome. Across the Channel, plot and counter-plot were hatched, took their course, and died fruitless; while in England, the one man with an iron will, the privy seal, held on his even course, though the waves of popular fury, beating on the ship of state, threatened to overwhelm the pilot. Norfolk, whose heart was doubtless more with the rebels than with the king, was driven against them. The unhappy Northumberland died faithful to Henry, although the fate of Anne Boleyn had prostrated him. The great rebellion spent itself; one after another of its leaders were brought to the Tower. The unfortunate Darcy died, charging it all on Cromwell, and at last, in July, Robert Aske suffered a felon's death. The Pilgrimage of Grace was over; it had ended in a futile loss of life to the cause of the old religion. "Twice the children of Israel went up against Benjamin," wrote Cardinal Pole, "and twice they were put to confusion."

In the midst of trials and executions, Raby yet lingered in the Tower untried. Either overlooked in the great pressure of trouble, or held for stronger proof, he and the wizard languished, each in solitary confinement. The king's officers had taken possession of the strange house on the Thames and searched it, finding many curious contrivances for the execution of the mummeries which had confused the imagination of the magician's clients. Yet, so exuberant was the superstition of the times, that the exposure of paltry methods of deceit failed to destroy the dread of the small man who had held such sway there. Even the royal officers shrank from their duty, and no one occupied the house; the official seal was affixed to the doors and it remained empty. The shutters, taken down to admit the light for the search, remained so, and the windows blinked in the afternoon sun like evil eyes suddenly unveiled. No man ventured near it after sundown, and many who passed it, even at high noon, made the sign of the cross. A baleful influence seemed to issue from it; the vine that tried to climb up the door-post hung blasted in midsummer, and the grass did not grow, although no footsteps wore the ground about it. There was not an old wife in the neighborhood who had not a tale of how the wizard visited it every night, and how the smoke came from the chimney of his laboratory at the very hour when he had been in the habit of brewing the devil's tea.

Summer passed; Michaelmas came and went; all England waited in hope and fear for news of the birth of an heir to the throne, and on the twelfth of October, the vigil of Saint Edward's day, the bells rang out in wild peals of joy, the bonfires blazed from Land's End to the Tweed, the guns were fired. A prince was born; the hope of England lived.

CHAPTER XXVI

A PRINCE'S BAPTISM

IT was the hour appointed for the prince's baptism. It was night at Hampton Court; the king's equerries ran to and fro, the ladies of the queen were crowding the anterooms of the royal chamber. They had made elaborate toilets for the great occasion, and farthingales of satin and brocade spread wide on every hand; and more than one slender waist was girdled with costly pearls, while the great headdresses loomed up above fair faces, flushed and agitated with the haste and the unusual presence of the king; for Henry sat beside the state couch on which lay the young mother of England's future king. Pages quarrelled over comfits on the staircases; gentlemen-in-waiting ran against each other in their eagerness to excel in service at that hour; the doctors and nurses forgot the queen in their zeal for the prince. The heralds, armed with silver trumpets, stood waiting to proclaim the glad event; the sponsors were come, laden with

gifts, the Archbishop Cranmer, the Princess
Mary, the Duke of Norfolk — a strange company. My lord of Canterbury's spoons and
Mary Tudor's golden cup stood side by side;
the day was not yet ripe when she would sign
the warrant to send the archbishop to the
flames of martyrdom.

Into this scene of confusion came my Lady
Crabtree and Mistress Betty Carew. It was
an hour when all guests were welcome, and
the opportunity to reach the royal presence
was too valuable to be lost. Betty came with
a secret hope; she did not speak of it even to
her companion, but it was in her heart. She
had arrayed herself with more than usual care,
and she looked like a stately white rose as she
stood in the chapel waiting for the entrance of
the great procession. Her gown was of pure
white brocade, and on her head was the five-
pointed hood of white velvet, such as Anne
Boleyn had often worn; around her throat was
a single string of pearls. Months of anxiety
had stolen the color from her cheeks, but her
brown eyes were larger and more lustrous, and
there was a purpose, a resolution in her face
which made it beautiful in its intense animation. Old Madam, in a singularly ugly gar-
ment of copper-colored satin with a marvellous

headdress of black velvet, made a strange foil for the beauty, and many a curious glance was cast in their direction as they stood aside, watching, but taking no part in the festivities.

The torches flared in the royal chapel, the light shining red on the altar and on the solid silver font, which was guarded by four gentlemen, one of these Sir Francis Bryan, the cousin of Anne Boleyn. These four grand personages wore aprons, and towels were tied around their necks. There were Bryan, Sir John Russel, Sir Nicholas Carew, the master of horse, who was to lose his head in the matter of the Marquis of Exeter, and Sir Anthony Browne. The silver trumpets blew in the very chamber where Jane Seymour lay, and the procession came up between the torches to the silver font. There was the glitter of gold, the flash of jewels, the sheen of satin. Noble lords, great ladies, the peers of England walked in solemn company. The smoke from the many torches floated up to the roof and hung like a veil; below, the blaze of splendor dazzled the eye. Under a glittering canopy came the prince of England, borne in the arms of the Marchioness of Exeter, and behind walked the humble Mother Jack, the prince's nurse. The Princess Mary and the Duke of

Norfolk, Seymour, the queen's brother, bearing in his arms the little Princess Elizabeth, who held in her hands a chrisom, her gift to her infant brother. The father of Anne Boleyn, the Earl of Wiltshire, came with a towel about his neck and bearing a taper of virgin wax. Behind these, the lords and ladies of the court; a long and goodly procession, sweeping into the chapel and filling it with a gorgeous display of costly silks and jewels. And the music of the silver trumpets filled the air, while on every side beauty and magnificence vied with each other, and the blaze of many torches made the chapel light as day. The solemn service over, his serene highness, Prince Edward, Duke of Cornwall and Earl of Chester, was proclaimed by Garter, and the glittering procession took its way back to the chamber of the queen, where King Henry had remained all the while. It was midnight when, with the music of many trumpets, the throng came in to the great apartment where the pale-faced queen lay on a state bed with a canopy above it, resplendent with cloth of gold. There was the rustle of many sweeping skirts, the jingle of swords and chains, the flare of many lights, and all the room full of faces, looking eagerly toward the royal couch. The

Marchioness of Exeter bore the little prince to receive his mother's blessing; the king stood up, looking on, boisterous in his joy. Behind him were the pale, gentle face of Cranmer, the stalwart form of Norfolk, the sad and cold-looking Princess Mary, the daughter of Catherine of Arragon, and the little golden-haired Elizabeth, the child of such bright hopes, and now stamped with the mark of illegitimacy and shadowed by the fearful death of Anne Boleyn. The little princess, though only four years old, had a train borne by Lady Herbert as she walked into the room. The king had increased in corpulence, and the ulcers on his legs made his movements painful, but he was very merry.

"Sweetheart," he said to the queen as she kissed the child, after giving it her blessing, "the boy hath thine eyes and will have thy beauty."

"My lord," replied Jane, meekly, "I would rather that he looked like your grace."

"Nay," said the king, laughing, "I am willing that my successor should excel me in looks. What say you, my lords and ladies, is he not a goodly boy?"

There was a chorus of assent; it would have been a strange time to criticise the Prince of

England. Only one or two of the older women looked anxiously at the pale face and shining eyes of the queen, and nodded their heads at each other. Henry, overflowing with joy at the birth of a boy, moved about among the nobles present, talking freely to all, and with little thought of the nervous strain upon the young mother. His face softened by his happiness and his rich dress becoming his large and stately figure, the king recalled to many the handsome presence of his earlier manhood. He came down the long room, speaking familiarly and kindly to all whom he recognized, and showing his wonderful memory for small matters by his words to each one.

"Ah, John," he said to one tall nobleman, "how is that lame boy of yours? I will send my physician to look at his leg; the prince must have sound subjects."

Without waiting for thanks, he turned to another.

"Lady Harriet, you and I grow old; we are both limping; but we must mend our paces now." And to a younger matron, "Alice, I hear thy baby is a beauty; we must see if it can match mine."

A little farther on, he stopped beside a young couple who were standing together. "I have heard of your parents' opposition," he said with boisterous kindness; "I will see to it that it is ended; we must have a merry wedding before Christmas. Trouble ceased at this court when the prince was born!"

In his genial progress he had reached the end of the room where stood Betty Carew. Her tall, white figure and beautiful, sad face arrested his attention at once. It may be that he remembered her as an attendant of Queen Anne, for his own face clouded slightly and he looked at her with manifest interest. It was the opportunity for which Betty had waited, and she advanced with a beating heart. Her great beauty and something in her manner made a little stir as she came forward. A page was holding a torch near where the king stood, and the boy, attracted by her beauty, held his light so that the full radiance fell on her figure, outlining it in the white glistening folds of satin draperies and casting a wonderful glow in her eyes. She came forward with perfect dignity, pausing a little way from the king, her beauty causing a whisper of amazement to run around the circle. Henry, who was ever quick to recognize loveliness in woman, looked at her with evident admiration.

"'T is Mistress Carew, and I mistake not,"

he said graciously. "What will you ask of me to-night?"

"Your grace," she replied gently, "I have a petition, albeit a strange one for so joyous an occasion, yet I pray you hear it in the name of Prince Edward."

"My girl, thou hast used an appeal to which we may not turn a deaf ear," said Henry; "say on."

Mistress Betty drew a long breath; she was summoning all her strength to plead her cause.

"Sire," she said, "there is a prisoner in the Tower wrongfully charged with treason; an innocent man whom some enemy hath en-tangled. I pray your grace to hear his cause, to end this great suspense. Long, long he hath languished a prisoner without the oppor-tunity to establish his innocence. And he is innocent!" she clasped her hands together with a passionate gesture, "Simon Raby is innocent!" she cried; "and oh, my lord the king, I pray you to think of the terrible strain of this long suspense!"

"Simon Raby?" repeated the king; "once my equerry, I think."

"Ay, your grace," replied the Duke of Norfolk, "the son of old Lord Raby of Sussex;

an honest gentleman, who died nearly two years ago."

"An honest gentleman; ay, I remember him; he served my father well," said the king, thoughtfully. "Cromwell hath been eager trapping his mice, but I would not keep a true man in jail. Hath he not been tried, Mistress Carew?" he added, looking again at Betty.

"Nay, your highness," she replied sadly; "he has languished long, and with no hope, nor have they let his friends see him."

"How long hath he been in the Tower?" asked Henry, gravely.

"Fourteen months and more, Sire," she answered.

"'Tis too long," said the king, frowning. "I have no will to keep a poor gentleman without a trial; this shall be looked into."

Betty's heart beat high with hope, but she had yet a petition to make, and Henry saw it in her expression. Her beauty, her evident loyalty to the prisoner interested him.

"Speak, sweetheart," he said kindly; "what is in thy mind?"

"I pray your grace to give me warrant to see the wizard, Zachary Sanders, who is also in the Tower," she said; "they let no man see him, but I know that if he will, he can surely clear Lord Raby; and oh, I beseech your highness, to let me plead with him!"

Henry smiled. "You are not like to plead in vain, fair mistress," he said lightly; "for the sake of this blessed night, your petitions are both granted. Norfolk, bid my lord privy seal to give this pretty beggar a warrant to go into the Tower. But hark you, my wench, I charge you not to leave your heart behind you there," and with a laugh at his own jest, the king passed on, surrounded by an ever-increasing throng of courtiers until the apartment of the queen was gradually deserted, save by her own attendants.

The first white streaks of dawn were showing at the eastern horizon when Lady Crabtree and Betty left Hampton Court, and the mists of night obscured the scene.

"Thou didst have rare luck, my girl," said old Madam, drawing her mantle closer in the chill air; "and now there is a hope to end the matter."

"The king's grace was kind," replied Betty, "and I have good hope, for I believe that now they will hear Simon's cause; and if they do, all will be well."

"Mayhap it will," retorted Lady Crabtree dryly, unwilling to cast down the young girl's new-born hopes; "at least, Cromwell shall do more than shake his head at us. 'T is well that you struck while the iron was hot and the king was happy; for if they keep up that rout, they will kill both mother and child. Mercy on us, what a baptism! My lord of Canterbury and Mary Tudor walking together, and Norfolk, who loves the papists with all his heart. That ambitious prig, too, my Lord Seymour, who will rise on his sister's petticoats. It went to my heart to see Anne Boleyn's baby decked out to march behind this new toy! Well-a-day, 't is strange!"

A little farther on, she burst out laughing; a scornful laugh, too, which startled Betty.

"What makes you so merry, madam?" she asked quietly.

"Saw you not that fool, the Earl of Wiltshire," old Madam asked, "with a towel tied around his neck, and carrying my Lord Cranmer's silver pots, the christening present? Lord! why did he not go fetch his daughter's head? The drivelling idiot would dance at his own funeral, if he could crook his legs, with the hope to please the king's grace. 'T is such a courtier that upsets an honest stomach. Were I the king, I'd send him home with a merry flogging, as an ass."

CHAPTER XXVII

Superstition works its own miracles, and strangely enough, even in the Tower of London, its spell took effect. The royal officers had secured the person of the wizard and had suffered no harm from the contact. It was true that one young man had fallen in a fit at some strange vision in the wizard's house, but the others were unscathed. Yet the power of the little man's strange eyes and stranger manner worked upon them, and no prisoner in the Tower was better treated or with more reverence. The warder locked him in with shaking hands, his knees knocking together, and but for the sharper terror of the rope at Tyburn, he might have failed to turn the key upon his captive. The sentinels within the Traitor's Gate declared that at midnight the small man in a russet cloak passed between them, not in natural shape, but floating past them like a vapor, going through the close-barred wicket to the river and returning again at dawn. Of food, the wizard had an abundance; he had but to express the wish for some new viand, accompanying it with a gruesome prophecy in regard to his keeper's future, and the dish was immediately forthcoming. They denied him nothing; when other prisoners shivered, he had a fire; when better men languished in the dark, he had twenty tall tapers burning around his room. He was freely supplied with pen and paper, and he filled the sheets with cabalistic signs which froze the blood of his attendants. One of the bolder warders refused to tend his fire for him; the wizard looked up with a strange face and passed his hands before his eyes.

"Thy wife has a fit," he said calmly; "the baby is born dead."

The man hurried from the room, grumbling at the prisoner as an evil croaker, and at the door he heard the news confirmed. After that he almost grovelled in his anxiety to serve the evil little man who only laughed and mocked his terror. Nothing but a wholesome fear of Cromwell's anger kept such a prisoner in the Tower; a thousand times he could have escaped, but that, at the last moment, the thought of the privy seal stayed the hands of his would-be liberators. Cromwell could not be trifled with;

his arm was long, his vengeance swift, his eye that of a hawk looking for prey. Between the two, the magician and the king's minister, the warders of the Tower lived as men do between the devil and the deep sea.

It was the day after Prince Edward's great christening, and the wizard sat in his prison watching the blaze leap from the logs piled in his chimney. The wind was chill without, but he was warm, thanks to the terror of his jailers. He sat on a low stool, his elbows on his knees, his chin in his hands, gazing at the flames as if he loved them; the red glow of the fire flaring on his wizened face and in his wonderful eyes. He was dressed in russet-colored damask, a cape of Flanders lace about his neck, and on his head a pointed scarlet cap with an opal in the front, clasping the one stiff feather. He wore velvet shoes, scarlet like his cap, and on his thin, long-fingered hands were some curious rings, all strangely wrought and fantastic in design. He had but recently stirred the fire, and the blaze leaped up the chimney with a merry roar and crackle. So intent was he in his study of it that he never turned his head when the warder opened his door and admitted two closely muffled women. The visitors came in a little way and stopped, looking at him without speaking, while the warder, after staring in with wide-mouthed curiosity, retreated in fear of provoking the wizard's displeasure. When he had closed the door, the scene remained for some moments unchanged; the two women standing together, evidently watching the magician, though their mantles concealed their faces, and he still gazing fixedly at the blaze as if he read some story in it. There was no sound but the sharp crackle of the wood, and there was something unpleasantly awe-inspiring in the stillness of the gloomy place, where no light shone but the red one of the flames. Presently the wizard broke the silence. He had not shown by any sign or movement that he had seen his visitors, but he addressed them now, though without turning his head or glancing in their direction.

"My Lady Crabtree and Mistress Carew, you are welcome," he said calmly; "come to the fire and be seated."

Old Madam laughed harshly.

"What is the use to wear a mask?" she said; "the creature hath eyes in the back of his head like a spider."

As she spoke, she drew nearer the fire and seated herself on a settle opposite the astrolo-

ger, and Betty came over and stood beside her,
looking eagerly at the weird figure before
them.

"You came from Hampton Court," remarked
the wizard composedly, for the first time looking at them attentively, "with the king's warrant to visit the Tower in the matter of my
Lord Raby."

"We came to see you, sir," Betty said earnestly, "to learn the truth. We are convinced that you can clear him if you will.
In common charity, I pray you, help us un-
tangle this conspiracy against an innocent
man."

"Ay, I know the truth," retorted the magician; "'t is my business; but why should I
make my Lord Raby's affairs mine?"

"Tush, Sanders!" exclaimed Lady Crabtree,
who was unmoved by any awe of him, "do not
play the innocent. We all know that you are
knee-deep and elbow-deep in this conspiracy
and like to hang at Tyburn."

"Nay, I will never hang," replied the wizard
coldly, fixing his large and marvellously radiant
eyes upon her, "nor will the prince baptized
last night live to manhood."

"Pshaw!" said Lady Crabtree, with a laugh,
"it takes no magician to predict danger to the

baby with the rumpus they are making over it; any old wife can beat you there as a prophet!"

The strong-minded old woman had thrown back her wraps and sat by the fire, her hawk-like nose and square chin sharply outlined in the red light, and her great frame contrasting strangely with the diminutive one of the prisoner. The two natures, naturally defiant and antagonistic, recognized the qualities which made them so, and they eyed each other in mutual dislike and suspicion. But Betty Carew had only the one object and hope, and something in her beauty perhaps appealed to Sanders, for he treated her with more consideration than usual; he had, too, his own reasons for aiding her. She came a step nearer now and stood looking at him; her hood had fallen back and revealed her head, with its black hair uncovered, framing her pale but handsome face; her hands hung loosely clasped before her, and the firelight played in her deep brown eyes.

"I pray you," she said eagerly, "consider that he who so entangled Raby by placing that packet on his person, — in some marvellous manner, — he also must have betrayed you. Your cause is therefore identical with ours.

Surely you can think of some one who had the means to compass this — and the will."

The wizard looked at her thoughtfully; not a change of expression denoted that he felt any interest in what she said.

"Lord Raby had a servant," he replied, deliberately stirring the fire; "he can tell you all you wish to know."

"We thought of that," cried Betty; "but it is judged impossible that so ignorant a man could have had access to the papers which are now in the hands of Cromwell."

"Nevertheless, I tell you, find him," returned the wizard, calmly.

"He hath been already interrogated," replied Betty, sadly, "and now we know not where he is — since Lord Raby dismissed him."

"He is in a house in Cheapside," said the astrologer. "You may find it easily; the door is painted green and hath a rat-hole in the lower left-hand corner; there are three windows in the front of the house, each different in size and shape. He sleeps in the attic."

"He will tell us nothing," Betty answered in despair; "we have tried, and my Lord Raby is sure he knows nothing."

The wizard laughed, not mirthfully, but as if he relished some grim joke.

"He is in that attic," he said dryly; "take him and he will tell you all."

"I tell you," cried Betty, with impatience, "he will tell us nothing."

"Singe him," retorted the wizard, with a grin; "my lord privy seal can teach you how to entreat a prisoner to speak."

Betty recoiled with horror, but old Madam caught at the idea.

"The man is right," she remarked calmly; "'t is easy enough to screw out the truth. But verily, Sir Wizard, is there not more to tell?"

The little magician shrugged his shoulders.

"I have told enough," he said; "a woman who is near fourscore should know the rest without telling."

This reference to Lady Crabtree's age brought the angry blood to her face; she never admitted it to any one, and to find that this strange creature knew it, moved her to wrath. She rose and gathered her mantle about her.

"Come Betty," she said sharply, "we but waste time on this fool. Let us begone."

The wizard sat laughing silently, his sinister face lighted up with malicious enjoyment.

Betty lingered a moment, while Lady Crabtree hurried to the door.

"Is there nothing else?" she asked earnestly; "no other way?"

"If you follow my instructions," replied the wizard, "all will be well; if not — " He shrugged his shoulders.

CHAPTER XXVIII

MISTRESS BETTY left the Tower with a heavy
heart; she could not believe in the success of
the wizard's plans, and she had failed to see
Lord Raby. He was that day carried before
the Council to be examined, by order of the
king, who had not forgotten Betty's petition.
Thus, while she was thankful that the long
suspense was over, she was disappointed in
the hope of seeing her lover, after the months
of separation. She could but wait and hope,
in the mean time making every effort to establish his innocence. Her courage and determination so moved old Madam to admiration
that she lacked no aid from that quarter, and
fortunately, for their success, they found Sir
William Carew in London. He had come up
from Devon two days before and was in lodgings on the Strand, engaged in transacting
business with the Council. He was little
inclined, at first, to listen to their talk of
Lord Raby, having still his grievance in regard

to his packet, but at the mention of Simon's servant, he remembered his wager that the man was a rogue, and was more willing to undertake any matter that would prove the infallibility of his own judgment. He was not free of a superstitious awe of the wizard, and showed himself to be quite ready to follow his instructions, even without his niece's entreaties.

"Let be, let be," he said, in answer to Betty's suggestions; "I will take this matter in hand. I have two stout knaves with me, and they should be enough to catch the varlet. It shall be done secretly too, that those who employ him may not take warning and so escape us. Go to your quarters with my Lady Crabtree, and I will see that this business is executed in good time."

Betty was reluctant to leave the scene of action; she was eager for the first gleam of hope that might dawn with Shaxter's revelations, if he made them.

"Uncle, you will tell me what he says?" she asked. "I cannot endure this suspense so long."

"I will send for you," Sir William answered. "Your presence here now is more hindrance than help; but trust me, wench, I will tell you all there is to know, if indeed this rogue can reveal anything of importance."

Old Madam had been below stairs talking with an acquaintance at the door, and she came up now with a face of importance.

"There are bad tidings from Hampton Court," she said; "the queen hath taken cold; was ill last night, and to-day is reported dying. Saint Thomas! what luck the king hath with his wives!"

"Now may Heaven save the prince!" exclaimed Sir William, baring his head reverently; "the hope of the realm is centered in that child. We have scarce had time to express our thanksgiving for his birth, and cruel indeed would be the blow that took him from us."

"Ay," retorted Lady Crabtree; "the papists would have then the merry stirring that they have looked for these long years, and James of Scotland might use the nightcap that the pope sent him for Christmas. Happily, the queen's death need not now mean the loss of the prince; but they do say that it is a sickly child, and like to be, with such a father."

"I remember the days when the king's grace was the very type of English manhood," Carew remarked thoughtfully, "and as gallant a knight as ever wore harness; of goodly stature and amiable countenance, wise in council, learned in philosophy, and as gracious a prince as any man might desire."

"A wise man now, save with women," replied old Madam dryly; "but carrying too great a load of flesh and with the disease settled in his legs, no longer like to be a great soldier, or to live long. Well, well, this is his third queen, and she will not be cool before the Council will prefer suit to his grace to take another."

"It may be that another woman will not long for such an unlucky place," remarked Betty, quietly; "there seems to be death in it."

"Cromwell can send abroad then," said Lady Crabtree; "he will even get Master Friskyball to help him find an Italian princess; but look you, my girl, the applicants here will be as thick as cherries. Do you know your sex so little as to think that they will lose the chance of a crown? If a man looks like a wild boar, he will yet find a woman to marry him; some fool who will imagine that his heart is not indicated by his snout. I tell you women are all fools once; more's the pity!"

She was putting on her cloak as she spoke,

and having muffled it about her, she gave some parting instructions to Sir William; and then taking Betty, went down the stairs to the door where her attendants waited her.

"You will go to my lodgings," she said to her young companion; "but I have other business, and it may be late this night before I come. Content yourself, however, with the recollection that I will keep Sir William spurred up to the pitch."

Reluctantly enough Mistress Betty resigned herself to the wishes of her elders, and was escorted to Lady Crabtree's lodgings by one of her attendants. It was dusk when she passed through the gates, the porter closing them behind her. She crossed the little court, and entering the house, dismissed her follower and went alone up the stairs to the rooms where they were lodging. One of old Madam's women was there and had made the place cheerful. A fire burned on the hearth, the tapers were lighted, and a supper was laid for two upon the table in the center. It was a fast day, and there were some salted eels, a gurnet and a chet loaf set out, with a tankard of ale; for my Lady Crabtree always did good trencher duty even when fasting, which she did after her own fashion.

Betty Carew could not eat, she was far too anxious for the fate of the man she loved, and she walked to and fro, wrapped in her own thoughts and alone, having dismissed the woman. Lord Raby had been before the Council, but doubtless, by this time, was back in the Tower. How had it fared with him? she wondered. Had his innocence shone out clear as noonday, or had he been entrapped by the skilful cross-questioning and false accusations of his enemies? Believing in him with all her heart, she was yet fully conscious of the pitfalls in these secret proceedings, and she trembled for him. It was in her nature to love him more dearly in the hour of his evil fortune; she possessed that loyalty which is unshaken by the sharpest trials, and her greatest sorrow now was her own inability to fight his battles for him. Her persistence had won the king's attention to his case, had roused even her uncle from his angry apathy, had stirred old Madam to energetic action; but now, at the supreme moment, being a woman, she was powerless to help him. She longed for Sir William's summons, which would mean that something material had been accomplished, and in her eagerness, she ran twenty times to the window and looked down into the street; a light burned in the court, and this showed her that there was no one at the door. The time dragged wearily; Lady Crabtree came not, and there seemed little hope of any decisive action that night. Weary of her restless walk, she sat down by the fire, which was beginning to burn low, and waited. Every sound in the house, every step in the hall made her start with impatience; yet she scarcely knew what she expected. Nature has strong claims upon the young and healthy; no matter how great the anxiety, sleep comes at last, stealing over the senses, pressing down the lids, stilling the eager heart-beats. Betty had been under an almost continuous strain, and the warmth of the fire relaxed her nerves, comforted her physical weariness; her head drooped on her hand, her eyes closed, her breathing became soft and regular, in a few moments she would have drifted into unconsciousness. But suddenly there was a stir below, the sound of feet on the stairs, and Lady Crabtree's woman came hurrying in. Betty started up at once, alert and eager.

"'T is a message from my uncle!" she exclaimed; "from Sir William Carew?"

"Two men with a litter below, mistress," the woman replied, "and a message from Sir

William that you come at once to his lodgings."

Betty's fingers trembled with eagerness as
she fastened her cloak with the attendant's
aid. Something had happened, something was
known; she could not brook a moment's delay.

"Shall I go with you, Mistress Betty?" the
tirewoman asked.

"Nay; you must stay for Lady Crabtree,"
Betty replied; "and tell her where I am. It
does not matter; I can go alone with my
uncle's servants."

Without further delay, she ran lightly down
the stairs, where she found two serving men
in Sir William's livery, and at the door a
litter carried by four others, and there were
two pages with lanterns. She did not recognize any of the men, but observed that
one was cross-eyed, a powerful fellow, standing by the litter. She asked no questions,
but sprang into her place, dropping the curtains to keep out the chill night air, and in
a moment they were off upon their journey.
Her attendants said nothing, but walked so
rapidly along the streets that she was jolted
from side to side; but they could not travel
fast enough to keep pace with her eagerness.
Twice or thrice she peeped out from behind

her curtains, but the night was so dark that she could not see beyond the small circles of light made by the lanterns. They passed the watch, for she heard them answering his challenge, and it seemed to her that it took longer to reach Sir William's lodgings than it had taken to come from them earlier in the evening. Yet no doubt crossed her feverishly excited brain, and she was all hope and expectation when at last the party halted, and the men helped her to alight. She had been but once to her uncle's quarters, and was not sufficiently familiar with them to be startled when she found herself at the door of a tall house; but something in its aspect roused her first suspicion. Before she could realize where she was, the door opened, and partly because she was not yet aroused, and partly, too, because the men gathered behind her, leaving no retreat, she entered, and seeing a staircase like the one at Sir William's lodgings, began to ascend. Stopping half-way, she asked the man who followed her, the cross-eyed escort, where her uncle was? He pointed to a door before her without speaking, and she opened it and walked in. It was dimly lighted, and at the farther end was standing a tall man with his back toward her.

"Uncle, I have come," she exclaimed; "what tidings have you?"

He turned and came slowly forward; as the light of the solitary taper that burned on the table fell on his face, she recognized Sir Barton Henge.

CHAPTER XXIX

MASTER CROSS-EYES

THE instant that Betty Carew recognized Sir Barton's dark face, she recoiled with a cry of terror. Her first thought was of the door by which she had entered, but when she ran to it she found it fastened on the outside. There was another entrance, but that was behind Henge, and he stepped back, and locking it, put the key in his pocket with a grim smile. She was a prisoner; but after the first moment of dismay, she collected herself and confronted him with spirit. She was angry at his insolent daring, and her cheeks flushed and her eyes sparkled.

"Sir," she said proudly, "what means this? How dare you so insult me? Undo the door and let me go or you will answer for it to my uncle!"

Henge laughed and sneered.

"You take a high tone, mistress," he said tauntingly, "but it will be long ere Carew finds you; you are safe enough at last!"

Betty's anger for the time conquered her womanly fears; her hatred of the man, her contempt for an act that seemed to her one of cowardly wickedness, made her forgetful of her peril.

"You villain!" she cried, her form quivering with passion, "have you no better employment than to make war on a defenceless woman? It is like you! He who would strike a man from ambush is capable of any shamelessness. Undo the door, sir, or I will call the watch and make your name a byword in London!"

"Scream your loudest; it will not aid you," he retorted coolly. "Come, come, my pretty shrew; I have you now, and you shall rue the day you struck my face with your whip."

In spite of her anger, a feeling of dismay was beginning to shake Mistress Betty's resolution. She remembered that there was a little dagger in her belt that she had thrust there in the morning when she set out to the Tower. The thought of it was some small comfort; she had, at least, a weapon. She would not let him see any wavering; she held her head high and faced him like a beautiful fury.

"If you dare to harm me," she said haughtily,

"Sir William Carew will leave no stone un-turned until you are brought to justice."

Henge laughed again his unpleasant laugh, that rang in her ears with the sound of triumph in it.

"Look you, fair mistress, is it well to flaunt your influence in my face?" he asked her. "You and your precious lover defied me. Where is Simon Raby now? Safe, where he can neither save you nor himself. A traitor in the Tower! Beware, lest Carew falls in a like trap."

"Ah, now I know!" cried Betty; "a fool I was, and blind. 'T is you who ensnared Lord Raby! 't is you who would ruin my uncle. Villain! liar! coward! I defy you!"

"You young she-devil, you!" exclaimed Henge, advancing toward her, "I would wring that white neck of yours for your insults, did I not know I could invent a slower, surer punishment. I have you, my shrew, and you shall not escape me."

At his first step toward her, Betty retreated to a window, and now she tried to unfasten the shutter, crying out for help at the top of her strong, young voice.

"Scream away!" said Henge bitterly, his face full of dark enjoyment of her despair, "no one will help you; a screaming woman in this quarter of the town is no novelty. Do you look for your lover from the Tower to rescue you? You pretty fool!" he added contemptuously, "you are mine, mine as sure as death!"

Betty was no coward; she put her hand to her girdle and felt the little knife there safe. She meant to kill him — or herself. She had a firm, strong wrist and she could strike; he was a powerful man, but he did not know that she was armed, and an unlooked-for blow might end the matter. She saw the evil triumph in his face and set her teeth; she would kill him. He, unconscious of her purpose, looked at her and smiled, as a devil might, who saw his prey before him.

At this moment there was a strange interruption; the door that Henge had not fastened, the one that had been secured from without, opened, and the cross-eyed man entered, and closing it behind him, stood, with his arms folded on his breast, staring at Sir Barton, who, in turn, glared at him in furious surprise.

"What are you here for, Master Cross-Eyes?" he exclaimed. "Get out, you rogue, or I will break a rod on your bare back and slit your ears, to boot."

The groom pointed at Betty.

"She screamed," he said sullenly; "if you hurt a hair of her head, I'll cut your throat, my master!"

"You accursed villain, you!" cried Henge, in furious anger, "how dare you threaten me? Is it for this that I dragged you from the gutter?"

"Nay," retorted Master Cross-Eyes, unmoved; "you picked me up from the slums because you wanted desperate men to do your bidding; and so I would, if the case were different, but Mistress Carew you shall not hurt."

So amazed was Henge at the varlet's courage, that he did not spurn him from the room at once, but stared at him as if he doubted his own senses.

"And wherefore?" he asked harshly; "what is Mistress Carew to you, you hound?"

"One good turn deserves another, Sir Barton," the groom answered curtly; "this young mistress saved my neck from the halter at Deptford when old Lady Crabtree would have hung me as a valiant beggar. The young lady saved me, and, by Saint Michael and his angels, you shall not harm one black hair of her pretty head!"

"The devil take your insolence!" retorted

Henge violently, drawing his sword and raising his arm to strike the man on the head with
the flat of it, intending to administer a lesson.

But Master Cross-Eyes was more than his
match in strength; he caught his arm, and
twisting it back, sent the sword flying across
the room, pushing Henge toward the wall as
he did so.   Sir Barton, now fully roused to his
peril, grappled with his powerful adversary,
calling loudly for help as he did so.

"What ho!" he shouted, "John! Andrew!
Here, you villains, take this fellow to the
gallows!"

Master Cross-Eyes laughed, much as Sir
Barton had at Betty's cries for aid.

"I sent them all below," he said grimly;
"you may scream as loud as my young lady
now, and get no aid."

The two men swayed and struggled, the
vagrant having the advantage, yet closely
pressed by Henge, who was no mean opponent
and had the strength of wrath.   They overturned the table, and the taper being extinguished, the struggle continued in darkness.
Sir Barton was striving to reach the door and
Cross-Eyes was pressing him away.

At first Betty was so wholly fascinated by
the contest, so amazed, that she stood gaz-

ing, completely unnerved, her courage desert-
ing her now that a champion was so suddenly raised up for her. But in a moment
the full peril of her own situation returned to
her mind, and she looked for a way to escape
while the two were fighting. However, this
was not easy; one door was still locked, and
before the other the men were struggling; she
could not pass them and get out, for they
swayed to and fro before the entrance, and
when the taper was extinguished, she could
not see to move. In her extremity, she put
out all her strength, and undoing the shutters
at last, threw them open, and leaning from the
window, screamed for the watch. In spite of
the noise that the two men made fighting, she
heard an answering shout, and cried out again
that there was murder being done. As she
did so, there was a groan of pain from Master
Cross-Eyes and he fell heavily to the floor;
Henge had wrenched his hand free from his
adversary's grip, and drawing his dagger,
stabbed him. With an oath, Sir Barton threw
open the door and snatched a taper from its
socket in the hall and brought it into the room;
the sudden light revealed to Betty the prostrate figure of her defender and the furious
aspect of her enemy. He kicked the groom as

he passed him and then picked up his sword. Seeing her last hope of escape cut off, Betty again leaned from the window and called for help. This time the reply came from the court below, and there was a noise at the door. Expecting the watch, Sir Barton turned with a curse to confront him, his naked sword in his hand. The scene was one of wild confusion; the taper he had brought, and the light from the hall showed the scene of the struggle, the overturned table and chairs, the unconscious body of the vagrant, and in the window Betty's tall figure and white face. Henge himself stood waiting defiantly, his dress wildly disordered, and his breast heaving from his recent struggle. Footsteps came up the stairs, paused as if a stranger were looking about for the room from which the screams had issued, and then came across the hall. The next moment a man stood on the threshold, and at the sight of him Betty uttered a wild cry of amazement and joy, while Henge swore a deep oath, but recoiled a step as if he saw a ghost.

It was Simon Raby.

CHAPTER XXX

SIR WILLIAM WINS A WAGER

SIMON RABY stood only a moment on the threshold; a single glance at the interior of the room, at Betty, at Master Cross-Eyes, lying prostrate, and at the furious face of Henge, sufficed to tell him all. The next instant his sword flashed in the air like a ribbon of steel, and he sprang upon Sir Barton with the fury of revenge.

"You villain!" he cried, "was it not enough to send me to the Tower, but you must also insult and injure women?"

"Curse you!" answered Henge, between his teeth, "this shall be the end of you, you fool!"

"By heaven!" exclaimed Raby, as their swords crossed, "'t will be either you or I!"

Both were powerful men and good swords-men, and it being the second time that they had fought, each knew something of the other's play. Henge was spent from his struggle with the groom and Raby had felt the effects of the long imprisonment, but both fought with furious zeal, and knowing that death was in the issue, they put out all their skill. Foot to foot and eye to eye, they thrust and parried; Raby taking the offensive and using the point as he endeavored to strike under his adversary's guard, but Henge was one of the finest swordsmen of the court and parried every blow with marvellous rapidity and skill. The breath of both came short, the drops of perspiration gathered on Henge's forehead, while Lord Raby's face paled about the lips. It was but the different way in which each showed the strain. So determined was Simon's onset, that he drŏve Sir Barton back step by step toward the table, meaning to trip him and so have him at his mercy; but Henge knew the trap that was set for him and swerved to one side, dealing at the same instant so dexterous a blow that he nearly disarmed his opponent. There was no sound in the room but the clash of swords and the labored breathing of the two combatants. It was a spectacle worth seeing, the equal contest of two expert fencers. For a few moments Betty Carew had remained at her post by the window, so amazed at Raby's entrance, so alarmed for his safety, that it paralyzed her senses. But at the sight of Sir

Barton's apparent gain, she awoke from her trance and ran to them, throwing herself on Henge's sword arm with all her strength; but he took his weapon in his left hand and parried Raby's blows while endeavoring to shake her off.

"Let be, my darling!" Simon cried; "I dare not strike freely with you in the way; let be — and I will end it."

But Mistress Betty would scarcely have obeyed him but for the sound of footsteps on the stairs. She ran out into the hall to learn whether it was friend or foe, and saw, to her amazement, old Madam's hawk face upon the landing, and behind her the captain of the watch and two more armed men. Betty cried out with joyful surprise.

"Help, help!" she exclaimed, "here is the villain Henge trying to murder Simon Raby."

"This all comes of Raby's mad haste!" retorted Lady Crabtree; "'t is ever so with fools and lovers."

But while she stayed to scold, the captain of the watch and Betty had hurried back into the room. As they reached the entrance, however, there was a heavy fall, and they found Simon Raby standing with his foot on Sir Barton's breast and the point of his sword at his throat, while Master Cross-Eyes, who had recovered from his swoon, sat up, staring blankly at the changed scene. The captain of the watch uttered an exclamation and hurried forward.

"Have you killed him, my lord?" he asked.

Henge lay so still that Raby stirred him with his foot.

"I know not," he answered; "he has a thrust below the collar bone, but I think 't is too high for his heart. I got a blow under his guard and he went down like a sack of salt, and has not opened his eyes since."

"'T was a pity to kill him," the officer said, laying his hand on the fallen man's heart; "my lord privy-seal would have him taken alive at all costs."

The room began to fill with strangers, twenty torches and lanterns were about it and on the stairs; the court was thronged with a gaping crowd that fell back to let two new-comers pass, Sir William Carew and Cromwell. Some one had run for a leech, and the little man came hurrying in with his bag and knelt on the other side of Henge, opposite the captain. Old Madam was there, her farthingale tucked up and her great boots showing, and Betty Carew stood leaning on the arm of Lord Raby,

who had no eyes save for her, and was whisper-
ing in her ear fond and joyful words while the
others gathered around Henge. There was
silence and confusion, however, when my lord
privy seal entered with Carew.

"Ah, this is blundering work!" Cromwell
exclaimed, at the sight of the prostrate figure;
"this man was needed by the State. "Who
did this?"

Raby stood forth, and in a moment the light
of all the torches was centered on his pale face
and disordered dress.

"My lord," he said, "'t was I who disobeyed
your instructions. When I received the warning, sent by one of this villain's grooms, I ran
with all speed to the house, and hearing a cry
for help, came in, the door being unlocked, as
had been promised. I found this devil here,
trying to keep this young lady a prisoner.
We fought and he fell; I knew not that I had
seriously hurt him."

Cromwell was watching the doctor, who had
his ear against Sir Barton's breast.

"Is he gone?" he asked sharply.

"Nay, my lord," replied the physician, looking up; "he lives, but he is sorely wounded
and stunned too, by striking his head on the
table as he fell."

"Use your skill to save him," said Cromwell, coldly; "the State requires this witness." Then turning to Raby, "My lord, matters standing as they do, I pardon you; but never try to cheat the headsman, albeit 't is the natural office of a good knight to rescue distressed demoiselles, and this fair lady merited the service at your hands, having ever been a suitor for you, even to the king's grace. Sir William," he went on, "how came this ending to the muddle?"

"My lord, I caught Raby's servant, Shaxter, early in the evening, and, as you know, my Lady Crabtree and I soon found a way to make him confess that Henge had bribed him to change the packet that I gave to Raby for one that Henge had full of treasonable matter. Shaxter changed the packets when he helped his master to dress, just before he was arrested."

"Ay, arrested at the complaint of Henge, who came to me with every protest of loyalty; not that he deceived me," Cromwell added, "but the papers found on Lord Raby did mightily confirm his words. I know how you brought the villain Shaxter to me when I had Raby at my house for private examination; it was a happy matter that I could at once release him, but how came this villain's schemes to-night to miscarry so?"

"His servants were all false to him," Sir William answered, "and one of them sent us warning that he intended to carry off my niece, whom he has ever claimed as his affianced wife because of an old contract made when she was born. I know not yet which varlet of his did us this signal service."

Cromwell's keen eyes alighted on Master Cross-Eyes, who sat leaning on the table, too badly hurt to rise, but overlooked in the tumult.

"Ah, who is this?" asked the privy seal; "how many were in this affray?"

Betty Carew came forward now and answered for her champion.

"Sir," she said eagerly, "but for that man I should scarcely have escaped so soon. He took my part, and fought with Henge in my behalf, and from my heart I thank him."

"Is it so?" exclaimed Cromwell, glancing in some surprise at the unpleasing aspect of the man; "what say you, knave, how came you to serve this lady?"

Master Cross-Eyes looked up without any change in the sullen expression of his face.

"The young mistress saved me from the hangman when yonder big-nosed woman would have put a halter on my neck," he retorted bluntly, conscious that his night's work would protect him; "and I sent the warning to Sir William, despatched my comrades, who hated Henge, for he was ever a hard master, full of blows and curses and slow to pay, and I stayed to protect Mistress Carew."

"By Saint Thomas, 't is the valiant beggar that I had scourged at Wildrick!" cried old Madam; "may Heaven forgive me for it! You shall have a gold piece for every blow and more," she added. "Here, Sir Leech, look to his wounds at my cost."

"His service has atoned his fault," Cromwell said gravely; "but look you, varlet, being strong enough to fight and shrewd enough to catch a traitor, if you do not work henceforth, you shall hang at Tyburn."

"My lord," interposed Raby, "he will be taken into my service for his lifetime, and that is not enough to pay the debt."

"Ay," said Carew, "and he is like to make a better servant than the knave we have in jail, who served you as I foretold. My lord, you owe me the wager."

"It shall be paid," Raby answered heartily; "yet do I think you never dreamed that he was as bad as he has proved."

"'T is as I told you," Sir William retorted dryly.

While this was passing, Cromwell gave some brief directions to the captain of the watch and his assistants, who were lifting Henge's still unconscious form upon a stretcher.

"To the Tower," said the king's minister, "and keep him safe; to-morrow he will have to answer to the Council if he lives, — he and Zachary Sanders."

Lord Raby had tenderly placed the mantle about Betty's shoulders and drawn her arm through his, for they were all preparing to leave the house. Cromwell, turning from his talk with the officers, looked at the lovers, and a smile lighted up for a moment the stern reserve of his strong face.

"My Lord Raby," he said quietly, "never, I think, had man better cause to bless his fate for giving him a faithful heart. This lady hath been untiring, brave, and loyal in her suit for you. Save for her, the king's grace would scarcely have thought of your cause in this sad hour, when the Queen of England lies dead at Hampton Court. Fair and faithful Mistress Carew," he added, bowing low over Betty's hand, "I have had to fulfil an unpleasant office;

the king's servant must do his duty even though he should break a woman's heart; but never yet have I done mine so heavily as when I turned a deaf ear to your suit. I shall take it ill if you ask me not to the wedding."

CHAPTER XXXI

THE WIZARD'S FATE

In the trial that followed, the lost threads of the great conspiracy were found; and more, it was said that the secret examination of Henge gave Cromwell the first clue to the treason of Exeter and Lady Salisbury, and more noble blood flowed on the scaffold. Sir Barton suffered a traitor's death, dying as impenitent as he had lived, and cursing his fate that Zachary Sanders did not share it. And he did not, although the case against him was far stronger than against his more violent accomplice. The wizard was tried and condemned to be hanged, but no halter was placed around his neck.

A strange thing happened. The day set for his execution came, and he was led out of the Traitors' Gate into a barge to take him to the place where he was to suffer for his treason, which had been black enough to hang forty men as well as one. He was bound, at least, so said the Lieutenant of the Tower, and went under strong guard in the king's boat, yet in mid stream he leaped overboard and disappeared. His keepers swore that it was magic; one smelled sulphur and one swooned with horror at a vision he saw in the water. The truth of the matter no man ever knew, except that six stout yeomen of the Tower suffered for the prisoner's escape, and the wizard was never seen alive again. But for years afterwards there was a story that he haunted his house upon the Thames, and that at night a red light shone from every window, and his small figure was seen flitting about on the flat roofs of those two upper stories. The shadow of the little man in the russet cloak haunted every old wife's memory in that neighborhood, and whether he lay dead at the bottom of the river, or lived in some other region, he was still a terror to the imagination of many of his old-time clients, and his name hushed many a crying child with terror when all else had failed. It was even whispered that had he been set free, Queen Jane would not have sickened and died, and Prince Edward would have been a baby of better promise, and not with that look which made the old women shake their heads in grim foreboding.

At Christmas of that year, the bells rang

merrily at Mohun's Ottery, and my lord privy
seal came there to grace the wedding of Lord
Raby and Mistress Betty Carew; and the
bride wore on her neck a splendid jewel, sent
by the king's grace in memory of her petition
for her lover. Nor was she portionless,
although the child of Sir Thomas, for my Lady
Crabtree gave her a dowry, and it was said
that in old Madam's will she was the heiress
to the vast fortune that had accumulated and
doubled under Lady Crabtree's shrewd manage-
ment. Sir William Carew gave away the
bride, who looked the great beauty that she
was in her white robes and with the light of
love and happiness, which is a wondrous beau-
tifier, in her brown eyes. It was said that
there had never been a more stately or handsome couple wedded in Devon, or a finer wedding; though some stared at the groom's
strange servant, for Master Cross-Eyes, even
in his wedding garments, looked a rough
attendant; but to Lady Raby he seemed an
angel in disguise.

Standing beside her husband, Betty looked
about the great hall thronged with guests in
her honor, and in her heart she remembered
the sad and penniless orphan who had come
there a few years before. In her happiness

she did not forget her thanksgiving to Heaven for the wonderful change which had come into her life, which, stretching out before her in a golden vista, seemed to hold only love and hope.

THE END.

ON THE RED STAIRCASE.

By M. IMLAY TAYLOR.

With Frontispiece. 12mo, 352 pages. Price, $1.25.

The scene of this thrilling story is Moscow, and the time, the boyhood of Peter the Great. Much of the action takes place "On The Red Staircase" in the palace of the Kremlin.

It is a thrilling tale of intrigue and barbaric plot. A French viscount visiting Moscow on a diplomatic service is the hero; and his adventures while trying to rescue the beautiful Zenaide from a cruel uncle, who is bent upon marrying her to a profligate, are constant and of an intense order of interest. . . . The scenes are exciting. Escapes follow escapes. Secret missions with packets (stolen by hidden pursuers) are incidents of the plot; while sword-cuts, pinionings, attacks of all kinds, kidnapping, and desperate acts fill the pages. . . . The book is exciting, well sustained and excellently written. . . . Another "Zenda" story. — *Chicago Times-Herald*.

A most vivid and absorbing tale of love and adventure. . . . Miss Taylor has certainly an unusual gift of vivid word painting; and as we read, we can almost see the savage mob, and feel ourselves to be in danger. "On the Red Staircase" will give a far truer, because more striking and life-like, picture of early Russian history than a multitude of laboriously written and ponderous histories of the time, and the authoress has apparently a most promising future before her. — *The Churchman, New York*.

After the many problem-novels and the myriad psychological disquisitions disguised as fiction, a wholesome, breezy tale like this, honestly and brilliantly told for its own sake, is a real treat to be enjoyed without thought or criticism. — *The Bookman, New York*.

A strong, bracing story it is, and one which gives us a clear view of an exceptionally interesting epoch in Russian history. — *New York Herald*.

Sold by all booksellers, or mailed, on receipt of price, by

A. C. McCLURG & CO., Publishers,

An Imperial Lover

By M. IMLAY TAYLOR

With Frontispiece. 12mo. 377 pages. Price, $1.25

Miss M. Imlay Taylor will be remembered as the author of a spirited Russian historical novel called "On the Red Staircase," which has attained a wide reading the past year. She has now written a second novel of the same general description, called "An Imperial Lover." Again the scene is the Russian court, this time in the reign of Peter the Great, who plays a very important part in the plot. The tale is one of love, of intrigue, and of adventure, and seems to us even better than its predecessor.—*The Outlook*, New York.

The setting is admirably adapted to development under a skillful hand, and the author has succeeded in this undertaking.—*The Washington Star*.

M. Imlay Taylor has the story-teller's gift in perfection. Every word of her new Russian romance, "An Imperial Lover," is as captivating as was every word of "On the Red Staircase."—*The Times-Herald*, Chicago.

The story abounds in exciting incidents and has no dull pages.—*The Inter-Ocean*, Chicago.

M. Imlay Taylor gives us a picturesque and interesting sketch of Moscow society during an eminently interesting period, and tells a capital story.—*The Scotsman*, Edinburgh.

The novel not only shows careful and intelligent study of the period, but it is skilfully constructed, well written, and thoroughly interesting.—*The Spectator*, London.

Sold by all booksellers, or mailed, on receipt of price, by

A. C. McCLURG & CO., Publishers

Chicago.

A Yankee Volunteer

By M. IMLAY TAYLOR

12mo.   383 pages.   Price, $1.25

A painstaking chronicle of the principal incidents in the sanguinary struggle between Great Britain and her North American Colonies. . . . There is not a dull page in this excellent historical romance.—*Daily Telegraph*, London, Eng.

It is a far cry from Russia to the United States, yet Mary Imlay Taylor, who has written some most interesting stories of intrigue and fighting at St. Petersburg, shows in her latest romance, "A Yankee Volunteer," that she is quite as much at home in America as in the Czar's country. Her new book has for historic background the events of the first half of the Revolutionary War, and it tells a love story which is charming and quite a part of the stern adventures that make a hero.— *Evening Bulletin*, Philadelphia.

It is a good story — this of the Yankee rebel — "so gallant in love and so dauntless in war," and of the sweet Royalist who at last became a "rebel" for love of him. — *Living Church*, Chicago.

"A Yankee Volunteer" is indeed a story fraught with such exquisite beauty as is seldom associated with history.— *Boston Times*.

The story is beautifully written, and moves with the dignity and quaintness inseparable from the successful historical novel.—*St. Paul Pioneer Press*.

A fascinating picture of the royalist and patriot social elements of revolutionary days.—*Boston Globe*.

Sold by all booksellers, or mailed, on receipt of price, by

A. C. McCLURG & CO., Publishers

Chicago.

THE · BEVERLEYS.

A Story of Calcutta.

BY MARY ABBOTT,

Author of "Alexia," etc.

12mo, 264 pages.   Price, $1.00.

THE uncommonly favorable reception of Mrs. Abbott's brilliant novelette, "Alexia," by the public bespeaks in advance a lively interest in her new novel, "The Beverleys." It is a more extended and ambitious work than the former, but has the same grace of style and liveliness of treatment, together with a much more considerable plot and more subtle delineations of character and life. The action of the story takes place in India, and reveals on the part of the authoress the most intimate knowledge of the official life of the large and aristocratic English colony in Calcutta. The local coloring is strong and unusual.

A more joyous story cannot be imagined. . . . . A harum-scarum good-nature; a frank pursuit of cakes and ale; a heedless, happy-go-lucky spirit, are admirable components in a novel, however trying they may be found in the walks of daily life. Such are the pleasures of "The Beverleys." To read it is recreation, indeed. — *Public Ledger, Philadelphia.*

The author writes throughout with good taste, and with a quick eye for the picturesque. — *Herald, New York.*

It is a pretty story, charmingly written, with cleverly sketched pictures of various types of character . . . The book abounds in keen, incisive philosophy, wrapped up in characteristic remarks. — *Times, Chicago.*

An absorbing story. It is brilliantly and vivaciously written. — *Literary World, Boston.*

The author has until now been known, so far as we are aware, only by her former story, "Alexia." Unless signs fail which seldom *do* fail, these two with which her name is now associated are simply the forerunners of works in a like vein of which American literature will have reason to be proud. — *Standard, Chicago.*

Sold by all booksellers, or mailed, on receipt of price, by

A. C. McCLURG & CO., PUBLISHERS,